Prai[

"... a clever, touching, and who reads!"
—Nancy Thayer, NYT bes.

"A luminous tribute to love, art, fateful choices, and the indestructibility of the human heart. Its heartbreakingly real lovers, backlit by the silver screen, front a supporting cast of ghosts right out of vaudeville and old Hollywood—a trick roper, a raconteur, an escape artist, a folk singer, and the starriest of movie stars—but they all take a back seat to the unforgettable Harry and Sue. You'll want to ride with Harry in his taxi, wrapped secure in the knowledge that lovely Sue is flying right beside you."
—Mary Anna Evans, author of *The Traitor Beside Her*

"Most ghost stories are scary campfire tales that make you huddle close and fear the night. In Larry Baker's seventh novel, *HARRY AND SUE*, the ghosts exude tremendous personality and charisma and endless charm — but then of course they would. They are all dead celebrities returning to an old theater in downtown Oklahoma City where they proceed to bamboozle each other to the great delight of the narrator Harry, a man down on his luck and needing a friend in the worst way, even if she is a ghost. No scary campfire tale this, but an exuberant immersion into Americana from ages past, a bonfire of delight with Baker's own unique twist at the end. Enjoy."
—Mike Lankford, author of *Becoming Leonardo*

"A nostalgic tale of love gained, love lost, and, ultimately, love re-found, *HARRY AND SUE* offers readers a true everyman in Harry Mason - who, with the influence of several iconic celebrity "ghosts," can properly take stock of his actions and ensure the narrative of his life culminates in a true legacy. Whether standing up to Harry Houdini, seeking emotional solace from Marilyn Monroe, or discussing the nuances of human nature with Harry Chapin, protagonist Harry is equal parts vulnerable and humanly relatable. Larry Baker's new book makes for a truly unique ride; climb on in with Harry M. at the wheel ... and don't worry about the fare."
—Ira Kantor, author of *Hello, Honey, It's Me: The Story of Harry Chapin*

HARRY
and
SUE

A Story About Love and Ghosts

Larry Baker

Ice Cube Press, LLC
North Liberty, Iowa, USA

Harry and Sue

Copyright © 2023 Larry Baker

ISBN 9781948509411

Library of Congress Control Number: 2023931949

Ice Cube Press, LLC (Est. 1991)
1180 Hauer Drive, North Liberty, Iowa 52317
www.icecubepress.com steve@icecubepress.com
Check us out on Facebook and Twitter

No portion of this book may be reproduced in any way without permission, except for brief quotations for review, or educational work, in which case the publisher shall be provided two copies. The views expressed in *Harry and Sue* are solely those of the author, not the Ice Cube Press, LLC.

The paper used in this publication meets the minimum requirements of the American National Standard for Information Sciences—Permanence of Paper for Printed Library Materials, ANSI Z39.48-1992

Manufactured in USA with recycled paper.

Photo Credits: Back cover image of King's Theatre in Brooklyn, Max Touhey, photographer. Centre Theatre photos courtesy of the Allen Brown and Metropolitan Library System Special Collections.

This is a work of fiction. Any resemblance to any person, living or dead, is purely coincidental. The above statement is true, but with a caveat. This entire story is filled with the ghosts of dead people who were once living. All of them have been dead for at least forty years, some of them for over a hundred. But I bring them back to life. I have used facts about their lives that we all know. You will find bits and pieces of their actual words woven into the fictional dialogue I have written, lifted from multiple sources in the public domain. My goal was to make their ghosts compatible with who they were when they were alive. But I have a theory: being dead makes you a different person. You are you, but freed from being you. You have more power as a ghost, more insight about yourself, than you did when you were alive. In my story, Marilyn Monroe is the essence of this idea. You will recognize her, but her ghost is my creation, and her ghost is very different than the victimized Monroe that you have seen in recent books and movies. In my story, Monroe is heroic, and wickedly funny. I think that if we could resurrect Monroe and have her read this book, she would surely say, "Yep, that's me. And you, Larry, are a genius." (Okay, I might be loosely paraphrasing her reaction.) At the back of this story is a picture gallery: "The Cast of Characters." I have done my best to use only pictures that are in the public domain; or, for which I was given permission to use. But if you spot a picture that somebody still has a copyright on…let me know and I will have it removed from any future editions. I am still looking for a picture of Harry Ducharme. If you find one, please send it to me.

For Every
Harry and Sue
Wherever They Are

"Now I know what a ghost is. Unfinished business, that's what."
Salman Rushdie, *The Satanic Verses*

LET ME INTRODUCE MYSELF

"It's like a ghost is writing a song like that.
It gives you the song and goes away.
You don't know what it means.
Except that the ghost picked me to write the song."
—Bob Dylan—

My name is Harry Mason, and I drive a taxi. This is a story about when I kissed Marilyn Monroe, sang songs with Harry Chapin and Patsy Cline, did rope tricks with Will Rogers, swapped tales with Mark Twain, and watched Harry Houdini die. All that, and more, but they aren't the important story. No, that's about Sue, how I lost her, how I got her back. This is a love story. But I should warn you . . . it's also a ghost story.

THE PAST

A few years after Sue and I split, I started dating again. Life goes on, right? Sooner or later a pseudo-serious conversation would veer into "the past." I always made the mistake of believing the other person when she asked for an honest answer. I once had a girlfriend who was different from the others. She had her own past love, but she refused to discuss him. I liked her a lot. I looked forward to seeing her again. I never loved her. I wondered if she felt the same about me. If we had tried, could we have fallen in love? She liked to talk about having to "shed skin" to survive. On our worst night, our final night, she had stopped being patient and understanding. Who could blame her?

"Harry, I feel like I'm stuck in some country song about a threesome, you and me and some ghost named Sue. You're not shedding skin. You're wearing her like some goddam suit of armor. Keeping me out, keeping you trapped inside."

She was right. I lived on a stage with one other person, and it wasn't her.

Yes, I might be a stoner, but I'm not a drunk. I know the difference. I'm not an addict. I've gone weeks at a time stone cold straight. I've never been arrested. Always paid my bills. Except for buying drugs, never broke the law. Never physically assaulted anybody, except once, and he deserved it. I never wrote a book or composed a song, never flew a plane. I did read a lot of books a long time ago, but I never graduated from college. I've been in love once for sure, with Sue, and she loved me, a million years ago.

I weigh almost the same now as I weighed in high school, back when Sue kept trying to feed me all the time because she thought I was too skinny. She came from a poor family, much poorer than mine, and she was always hungry, so I guess she assumed that all skinny people were hungry too. I'm not skinny now, but I am thin. I have great hair. Probably the only thing on my body that time has not touched. Thick and wavy, and barely gray. Sue loved my hair. We would lay together and she would rub her fingers through my hair as we kissed. I think about that a lot. How she loved my hair. How she kissed.

I was born in Oklahoma City on Pearl Harbor Day, but four years earlier. I'm now pushing sixty, too old for a midlife crisis but too young for Social Security. My parents are dead. Evidently, I don't have a pedigree gene pool. My father dropped dead from a heart attack as he was watering our lawn. My mother stepped in front of a bus a year after that. *Distracted*, the police said. She was distracted. So was the bus driver. I joined the Air Force.

In the worst of cosmic ironies, my older brother Frank became a bus driver in Tulsa. He was the essence of my gene pool. Probably bipolar, probably schizophrenic, definitely crazy. He was fired after he revved up his engine, ran a red light, paralyzing his passengers with fear, and rammed his bus into a Cadillac that had just entered the intersection. Told his boss and the police that Jesus had told him to do it. They were skeptical. But I knew my brother. He had been talking to Jesus for years. The difference between me and my brother? Ambition. I coasted. Always did. But my brother dreamed of being rich. Jesus encouraged him. Lose his job driving a thirty-thousand-pound bus, he would go get a job as a janitor. Lose that, he would lie on a job application and get a garbage collector job in Sapulpa. Never get married, grift as much as he could, perfect the art of petty theft, small bits of money add up. Take that money and buy South African Krugerrands. One at a time, thousands of them in thirty years, bury them somewhere and not tell anybody because he didn't trust anybody, not even me. I saw a trunk full of them one time, on his birthday. Swearing me to secrecy, he had opened the trunk up after closing all the shades in his house. You would have thought that he was showing me the Shroud of Turin. Every birthday he would dig up his treasure and go find somewhere else to bury it. Jesus told him to do it. Once a year, that was his annual accounting ritual. I was actually stunned. I had tended to discount my brother's story about becoming rich. But there it was, probably hundreds of thousands of dollars in gold. Method and madness were in perfect sync. I wished him and Jesus the best of luck, but it never occurred to me to ask him for money. A month after I witnessed his wealth, my brother killed a man back in Tulsa. A stupid drunken argument, a knife, and a life sentence in McAlester. That life sentence only lasted a month until he met another inmate who claimed to be privy to the inner workings of Jesus, so the two disciples settled it as the truly religious do . . . they killed each other. Somewhere between Tulsa and Sapulpa is my brother's stash, which only I knew existed, buried in red clay, location unknown.

So that left me as the last of the Masons. I have some distant cousins I've never met, including a second cousin who is a city councilman in Tulsa. But he's a Republican and I'm a Democrat. I'm not political. I haven't voted in twenty years. The Republic has rolled on without me.

My Air Force stint was in the mid-fifties. Two years in the motor pool, driving trucks and jeeps, fixing engines, pretty much protecting Cold War America from godless communism. I was stationed in El Paso, so it might be more accurate to say that I was protecting Texas from Mexico.

I knew I had made a mistake, so I didn't re-up. I didn't like living in barracks, sharing air or laundry with other young men who were as ignorant as I was. But I did do one thing religiously. I wrote to Sue almost every day, and I called her every Sunday. Once a month, I could afford to buy her a bus ticket and we would spend a weekend together.

We met in the eighth grade. By classroom standards, neither one of us was a good student. WWII was over and we were surrounded by kids with fathers who were home from Europe or the Pacific. Not the rich kids. They went somewhere else. Not any black kids. They ended up at Douglass. But even in our own underfunded educational universe, there were smart kids and dumb kids, and then me and Sue. It was her distinction. Me and her, and everyone else. My parents weren't dead yet. She was raised by a single mother with four kids, and she was always hungry. But she always shared her lunch with some kid who was even hungrier. She helped other kids with their school work too. That's how we officially met. I was having trouble reading and asked her to read a line to me. It was not a coincidence. I had wanted to talk to her for a long time, more than school talk, more than recess talk. She was different. I didn't know that I was different too, until she gave me that tilted-head look.

"Open your book," she had said. "You read it first. Tell me what's there."

I muttered something about how I wouldn't have asked her to help me if I could already read it. But then Mrs. Butthole, our teacher . . . no, not her name, just what we called Mrs. Butler out of the classroom . . . said the magic words that turned me and Sue into a couple.

"Susan Alden, Harry Mason, both of you be quiet or I am going to have to separate you."

How did we both know it at that exact moment? We looked directly at each other and both knew what the other was thinking.

No, I will die.

I felt it right then, but I didn't know how to say it. I didn't have the words for how I felt, but Sue knew. She put her finger over her lips to shush me, arching her eyebrows, and then turned to face the front of the room, the model of decorum and obedience. Her acting debut for me.

Lunch period couldn't come fast enough. Thirty seconds after the bell rang, we skipped the cafeteria and ran outside laughing, running toward the farthest corner of the fenced-in grounds. We had thirty minutes. She was breathless.

"I thought I would cry right then, Harry. Separate us, how stupid is that? She really is a butthole."

"I don't know what to say, Sue. I mean, I mean . . ."

"You mean, Harry, that we are never going to be separated, ever. That we will die first."

I was gob-smacked and star-struck. Overwhelmed. I was fourteen years old. Sue was thirteen. I was going to be a pilot. She was going to be an actress.

"Will you still help me to read?"

She laughed hysterically. I thought she was about to hug me, but she stopped, threw out her arms as wide as she could and twirled around.

"Harry Mason, you dope. Everybody in class knows you're as blind as a bat. Mrs. Butthole probably thinks you're a retard. Read with you? Harry, you go home and tell your parents to take you to an eye doctor. But you have to promise that I will help you pick out the frames, okay? I think you'll look cute in glasses, and I always wanted a brainy boyfriend. We will read everything together."

I can remember that day in every detail. If she was acting, I didn't care.

Did I tell my parents about the girl who told me I needed glasses? Did she tell her mother about her blind-as-a-bat new love? I told my parents that my teacher had suggested that I needed glasses. She told her mother that she had a new "project" that required her to stay after school a lot. Her mother was burdened with three younger children and knew that Sue could take care of herself. My parents were oblivious to my existence most of the time. Truth be told, my brother Frank had always sapped all their attention, already bringing home "lost" cat collars that he seemed to consistently find in the neighborhood.

Not even Mrs. Butthole knew about us. Sue taught me how to act like we were just casual friends. Sue had lots of friends. Classmates were still skeptical about my "friend" potential. Too much of a loner. But, if Sue liked me, others started to see me differently. Sue was popular, but not with the popular kids. Her domain was peopled with the junior high cast of emotional cripples and late-blooming flowers. She insisted that I was in the late-bloomer crowd. After a year together, she upped my status to "blooming."

In her world, the worst thing you could be was a bully. Norman Rochester was the bully in our class, and I was terrified of him, especially in gym class. His friends called him "Rocky." The smart thing to do was be his friend. Sue was not his friend, but she was a girl and Rocky ignored girls. He went for the low-hanging fruit of nerds and the physically weak. But I was there when he made the mistake of cornering Larry Mohn, a slow-witted boy half his size. Larry was one of Sue's projects. He had a dime and Rocky wanted the dime. I was probably thirty feet away in the hallway, waiting for Sue, telling myself to go help Larry, when she came out of the art classroom and steamed over to Rocky, a little bottle of paint in her hand. I thought she was going to hit him with it, but in midstride she had the lid off and soon enough the back of his new jean jacket was covered in red. Rocky turned, realized that he had been splashed, and stepped toward Sue. I then shocked myself and everyone else by stepping between him and Sue. It was soon a Mexican standoff, but I was probably doing Rocky a favor by keeping Sue away from him. Order was restored when Mr. Schenker, the principal, arrived, asked a few questions, looked at Rocky, who I am sure was already on his radar, and then at Sue, and announced, "Norman, go to my office."

After school that day, Sue finally took me to her house and introduced me to her mother, announcing, "Meet Harry, my hero, your future son-in-law." Was she being a bit theatrical? Of course, she was. She was Sue. She asked her mother if I could stay for dinner. It was that night when I fully understood how poor her family was. It was the hesitation, the awkward look on her mother's face, as if trying to answer without saying words, to remind Sue that meals at their house were already sparse affairs, and the five Aldens always left the table still hungry. It was in her face. The embarrassment. Sue knew it, but she had a Plan B. "I have some babysitting money saved up. Harry and I can go to the Piggly-Wiggly and get some stuff. Come on, Mom, it'll be fun. I'll get some hamburger meat and noodles and we can have spaghetti. Okay?"

"And I'll get some ice cream for dessert," I added. Sue looked at me like I had just announced I had found a cure for polio.

"Didn't I tell you, mom? He's my hero."

How do you describe your first kiss? Not your first clumsy peck on the mouth. A real kiss, the first kiss with your first love. Sue and I went shopping and walked out of the store with a feast of ingredients in a bag, including French bread and chocolate ice cream. We had to walk fast to keep the ice cream from melting. Her house was six blocks away. When we got to the corner a block away from her house, she pulled me into the alley next to Mr. Tubridy's shop, and she told me to put the groceries down. I was clueless. She was not.

"Kiss me, Harry. Here and now, and let's always remember this spot, okay?"

We had been "dating" a year. We had never kissed. I know, I know, then we weren't really dating, right?

Next to a dry-cleaning shop in south Oklahoma City, at that moment of the day when it is not quite light and not yet dark, we kissed. Holding each other close, she whispered, "I want you to be my first, Harry. When the time is right." We kissed again, and she ran her fingers through my hair. We looked at each other and I could see her almost smiling. "And if I ever have breasts, you can start there." Then we went to feed her family. Her breasts didn't arrive for another two years.

Sue was consistent. She lived her life around three passions: drama, art, and me. I was happy being third in the pecking order. Me, I tried to be a jock, and I was good enough to be on the varsity swim team. Knowing her, my grades went up, but my athletic career peaked in my junior year. I won a state swimming championship in the 800-freestyle. In my senior year, a sophomore broke my record, but I was still captain of the team. Sue still loved me. I still talked about being a pilot. Sue was destined to be an actress.

I suppose we can all blame either our parents or our teachers for how our lives turned out. They can destroy us, or they can motivate us by trying to destroy us. Sue had an art teacher who tried to fail her. Not in grades, but in desire. I loved her drawings, but, of course, I loved her, and my objectivity was gone. She could do charcoal sketches, portraits, and caricatures. But she always hated any assignment that required realistic colors. It was the Sue Alden "contradiction." On the most meager of budgets, she was a colorful dresser, mixing and matching skirts and blouses in color combinations that had no point of reference in the known world, but she walked into school and boys turned their heads while girls would ask her to help them pick out their own clothes. In the school stage productions, she demanded that she make her own wardrobe decisions, and she was consistently dazzling. But she refused to use color in her art to satisfy the teacher. That art teacher, the woman who failed her, would look at her paintings of flowers or anything else in nature, and insist, "Roses are red, Susan, or yellow, sometimes white. The stems are green. Grass is green. Dirt is brown or black. You can't change the way things are in real life."

Sue told me later, "Do you know what I wanted to tell her? I wanted to say that there were so many colors in the rainbow and that I could use them any way I wished."

"But, you didn't," I said.

"No, I didn't. But when I'm a star and you write my biography, you just make sure you put that bitch in my story. And you fucking crucify her. I plan on winning an Oscar and thanking her in my acceptance speech for all her encouragement. Somebody else must have already said it, but you heard it from me first. Success is the best revenge."

How could I not love her? But I never wrote her story. I should have, but she went away and I stayed behind. I knew we were over the first time we didn't celebrate the anniversary of our first kiss. For eight straight years we always went back to Mr. Tubridy's dry-cleaning shop on that date and at that time of the day. Even when I was in the Air Force, I planned ahead to have Leave so I could be back in Oklahoma City to be there. Eight straight years. There was not a ninth.

It was our second anniversary, both of us still virgins, when I first saw her cry. We were kissing in the dim light when we heard singing from inside Mr. Tubridy's shop. I could see her eyes widen. "Do you hear that?" We walked to the front door, surprised to find it partially open. We looked through the windows, but the inside looked pitch black, or so I thought. "Look, Harry, there's a light coming from the back of the store." It was there, a sliver of light seeping out of a door in the back of the shop. We just stood there and listened. A baritone voice, singing in a language I did not understand, like an angel, or a god. On an impulse, I pushed open the front door. Sue looked at me and then nodded in the direction of the light. We slipped into the store as if we were spirits ourselves, soundless and invisible, and we stood there in the dark listening to Mr. Tubridy sing. Sue put her arm around my waist and pulled me closer, leaning her head on my shoulder, and cried. "Harry, I just want our life to be as beautiful as that voice."

My brother Frank taught me to swim. All the kids around me were swimmers and they would ask me to go with them to a pool or a lake, but I was a rock in the water. Frank's method? He was a believer in the "sink or swim" school. He pushed me in a pool when I was seven and I was terrified. But he was also in the water right after me, scooping me off the bottom, dragging me to the edge of the pool, hoisting me up, and then, as I was still trembling, he pushed me back in. He was older than me, bigger than me, and crazy as a loon. But he had a soft side that nobody ever saw, not even my parents. I think he actually cared about me. It took a week, but I learned to float and then to swim. He would stand in the shallow end of the pool and put his hands under me, coaching me, relaxing me, and I would feel myself floating, never noticing that he had removed his hands from under me. Soon enough he would flip me over on my stomach, his hands under me again, and make me practice breathing, take a breath, hold it, put my face under water, wait three seconds, always count to three he said, and then come up for air again.

For some reason, Frank thought that his swimming would attract girls, and he told me that was enough reason for me to learn how. At my age, attracting girls seemed an odd goal. But I learned anyway. Within a year, I was beating him in races. As young as I was, I knew what his problem was. Frank was one of those swimmers who attacked water, slapping his arms into the water rather than stroking the water. He forced his arms to do most of the work, not his legs. Splash, splash, splash . . . Frank was a splasher. By the time I was a teenager, I could see that Frank's splashing was a major turn-off for girls at the pool. But Frank splashed all his life.

By the time I met Sue, I was already a lifeguard. I had lied about my age. The newly hired pool supervisor had seen me swim a lot the first month he was there. He assumed I had been doing it since birth. Frank left home when I was ten. My parents were averse to sunlight (my private joke to Sue), so I went to the pool almost every day when it was open, even in cool weather. I liked to swim, and I liked to float. After we started seeing each other, Sue would come to the pool in a bright red one-piece suit, spread her towel on a lounge chair near my station, put on a straw hat and sparkly framed sunglasses, and read a book. Her breasts had still not arrived, but she made sure the red suit was padded. I thought it was weird that she read her book out loud, but she told me that she was not really reading.

"I'm practicing lines, Johnny."

She called me "Johnny" at the pool because she always compared me to Johnny Weissmuller from the movies.

"I read the dialogue out loud and become that character. Practice, Johnny, practice will make me a star. And when do I get to see you rescue somebody?"

I tried to joke with her. "I could always rescue you, Sue. You know, you go out to the deep end and start acting like you have a cramp or some undertow is sucking you to Tulsa, and I would rescue you."

It was as if a lightbulb went off in her head.

"I could do that! I could act like I was drowning. I could be drowning and you could save me, and you would be a hero and then I could act like I was in love with you for saving me."

"As I recall, you *are* in love with me."

"Johnny, you do realize that it is harder to act like you're in love than to actually be in love, don't you? Acting takes talent."

I wasn't sure how to interpret that, back then and for years afterwards. But I kept swimming for the rest of my life. In high school, Sue came to all my meets and cheered for me. I went to all her plays and clapped for her. When we were seniors, after her breasts arrived, after we started to have sex, we would sneak into the city pool at midnight on hot summer nights, and we would swim together. No diving, no splashing, no shouting, just being together in the water. Soon enough, she dared me to go skinny-dipping. Did she really believe I wouldn't do it?

Sue had us all figured out.

We were on our bicycles headed to church on a cold November morning. I was a sophomore. She was a freshman. I wasn't a churchgoer, but she was in the choir. We had our life organized around the other's schedule. Well, hers mostly. I would endure her Baptist preacher as long as I could hear her sing.

I was pedaling too fast that morning, forgetting about her behind me. I bicycled a lot that year, working on my endurance for swimming.

"Harry, you gotta slow down," I heard behind me.

When I slowed and turned my head back, I could see that she had already stopped about twenty yards behind me, one foot on a pedal, the other on the ground, her breathe a steamy cloud. With me fully stopped, I assumed she would catch up. But she just parked herself in that spot and waited for me to come back to her. Looking at her breath in the air, looking at how her knit hat was too big for her head, covering her ears and slipping down to her eyebrows, I wished I had a camera. But I pedaled back to her.

"Harry Mason, you are a giant butt-hole."

"And you are a giant buttette-hole."

My idea of humor.

"If I have to pedal so fast to keep up with you, I'll get a sore throat. I have a solo today. If I sound like death eating a cracker, it will be your fault, and I will kill you."

"I'm sorry, Sue."

"You're forgiven."

An hour later, I was sitting in the balcony listening to her sing "On Eagle's Wings." I was thinking that all those Baptists did not deserve her. Hell, neither did I. We were still a year away from having sex. She had given me her heart and voice, that was enough. Two hours later we were back on the road, headed back to her house, when she informed me that her bladder was not going to wait until we got back to her place, so we stopped at the new Denny's. Bladder empty, we decided to eat there but had to wait for a booth. Sunday lunch crowd. Sue and I were going to buy one breakfast and split it.

Sitting on that bench in Denny's, she explained us to me.

"Harry, girls have categories for boyfriends. They can be the *Oh my god he is so handsome and I am so jealous* or they can be the *Oh my god he is such a loser and so not you, how can you do it* kind."

I waited. She stopped talking and looked around Denny's, as if she was there all by herself.

"Sue?"

"Oh, right, you and me. I forgot."

"So funny I forgot to laugh."

"Harry, I invented a category for us, more for you actually. It seems to me that you are the *I have no idea what you see in him, but the two of you seem perfect for each other* category."

I decided that we should come to Denny's every Sunday forever. She slid closer to me, locked her arm in mine, and leaned her head on my shoulder.

"Sue, can I ask you a question?"

"Harry, you are always asking me questions. For the record, I am not an encyclopedia."

"Do you believe all that stuff they talk about in church?"

"All I know, Harry, is that if God exists, he is doing a crappy job taking care of all us sparrows down here. So, how about you, do you believe it?"

"I'm not sure."

"Well, lemme know when you figure it out."

"I don't know. Something about going to church doesn't feel right."

"It must be a Baptist thing. All I know is that I'd become a Catholic except for one hitch. I mean, Jesus, you ever go to a Catholic Mass? I love the drama, the costumes, the rituals."

"But, I hear a 'but' coming."

"But their taste in music is awful. I'd be wasted as a Catholic singer."

Sue and I both agreed that the funniest moment in our time together was when she ruined my political career.

I was a junior, and I have no idea why the idea hit me, but I wanted to be the student body president. The problem? I had to get elected. Getting elected required popularity. This was not the United Nations. It was Grant High School in Oklahoma City, Oklahoma. I was not unpopular; I was simply a good swimmer with zero charisma. But I had Sue.

"Harry Mason, I am shocked. You actually have ambitions."

"I'm just trying to keep up with you."

"That is so sweet, sweetie, but it ain't going to happen."

"You'll help me, right?"

"Harry, help? I will run your entire campaign. I will make you the Ike of Grant High School. Go Big Red. Go Big Grey. Go Generals."

"What do you know about running a campaign?"

"What do *you*?"

A match made in heaven. We laid siege to the citadels of power. Everything depended on one thing: the big rally at the end of the year in which all the candidates had to get up in front of the student body in the auditorium and make a speech about goals and aspirations for the coming year and how the candidate all by himself was the embodiment of Grant tradition and honor. The office itself only had one responsibility . . . to Chair the Student Council meetings. But you got your own page in the yearbook. I might have been able to make that kind of speech, if I practiced a hundred hours before. But I *could* do it. The other requirement was totally beyond me. Every candidate was expected to have some sort of skit at the rally. You were expected to not only inspire the masses, but to entertain them too. I was clueless.

"Harry, leave that to me."

"And you can do a political skit?"

She did one of those pucker-mouth skunk-eyed expressions that always told me that she was exasperated with me.

"Harry, I am Sue Alden. I am the Queen of the Drama Club and fifty drama nerds, Queen of the Choir, the Queen of Grant High, the Queen of your peasant life. I will handle the skit. You go write some sort of proclamation or something."

The problem? She wouldn't tell me what the skit was going to be. She would organize it, rehearse it, and then perform it with her drama and musical minions. "Trust me," she said.

Lucky for me, the candidate speakers were arranged in alphabetical order. Through some sort of serendipity, Mason was the last name on the list of five. Sue's reaction to that news? "Perfect." When it came time for me to speak, I was feeling good about my chances. The other candidates' speeches were as bad as I expected mine to be. No front-runners. Their skits? I could almost hear Sue's voice. *Lame-butts! That's the best they could do?* She would have been right. Four skits of lame songs, rip-offs of football cheers, unfunny satires of some of the teachers, and, in general, yawners. Then it was my turn. I was the best speaker of the bunch. I might not have been Winston Churchill inspiring, but I was better than Donnie Bledsoe, quarterback of the football team, drop-dead handsome, and the odds-on favorite. As I finished, I waited for Sue to seal the deal.

In the back of the auditorium, a trumpet blared, badly. But it got in tune soon enough and was joined by a half-dozen snare drums. The parade began, and I immediately realized what Sue had planned. She was going to re-create one of those political convention demonstrations that erupted as soon as a candidate was introduced. A "spontaneous" parade and music. Within a minute, each aisle of the auditorium was filled with marching band and drama nerds, bedecked in gray and red sparkly pointed birthday hats, half of them carrying posters on sticks, all about some guy named Harry Mason. The music was enthusiastic, but still out of sync. The song they were playing? "I'm Just Wild about Harry." And then, as if on cue, the music softened and the auditorium was filled with Sue's voice, singing about how wild she was about that Harry Mason guy. Everybody else in that auditorium, me too, was a pimply faced kid in Oklahoma. Not Sue. She was a star on stage on Broadway, belting out how some guy named Harry had kisses that were like heavenly blisses. My fellow Grant Generals were on their feet. I was headed to victory. If only we had stopped there.

As soon as she stopped singing, she disappeared and her entourage started marching out, but then I saw her and four other nerds come back into the auditorium along the side aisle, each with a giant poster in their hand. They stood against the wall, thrusting their arms up and revealing my name. One letter per poster. H-A-R-R-Y. Sue was the H, and she started chanting "Hair-eeee, Hair-eeee, Hair-eeee" and was soon joined by the other four. She had plants in the audience who started chanting along with her. I was spellbound. I was also still standing at the podium. I inexplicably started to ad-lib a thank you for everyone's support. As I opened my mouth, I saw the five signs flipped around in unison. On the back M-A-S-

O-N was spelled out. Sue was the H *and* the M. Flipping back and forth, HARRY and then MASON. The chant tempo picked up. "Harry Mason Harry Mason Harry Mason." I wanted to keep talking. I tried to speak over the chants, one last vote-for-me plug. As my voice rose, my dreams of the White House went poof. Sue got out of sync, flipping her card one beat off. Harry Mason became Marry Hason, over and over, Marry Hason Marry Hason Marry Hason. Cheers became jeers and laughter. But Sue kept flipping that card out of sync.

Until she realized something was wrong.

She looked up. I didn't want to be student body president anymore. I wanted to go save her. I wanted to take her away. She was devastated.

I lost that election, by a hundred votes, to that bastard Donnie Bledsoe. Sue blamed herself. She seemed inconsolable that night. As much as I tried to tell her that it didn't matter, that I would have been a lousy president anyway, that Donnie Bledsoe would screw up and the other kids would regret not electing me, that she was still the Queen of my life. . .she kept crying. That night, we went all the way for the first time. When it was over, we were both laughing. We weren't sure which was funnier. . .the skit fiasco or the sex.

I live in a boardinghouse room now, and I swim at the Y across the street almost every day. I drive a cab twelve hours a day, sleep six, and simply try to fill up the remaining six. I keep a box of memories under my bed. Pictures, letters, movie ticket stubs, a few LPs. I try to remember everything about those eight years, even the end.

The day after we went to a Marilyn Monroe movie at the Centre Theatre downtown, Sue told me her plans about going to Hollywood. Had I been that oblivious all those years? Of course. I was Harry Mason. All her talk, even me knowing that she was a wonderful actress, I had always assumed it was a long time away. But she was not thirteen any more. She was twenty-one.

"Harry, don't be so stubborn. You know you can come with me. I want you to come with me. I thought about New York, about the stage there, but last night made up my mind. I want to be in the movies. You know I've been planning this forever. I contacted an agent in each place, sent them photos and credits. They were both interested. And I have been saving my money since I was in diapers. I have enough to tide me over for at least six months. Harry Mason, do . . . not . . . act . . . surprised."

You go back in time and look at yourself? You in the past? I've gone back to that moment a thousand times, hating myself, wondering why she loved me. Who the hell was she in love with?

"Harry, you need to come with me, get out of this town. There's a flight school in Los Angeles. You're twenty-two. You've been in the Air Force. You can get in. We can do this together. You can learn to fly while I start practicing my Oscar acceptance speech. I'm going to have my own private plane and you can be my pilot." She leaned forward and whispered to me, "And we can have sex in the cockpit. If we can do it in your car while you're driving, we can do it while you're flying."

It seemed so simple to her, so obvious, so inevitable. All we had to do was *do* it. Me, I was suddenly scared to fly. As that paralysis began to set in, I managed to say the wrong thing.

"Sue, let me think about this. I've got a good job now, working at the Sheraton. Enough to support us both. I'm not sure I can go out there and let you support me."

That look you never want to see in the face of somebody you adore? The *Have I been wrong all these years* look. We were sitting in the front seat of my car. She scooted away from me and leaned her back against the door.

"Harry Mason, I am going to be an actress. Whatever it takes, I am going to be an actress. And then I am going to be a star."

A month later, she was in Los Angeles. I was still in Oklahoma City. We had spent that month going back and forth with each other. Angry, conciliatory, disappointed, optimistic, compromises offered, compromises rejected, more anger, sadness. We were both actors, pretending that we would always be in love. No, that is wrong. We weren't pretending to be in love. We were pretending that we would find a way to remain a couple. Perhaps she could go and I could come later? If she waited a year, then we could go together? Get some more local acting credits to get her more attention in Hollywood? In the end, she was still gone.

It wasn't as if we officially broke up. She compared it to when I was in the Air Force. Separated, but we wrote all the time and I would come home once a month. She could do the same, right? Come see me once a month, or I could even go see her? But the letters from her slowed down. She came home twice, but then a letter about her schedule being so hectic, so many contacts to make, having to be available all the time in case her agent got her an audition or a reading. I was still young then. I thought I was the first person who had ever had his first love disappear. But it was all a cliché. Sue and me. Hollywood was full of Sues or the male version of Sue. I was the small-town lover left behind. A star was ascending.

And then the inevitable final letter: *This is not going to work anymore. Not fair to either of us. I will always love you . . .* that letter.

I tried to call her. No longer a working number. I sent a letter. Returned as undeliverable.

She did become an actress. She did not become a star. I've seen all nine of her movies. In only one did she have a spoken line. Four years, nine roles, one line. For ten years after that, I never heard of her again. And then I started driving a taxi. Old classmates became fares, sitting in the back seat telling me bits and pieces of her life. She stayed in Hollywood, worked on movies, not in them. She was doing well. Her wardrobe skills were appreciated. She worked in continuity. She was married to a director. Divorced. Married to an actor. Divorced. She was in the movie business, that was all that mattered. They were confident that she was happy. But I knew Sue. I knew what mattered to her. I waited for her to come back. She did, but not to me.

I was assured by my classmate passengers. *She's fine, Harry. Living in Nichols Hills. Met a lovely man in Los Angeles. He was an investor in a film, banker here. A big house in Nichols Hills. Too bad about you and her, but life goes on, right?*

Was it 1973? I went to a lot of movies when I was younger. Me and Sue, how many? They were cheap. But not the Centre. For me and Sue, it was a big deal to go to the Centre. It held on for as long as it could, when "downtown" meant something good and not something bad. Going to the Centre was a dress-up date. You paid more, but it was worth it. Was it 1973? I went to the Centre to see *The Way We Were*. It was the perfect date movie, but I was alone, surrounded by couples. I was invisible. I went three times, always sitting in the top balcony, top row. If I was lucky, and went on a weekday night, not a weekend, I usually had the balcony to myself. That should have been my first clue that the Centre's days were numbered. But you see where I'm going with this, right? Redford and Streisand in love. Me and Sue in love. But the four of us were doomed. Irreconcilable differences. The big flaw in this comparison, I have to admit, is that I could see Sue as the glamorous Redford character, but I was nowhere near the earnest Streisand character. I wasn't in the movie at all, get down to it, but the song was me and Sue. Those damn misty colored memories. Still, it was the end of that movie that kept me coming back. I wanted that ending for me and Sue. Redford and Streisand see each other from across a busy street, each in their own new lives. Their memories bring them together one last time. They are still in love with each other. Roll the credits, cue the song. But here I am, living in the same town as Sue, knowing our paths will never cross. Sue and I had eight years. We were stupid teenagers, then slowly evolving young adults, then we were a former couple, then we were strangers.

I suppose every newspaper has some version of the "Milestones" page. Births and deaths, sure, but I always wondered most about the anniversary announcements. Twenty was no big deal, but somebody could make it special in print. Thirty was noteworthy, but the fifty-year mark was breath-taking. A half century of love, I always hoped, of sitting across a breakfast table and sometimes not even talking, but in love. Was it just inertia? A life together. Always two pictures, then and now, wedding day and fifty years later. I always wondered what that couple saw when they looked at their wedding picture. The future? Themselves in a photo, same pose, fifty years later? Was their fifty years a seamless thread, or severed and tied back together again and again as their relationship had its ups and downs. Fifty years of knots?

APRIL 19, 1995

I made friends in high school, more after Sue and I started dating. Of course, I lost most of them after we split up. They took sides. She won. I even went to my ten-year class reunions, until I didn't. Too many times I was asked "How ya doing, Harry? What ya up to now?" and when I told them that I was a taxi driver you could see their eyes glaze over. But there were still some friends who kept in touch with me because I was a taxi driver. They would go out of their way to call me when they needed a lift. And we would talk about the old days or their current lives, their jobs and children. Their lives progressed. I was merely an audience for them, like a bartender. In time I became a multi-generational bartender. One of my fares was actually the daughter of Natalie Kimmel, a good friend of Sue's, and I would sometimes get bits and pieces of Sue's life from the daughter. Bits and pieces, but I could tell that she was not passing along anything really important about Sue's life. Just bits and pieces she had heard from Natalie. One morning, the daughter had had car trouble and needed a quick lift to her job in the Murrah Building, a few blocks away from the Centre. She was very happy that morning, telling me the big news . . . she was pregnant. It was April 19, 1995. Bits and pieces, two hours after I dropped her off, she and her baby were bits and pieces.

That night was the first time I heard Harry Ducharme on the radio. After I heard the news about the Murrah that morning, I had just kept driving around town, ignoring calls for fares, wishing I knew how to get in touch with Sue because I wanted to be the one who told her about Natalie's daughter, but it was hopeless. I was sure that Sue saw the news like America saw the news, on television. She didn't need me. Day into night, I kept circling. I'm not sure, but I must have passed the Centre a hundred times as I tried to get close to the Murrah. But the entire block was yellow-taped off and shattered glass was all over the nearest streets. Every building close to the Murrah had its windows gouged out.

I turned on the radio.

"Helluva day for me to start this job, my friends. Death and destruction and terror. But I think I can find some lines to put it all in perspective. Not my lines. I'm not that talented. But this has all happened before. Trust me."

Who was this guy? And how could he just . . . dismiss . . . all those people? Natalie's daughter, her baby, everybody else.

"My name is Harry Forster Ducharme."

He was named Harry, just like me?

"I'm not from here. I was born in Iowa. Adopted by Quakers after I was pulled out of a river. My parents are dead. All my people are dead. I was married once. I thought I was going to be a primetime dj, stack up money and buy my own record store. I used to be a drinker." An hour of listening to him, you knew he was lying about being a former drinker. "I have a son, but we don't talk. Husband and father, I was lousy at both. I used to work for NPR, did a lot of stories on *Morning Edition*. Had a future."

Was that the moment I felt a chill in the taxi? My body temperature seemed to drop as I listened to that mesmerizing voice. More than that, I had the feeling that Harry Ducharme was talking directly to me, that I was the only person listening to him that night. I could hear phones ringing in the background. So, I must have been wrong. Others were tuned in, trying to make a connection.

"Not tonight, folks, no time for chatter. Tonight is for grief and poetry. I'll do all the talking. This show is my dime. Until I get canned again. I coulda been a contender, but here I am talking to you, and you only."

He was talking to me.

"My parents died in the ocean, disappeared, on a trip that I had bought for them. A tour boat sank, the other bodies were found, but not my mother and father. I was adopted, but they were the only real parents I ever knew. I was eighteen when they died. I think that's how I want to die. In the ocean. Hold on a second, I need to pull a plug here." The phones stopped ringing in the background. "Now it's just me and you again. So, where was I? Where are you?"

That first night, two years ago, I wanted to call him and offer him a free taxi ride anywhere and anytime. I wanted to meet him. But the only time we would ever be together was that late shift from ten p.m. to two a.m.

"You think today was senseless, and brutal, and tragic. You're sad and angry. But today is not unique. You need distance. From a distance, things are clearer. Everything that happened today will happen again. Death will happen again. Love will happen again. Life will happen again. Where do you want me to start? Dylan Thomas? Go find his poem 'A Refusal to Mourn the Death, by Fire, of a Child in London.' Hell, hold on, let me find my own copy."

And then the air was dead for a full minute, until he returned with a huff and slowly read the poem. Twice, he read it twice.

"Pay attention to that last line. 'After the first death' . . . see, that's the key. There was always a first death, before you were conceived in the mind of God or your mother's womb. 'There is no other.' Nobody really died today. They are still among us."

Ducharme was right. Two years later, I started seeing ghosts.

HARRY MEETS HARRY
APRIL 19, 1997

I thought I was driving with a dead man. I didn't know he was dead for sure, but he was damn quiet. I had been driving by the Centre, the dead downtown theatre, probably a hundred years old, closed for a couple of years, headed for the wrecking ball soon enough. Urban Renewal had plans for gentrified high-rise condos. In the years after Sue and I had gone there, years after I saw *The Way We Were*, I had watched westerns at the Centre, Superfly and Shaft movies, porn, and midnight drug movies.

It was raining. He was standing under the darkened marquee. A tall thin guy. Raincoat too big for him. Wet red hair. He saw me and waved, but his hand never got higher than his chest. I pulled over to the curb and he got in the backseat.

"I need to go home."

I told him that I needed an address. That seemed to stump him. Where was home? He asked me how far a hundred dollars would take him. I've had stranger fares. Lord, the stories I could tell. I've had a lot of the *just drive for a while and I'll know it when I see it* kind of directions. Fair enough, the meter was running anyway. But this old guy seemed like he needed to be cheered up, so I asked him, "A hundred bucks? Depends on whether you want to go in circles or a straight line." I thought I was being funny, but he started crying. I apologized. I meant no harm.

"I don't have an address."

So, there we were, sitting in my taxi, the rain beating on the roof, windshield wipers swishing back and forth, graffiti-covered news racks tipped over at the corner, both of us wanting to go home. Well, my home was one room in a boardinghouse over near the YMCA. Him? Who knew?

"I'm sorry. I'm not sure why I stopped you. Can we just sit here a minute and let me figure this out?"

"No problem," I said. Hell, it was almost midnight. I was officially off duty two hours ago. I was just driving around in the rain, smoking a joint, listening to Harry Ducharme. A minute was all he needed? He could figure it all out in a minute? I was willing to sit there an hour if he could figure it all out. So, we sat there for longer than a minute, neither one of us talking, but at least I had my eyes open. I looked in the rearview mirror. He looked like he had fallen asleep, his head plopped back against the seat. I listened for him breathing, but nada. Thirty years a taxi driver, I've had people fuck in the backseat, punch each other, have babies too soon, puke, and pass out. But I've never had anybody die in my taxi.

"Mister, you okay?"

I reached back and nudged his leg.

"Mister?"

"I remember you."

Okay, whatever I paid for my weed this week, I got a bargain. I can hear dead people talking to me. It's his voice for sure, but he ain't moving, his lips are tight.

"You were a young man. You came to this theatre often, with a beautiful young woman. I envied you. And then by yourself."

"Mister, I think you might have the wrong . . ."

But he was right. I turned back and looked out the windshield. The marquee lights were dark, but the box-office was lit up. Me in a taxi in the rain, with a dead man talking to me.

"Harry is your name, as I recall. But the young woman, I apologize, I do not remember her name."

"Sue, her name was Sue."

I looked in the rearview mirror again. The old guy's eyes were open.

"Look. I'm a little confused here," I said. "Are you okay? I mean, I thought you had, you know, gone away."

"Died, you mean? No, I'm fine. As for being confused, such is life. But I am very tired, for sure. I had intended to simply take a walk, as I usually do every night, but this rain upset that plan."

"So, the question remains. Where would you like to go?"

"Oh, we're already here. This is where I live. Would you like to see my home? Perhaps some of my friends might enjoy meeting you, but don't be offended if they don't appear right away. It is late. They often travel."

"Mister, you said . . . forget it. I'm sorry, but I probably should go . . ."

"My name is Dwight Ferber. Call me Dwight, please. You are Harry Mason. So, Harry, I would be honored to show my home to you."

What the hell, I told myself. It wasn't as if I had anything else to do or anywhere else to go. I killed the engine.

How many times had I been to the Centre? A million? Back when it was a big-deal theatre and I was a kid, and then as a teenager dating Sue. A screen bigger than big. It was Grand Canyon panoramic. And I remembered how gorgeous the inside was, Arabian Nights gorgeous. But I wasn't a kid anymore. The Centre had become a dump, a "blight" according to the City Fathers. I was prepared to be disappointed, but Dwight sure as hell knew how to give a tour. He unlocked the front door and we went into the dark lobby. He pulled a giant flashlight out from under his raincoat and started shooting beams all over the place.

"Most of the power is off, switches pulled in a room backstage. Only the essentials left on. That was Peyton's idea back in the seventies. Trying to save money. He worked hard to keep the costs down. It never made sense to me, but I trusted him."

My eyes followed Dwight's beam of light as it slowly went around the lobby. Looking down at the carpet, I remembered how I had once marveled at how ornate the design was, almost Persian in its swirls and colors. It was still there, but faded and worn thin in spots. I took a deep sniff. How to describe the smell of stale popcorn, rotting carpet fiber, and tobacco smoke? He pointed the flashlight up toward three enormous crystal chandeliers, suddenly lit, dozens of shiny brass arms and flickering light bulbs reflecting light back at us, light bouncing off the walls. I remembered those chandeliers. I remembered Sue gasping when she first saw them, holding my hand. That quick intake of breath and then how she seemed to stop breathing for a long time.

I was standing still as he walked away from me and the chandeliers faded. The flashlight beam arced back toward me and then to the wall to my left, the wall separating the lobby from the auditorium, a wall with three floor-to-ceiling mirrors, encased in gold frames with red velvet bunting on three sides. How many times had I stood in front of one of those mirrors? The last time, with Sue standing beside me. Sue in the past. The night before we broke up. Just as I was about to walk toward one of those mirrors, Dwight switched off the flashlight.

I was in the dark again, or so it seemed at first, but then I saw him standing at the other end of the lobby, dimly illuminated by the light from the glass-topped concession counter. He was waving at me to come to him.

"These cases used to be refrigerated and illuminated, so we had to keep the power going all the time. But the refrigeration unit died years ago and there is only one light still working. You know, some theatres keep a light burning near the stage all the time. Called a "ghost" light. So, I guess this is our own ghost light, in an empty concession case, always on. This is where I first saw you and Sue. I was selling you popcorn. She suggested two straws for the Coca-Cola you bought."

"I'm still sorry, Dwight. I don't remember you."

"That's fine. Nobody else does either. And, besides, you were in love. I was merely an extra in your own movie. I was a nobody. You and Sue were the stars."

"But you live here? Isn't that what you said?"

"I'll show you my room later, but now you have to make a decision. Up or down?"

He pointed the flashlight beam up and I could see the railing of the second level mezzanine. Then the beam swung to the left and right and I could see the top of the wide red-carpeted stairs that began at each end of the lobby and curved up.

"And down?"

"Ah, as you enter the auditorium you begin to walk *down* the aisle, remember? To get to the stage, to get to your seat, you have to walk down. And down is where I live."

He opened the double door to the auditorium, as if an usher, and did a polite half-bow, sweeping his hand toward the dark auditorium.

"Dwight Ferber, are you real?"

I was still stoned.

"That's a good question. I used to get it a lot."

The first thing he did once we were in the auditorium was shine the flashlight toward the stage. I remembered those screen curtains, three of them, and all part of the nightly opening ritual. An organ would have been playing throughout the intermission, but as the overhead lights dimmed, leaving only the tiny star lights shining in the ceiling, you could hear the opening chords of the movie soundtrack begin, usually a familiar studio theme (Twentieth-Century Fox was the best), and the heavy dark first curtain would start to rise like a waterfall going backwards. It always reminded me of how old ships would have raised their sails with ropes and pulleys. As the first curtain cascaded upwards, a second curtain was exposed, a lighter shade but equally as gaudily trimmed as the first curtain, and it would split and slide to the edges, leaving the final curtain of sheer silky transparency. With the final curtain revealed, the film was already on the screen, seen first through that dreamy wave of material. That final curtain would split and the movie itself would appear in perfect focus as the opening credits began. I loved that moment.

But the empty auditorium was different from the empty lobby. We were not alone. As we walked slowly down the aisle, the flashlight beam focused on the immediate few feet in front of us, I thought I saw someone walk across the stage. Footsteps creaking on the old wooden stage. I could hear doors closing, and then I stopped cold behind Dwight. I felt something rub up against my ankle, sliding along for a few seconds. My first thought was that it was a rat, but then I heard a soft purr.

Dwight must have anticipated this.

"Cats, Harry. We have lots of cats here. The one you felt, it is real. Sam likes cats, so we let them come here to live. All of them have names, but I don't know them. But you must agree, we never have to worry about mice."

Knowing there was one cat rubbing my ankle, I soon began to hear other cats scurrying around the auditorium. I couldn't see them, but I felt them. How many? Hundreds? Dozens for sure.

"You'll get used to them, Harry. Everybody does, even though a few of us wish that Sam was less a cat person and more of a . . . well, anything but cats."

"Do I get to meet Sam?"

"In time, Harry, in time. I'm the only permanent resident here. At least, the only one who actually chooses to live here. Everyone else travels, and Sam is in great demand elsewhere. He's not here tonight, but if you wish to come again you might meet him."

Come again? I wasn't sure about that. Hell, I wasn't even sure I was there then. Me and a dead guy, who insisted that he was not dead, and phantom cats in a dark auditorium? Years ago, I had told myself that I wanted to be a writer. I also told myself that I wanted to be a pilot. A drummer in a rock band. Perhaps a fireman. I wanted to be a lot of things, but I ended up being a taxi driver. From day one, Sue said she wanted to be an actress. Everybody else knew it too. Nothing else, always an actress. She told me again after our last date, a movie at the Centre, and then she was gone. If I had become a writer, I could have told *that* story, but nobody would believe a story about invisible cats and a dead man. A dead man who was alive?

We were on the stage, and Dwight was pointing his flashlight down toward the empty seats, a circle of light going slow, as if he were counting each seat. Too slow. I started to worry about my taxi outside, parked at midnight in a bad neighborhood. At this rate, it would take a week to see the entire theatre.

"Dwight, I probably need to go."

"Yes, yes, I know. A lot to absorb the first time. Everybody has that same reaction. But, a few more things and then you can come again tomorrow night. Okay? Just a few basic rules first."

"There are rules? Rules for what? Walking around in the dark? I'm going to wake up later and none of this will have happened. Are there rules for that too?"

"Harry, I want you to be happy here, but you need to know a few things."

"A few? Jesus, Dwight, only a few?"

"Bear with me, please. Just the basics."

The next thing I know, he is pointing the flashlight to a spot at the center of the stage, right up against the first curtain, telling me to stand there. Standing next to me, he pulls the curtain up, then the second curtain, then the sheer curtain, and then he points the flashlight at the screen itself.

"Look closely and tell me what you see."

"I see a screen."

"Look closer."

I was never a detail person, but soon enough two odd things were clear to me. The screen was actually light yellowish-brown, and it was not solid. Even in the small area exposed to me, I could see thousands of tiny pores, tiny dots, each perfectly aligned with the others.

"A hundred years of tobacco smoke will cause that," Dwight said, reading my mind again. "The holes are to let sound come through clearly from the giant speaker horn behind it."

I started to reach out toward the screen when he grabbed my hand.

"That is the first rule, the most important rule. You must never, ever touch the screen. If you touch the screen, the Centre will disappear. Do you understand?" With that, he let go of the curtains and the screen was hidden again.

Did I understand? Of course not. I was willing to write it all off as more of, as I would soon call it, Dwight being Dwight, but we were interrupted by the sound of somebody clapping in the dark auditorium. Before I could speak, Dwight said, "Ignore him."

"Ignore who? Dwight, who the hell am I supposed to ignore?"

All he did was turn and shout at the auditorium, "Harry, go away!"

I kept thinking that this must be the moment that I wake up, that this was obviously a very weird dream, that I was asleep, and I had to wake up.

"Dwight, I'm right here."

He kept staring at the darkness. The clapping continued, and then a shout of *Encore, encore*. He grabbed my hand and said, "Follow me. There's more to see."

I had been on stages before, seen the apparatus required to stage live productions: the scaffolding, the dressing rooms, the costume rooms, the set construction rooms, the orchestra pit. The Centre had all those, plus a screen and sound horn, but it was also obviously different. There was more of everything, more levels, a labyrinth of rooms and doors.

Dwight started by showing me an apartment just off stage. "This is where Peyton lived."

"Peyton's *place*?" Again, prime humor by me which sailed right past him, and I had to finally accept that Dwight Ferber had absolutely no sense of humor.

Even though we only had the flashlight, I could see that the room was immaculate, down to every shirt in the closet being hung exactly two inches apart, every sweater folded and stacked on the shelves overhead.

"Do I get to meet Peyton?"

He ignored the question.

"It's exactly as he left it. All I do is dust it once a week."

Then the flashlight beam swept past three pictures on the wall.

"That's Peyton on the left," Dwight said. "When he was just starting in the business. Then there's him and Cori. And then the three of us, a few weeks before he died."

I stared at the third picture. "Dwight, is that really you?"

"We were very happy then, but he died and Cori went away."

The Dwight in the third picture was a giant, probably three hundred pounds with flaming red hair down to his shoulders. The Dwight beside me was a rail.

He talked to the picture.

"She's coming back, and I'll be here."

The flashlight stayed on the third picture as we stood silent for almost a minute. As we finally turned to leave, the flashlight swept past a door in the corner.

"Another room? Your room?" I asked. Seemed like an innocent question, but Dwight went on the defensive.

"That is private. Peyton's private room. I've never been inside. Cori had. She told me about it. Peyton's private library. I asked Peyton to let me see it, but he refused. All Cori would tell me is that it was the most beautiful room she had ever seen in her life."

"Dwight, Peyton's dead, you told me. Cori's gone. You have the keys to everything. You could go in there anytime you wanted."

"Rule number two, Harry. Peyton's room is private."

Why was I even trying? This was not happening anyway. Screens not to be touched, rooms not to be entered. Rules in a dream?

"I'm sorry, Harry, I'm getting tired. I'm not used to visitors from the outside world. My mind wanders. Let me show you one more thing and then you can go home if you want to, although you are certainly welcome to stay here until the morning. Plenty of rooms."

Leaving Peyton's room, we went through a long hallway to the opposite side of the stage, down some stairs, through some dark hallways, to a giant double door. "I think you'll find this room very interesting," he said.

I was more than interested. I was spellbound. We were in an underground garage with space for probably a dozen cars, but tonight there were only three, and all of them looked like they were parked there in 1940 and had not moved since: a black Cadillac limo, a brown Ford delivery van, and a yellow DeSoto cab, the model with the oversized wheels. Each was spotless.

"Many of the traveling shows had entourages of vehicles, so we used this space for parking."

"Why are these still here?"

"That's a good question. Now, let's continue."

We retraced our path back to the stage. He then went to a small black box and hit a few more switches to turn on the overhead lights and footlights. We were flooded in light, center stage, when the clapping started again. I stared into the dark auditorium but couldn't see anything. Dwight was upset, again.

Encore, encore, again.

"Go to hell, Harry!"

Offstage to the left, a man stepped out of the shadows. He was wearing a long frock coat and dressy shirt that looked like it was straight out of a Broadway musical. He walked toward us, miming the act of clapping. He had a high forehead, thick wavy hair, and piercing eyes. As he got closer, I could have sworn that he winked at me. Nearing us, he extended his hand as if to offer a handshake, but then withdrew it just as I was about to extend mine. Standing next to us, it was obvious that he was much shorter than me, and probably a foot shorter than Dwight. And he had an accent. English was not natural to him.

Dwight, cat got your tongue? They seem to get anything else they want around this place. And aren't you going to introduce me to your new friend?

Dwight was angry.

"Harry Mason, meet Harry . . . Harry Houdini. Trust him at your own peril."

I waited, but neither man spoke. Houdini pointed to the lobby, holding his hand in midair until Dwight huffed, "Enough for tonight."

They both walked me to the lobby, their silence maintained. The rain had stopped. Me? What the hell was I supposed to say? "Nice meeting you guys. We should do this more often." I was pushing sixty. I hadn't been un-stoned in probably a year. I had just spent two hours in a hallucination, tag-teamed by two men. One of them was dead for sure. The other was just weird. It would make a great story, I was sure, if I just had anybody to tell it to.

My taxi was waiting for me. I think it was my taxi. The taxi I had parked had been a fifteen-year-old heap. The taxi in front of me was just off the assembly line. Perhaps all I had needed all these years was a good rain to wash it off? The new un-dented yellow body was polished, almost dazzling under the marquee lights. I just stared at it. I had read somewhere in my past, back when I still read more than the morning paper, something in a short story about *A man with a good car don't need no justification.* I had more than a good car in front of me. I had the Mother of all Taxis. I walked around it, and then again, sliding my fingers across the body. Then, sitting behind the wheel, I was immersed in that new-car smell. The smell of the taxi I had parked two hours earlier would have been enough evidence in court to send me to prison for dealing dope. I vowed to never smoke in my taxi again, ever, but I also knew that I wasn't good at honoring vows. I reached over and opened the glove compartment. The first of a future of contradictions. My bag of weed was still there. It was my taxi. But new.

"Drive safe, Harry."

Drive safe, Harry.

Dwight and Houdini were standing side by side, waving good-bye. For some stupid reason, I just waved back and gave them a thumbs-up. And then I turned the key. The engine started, not with its usual shudder and clank, but with a purr. I was very tired.

I woke up, face down in my pillow. I didn't move. I simply wanted to go back to sleep. It was a dream. It had to have been a dream. I wanted to go back to sleep and back to that dream. But I lived in a zoo. Human animals stomping down the hall to the communal bathroom at the end. I was lucky. My room at least had a toilet and a sink, but a daily shower hadn't been in my routine for years, though I could bathe whenever I went to the Y across the street and took a swim. Swimming laps and driving a taxi, the yin and yang of my life. I should have gotten up and made myself some coffee, gone to the Y, piss the THC out of my system, go find a morning paper, but I lay there with my face down, listening to the parade of flatulence in the hall. Should have, could have, would have . . . I went back to sleep.

Harry Ducharme used to have a call-in format, but he stopped it one night as he lost his mind at the stupidity of a question from one of his listeners. Ducharme was probably drunk all the time, but he was interesting as hell. He would do news commentary, especially about politics and insane people in Florida, play nothing but golden-oldie rock, share Hollywood gossip, read poetry, especially Dickinson, sometimes read entire chapters from books, and generally talked like he was going to kill himself on-air. I loved his show. I missed the call-in exchanges, but I only had myself to blame. I was the one who had asked the stupid question. I wish I hadn't done it. Ask the stupid question. I realized that Ducharme might be the only person who would believe me if I told him what had just happened to me.

"Just when I think this country can't be any more stupid, we start getting crazy about the most powerful man in the free world having a blow job? I mean, at least he's not bombing Cambodia or selling guns to the mullahs in Iran. Those we tolerated. But he lets an intern polish him off, and we discover God? And, Jesus please Jesus, Newt is calling for his resignation. Hamilton and Madison must be weeping in their graves."

Ducharme was on a roll. Me, I just wondered how he kept his job. I wished he did less political commentary and more poetry reading.

You think that is his real name?

I looked in the rearview mirror. Houdini was in the back seat.

You might be Harry Mason for real, might be. Myself, I am Erik Weisz, a Hungarian Jew. I did have an agent named Harry Day in London, but then I discovered that his real name was Ed Levy. The name game. As for myself, I created Harry Houdini, last name from a French magician, first name from Harry Kellar, an American magician. The universe is full of Harrys. Names are like clothes, my young friend. They can be changed at will, for fashion or function. My name is both, of course, but you seem to be a very functional Harry Mason. Your radio friend? Harry Ducharme is not who he says. I would wager that.

"Harry, Erik, whoever, how the hell did you get in my backseat? You're not even real. And when did we become friends?"

I am as real as death. And I am here to protect you.

"You know, I thought Dwight was a bit overwrought, with all that talk about not touching screens and the Centre collapsing, but you're catching up."

Drive me around town, friend, and let me tell you the story of the Centre before Dwight does. His memory is not reliable. He lives there, I only visit, but I have heard his version dozens of times. He gets on stage every night and tells it to a captive audience. I only visit a few times a year. You were lucky to catch me this time, or you would be adrift in his world. He'll tell you about Peyton and Cori, but even he doesn't understand the real reason he lives there.

I looked at the gas gauge. A full tank, a shock to me. Enough to drive to Tulsa and back.

"I'm all ears."

I died on Halloween Day in 1926, early afternoon. I got tired of fighting the pain. How and why I died are irrelevant. Doesn't matter. I'm dead. But I am not a ghost. I spent the last ten years of my life debunking all that supernatural hocus-pocus con game. Do not call me a magician. Magic is supernatural. Everything I did had a rational explanation. I could teach you if I wished. I was also an illusionist, but even illusions can be explained and repeated. They just require an audience who wants to believe that magic and illusions are real. That's where Dwight comes in. He wants to believe. He does believe in magic. He believes in ghosts. I've been around him, off and on, for twenty years, but I have been in the Centre since 1926. The week before I went to Detroit and died, I performed at the Centre, in these very clothes. Perhaps 'perform' might be imprecise in my case. I lectured. I educated the audience about the sham that is spiritualism. If you choose to go back to the Centre again, at Dwight's urging, you will meet the others who "performed" there. They are dead, but they always return on the date they performed. They are allowed to wander away to other venues where they performed, but they are all obligated to return to the Centre on the specific date they originally appeared. It is one of Dwight's "rules," a rule which did not exist before he arrived. Over time, I have seen them return more and more at their own discretion, as I often do. I will admit, I have come to enjoy meeting my fellow performers and artists. Except for the cat-man. I hate cats, and I do miss my own two dogs, but the cat-man ruined any chance for the rest of us to enjoy our own pets. Another of Dwight's rules. Not only are they bound to return to the Centre on the date of their last performance there, the only other places they can visit are venues around the world at which they have performed. It is an absurd rule, of course, and I ignore it. For some reason, the others obey him. Unless they performed for a paying audience in their own homes, they can never go home again, never see the ones they love. For some of them, that is the hell they always feared. But Dwight has created that hell. Thusly, the only home they have left is the stage. They have become their own family. For myself, I sense that Dwight resents it when the others are on other stages. He is not a generous man, Harry. He has been entertaining to observe, but he was always harmless, until he brought you inside tonight. You are the first outsider, young Harry. You are a deviation that has an explanation, but, right now, I am not sure what it is. All I can tell you is that you should not return to the Centre. Dwight has plans for you.

This was too much for me to think about and drive at the same time. I pulled up in front of my boardinghouse. Years ago, I had painted the curb blue and posted a sign: TAXI PARKING ONLY. ENFORCED 24 HOURS. ALL OTHERS TOWED. I almost always had a spot waiting for me. My biggest regret was not finding a covered parking space near my boardinghouse. My new taxi deserved better treatment than my old one had gotten.

Houdini was waiting for me to respond, but I was fighting off fatigue and residual dope. I was no match for him. I needed to sleep. We sat in silence for a long time. He seemed to be in no hurry. But then it hit me, the flaw in his story.

"You say that everybody is trapped in the Centre and only allowed to go to other places where they have performed. One of Dwight's rules, right?" I watched him in the rearview mirror. He smiled and nodded. "But you're here in this taxi with me. You never performed here. So, you're able to go anywhere you wish, but the others can't, right?" Another nod. "How can you then do it? How are you able to break the rules? And you don't believe in ghosts or the supernatural, but you say you are dead, so what are you now if not a ghost?"

Harry, you must pay attention. I explained this to you. You forget who I am. I am more than a magician, more than an illusionist. I am more widely known as "The World's Greatest Escape Artist." No chain, no cuffs, no man, no water coffin can contain me, and certainly not Dwight's rules. As for me being dead but not a ghost . . . perhaps I am an angel. Your angel come down as Harry Houdini.

"I'm beginning to think you're a . . ."

I could not find a word. I looked in the rearview mirror. The backseat was empty.

It was a long time ago. First kisses, first loves, a long time ago. I should have written a book, but I hate sad endings. Sue and I were together for eight years, until we went to the Centre the last time. Of all the things I remember about our past, I cannot remember the name of the movie that night. I remember the theatre, the lobby, the balcony where we sat, her perfume. Was the future already there in that movie as we watched it? Dwight remembered us. I'm sure he would remember the movie too. But even if I understood the past now, saw the clues, it wouldn't change the past. Sue would still be gone, and I'd still be living in a boardinghouse next to the YMCA, talking to ghosts. Houdini told me to never go back to the Centre. To not trust Dwight. But Dwight told me to not trust Houdini.

Lying in bed, looking at a water-stained ceiling, listening to doors slam down the hall, I made a decision. I was going back to the Centre. Any place other than where I was . . . it had to be a better place.

DWIGHT'S STORY

Harry Ducharme was in love with a poet. I had heard variations of that love many times as I drove around late at night. Tonight, he was off the cliff.

"How is it possible for anybody to write a line like 'My Life had stood a Loaded Gun'? Whose mind works like that? I want to go back in time. I want to meet her. Hell, I want to buy her a drink. I want to get her on the phone and ask her a million questions. The world is full of poets who haven't written a single memorable poem. She wrote hundreds. I think I've read most of them on-air. Doesn't mean crap. Nobody listens to me anyway. Tonight is her night. If you don't want to hear more, turn off your damn radio. Wild nights are coming. Funerals in your brain. The blankness of pain. Flies buzzing when you die. Tonight is her night. Tomorrow is Flannery's night. There it is, my ideal threesome. Her and Flannery and me. A Loaded Gun, she wrote. Love as a loaded gun. Life. And pay attention to the last line, about having the power to kill but not the power to die. Who writes like that?"

Your friend Harry seems a bit overwrought tonight.

I was parked outside the Centre. Houdini was in the backseat.

And who is Flannery?

I ignored the question. I could see his face in my rearview mirror. He looked at me looking at him, and then he shook his head.

I am disappointed, Harry. You came back. You seemed like an intelligent man, albeit unfocused. There is nothing for you inside the Centre. But you came back.

"I just had some questions for Dwight, about the last time I was here. Questions you can't answer."

Houdini shrugged.

So be it. I'll accompany you regardless. Be prepared, however. Dwight will perform tonight. You and I will be his audience, perhaps others, although I have heard it many times before. I will give him credit. Unlike some others, Dwight does not change his story over time. But, and this is an important but, remember that consistency is not the same as honesty.

We went inside and sat in the front row. Dwight was alone on center stage, under a spotlight. No podium, no microphone, no papers in his hand, dressed in a baggy gray suit, but no tie.

"My name is Dwight Ferber, and I'm the person whose life you and your friends made miserable in high school. You were slim and muscular. I was six foot six and weighed 360 pounds. You were blond. My hair looked like a carrot-colored Afro. You were graceful or athletic. I was neither. I was named after my grandfather, who had won the Medal of Honor in 1918. You nicknamed me Dyke Furball when I was a sophomore, the same year my grandfather died. The Centre had been built in 1904 as a stage for vaudeville and dramas and public lectures, but was converted to a movie theatre in the Twenties. Two thousand seats, two balconies, a dozen chandeliers, and a stage that W.C. Fields and Will Rogers had juggled and jumped rope on. By the time that Peyton appeared, the Centre would not maintain its glory much longer. But I don't blame him. I was hired in 1950. I started as an usher, then worked the concession counter, and then I was made assistant manager. I assumed I would be manager when my boss retired. He did not retire. He was fired by the out-of-town owners. No explanation. A mystery. I came to work one day and met my new boss."

"Peyton Davis was twenty years old. I was forty. From that first day, the entire staff called him Mr. Davis. To this day, I still do not know where he came from, why he got the job over me. Another mystery. But it was only after he was made manager that I started seeing any of you. Not a lot of you, not often, but late at night when the doors were locked. I was terrified at first, and I told him, but he told me to ignore all of you, to do my job, to leave you alone. It was none of my business."

"The more I knew him, the more I understood why everyone called him Mister. He was already an old man who commanded respect. A movie theatre might be a small pond, but I could see Peyton giving orders to an army, not just a staff of fifteen people making minimum wage. He had those qualities that every great leader had: intelligence, charisma, courage, and the ability to bluff. The first time it was obvious, how different he was? He was about to get mugged in the lobby. The Centre was packed with stoned teenagers watching a midnight showing of *Reefer Madness*. Contact highs were cheap that night, but the stoned majority had a small hostile faction which had inhaled red and green pills as well as smoke."

"Seeing Peyton that night, I also saw how the moment was balanced between order and chaos. He was having two debates at once. To his right were three turbaned India Indians demanding their money back while encouraging the overhead mezzanine crowd to ask for theirs as well. To his left was the projectionist Mac, who had come out of his booth to tell Peyton that he was not going to stay past 1:30 a.m. because it wasn't in his contract. It was 1:15. I had stepped up behind Peyton and started glaring at the Indians. Usually, until I opened my mouth, I could intimidate most people. For the next five minutes, I did not say a word. Peyton calmly offered them a refund. But the Indians wanted it then and there. Peyton offered them double their money back. No deal. While that was going on, Mac interrupted, threatening to close down early. Peyton told him to get back in the booth . . . period . . . and then turned back to the Indians. They backed down."

"He was always here, surrounded by the hired help who ranged in age from thirteen to seventy-one. He knew the youngest girl had lied about her age when she filled out her application. But he also knew she desperately needed the money. The old man was a widower and wanted a clean, well-lighted place to spend his evenings. That's how Peyton explained it to me. A clean well-lighted place, from a book in his private library."

"Within a year, I had moved into the Centre with Peyton. He fixed up a storage room below the stage. In addition to my assistant manager work, I did maintenance and cleaning after the theatre closed. It was soon like living in the world's biggest haunted house. Peyton had his moods, those moments I would catch him just staring at something in his mind. Those moods when all of us knew it was best to simply let him be alone. Late at night, he would walk around in the dark, talking to himself."

"Cori? I found her in the Ladies restroom at midnight. She was unconscious and bleeding out her nose. We were showing *Zabriskie Point* and had another packed house. There must have been a hundred Oklahoma hippies who had stepped over and around her before I came in on my regular cleaning circuit. I thought she was dead, and my first thought was to run for Peyton. But then I knelt down and felt her neck. It was hot. I was holding her hand when he found us a minute later. He told me that we had to get her out of the building. I didn't understand. He picked her up himself, not waiting for me, telling me that the police had told him a week ago that if they got any more complaints about drugs or fights, they would shut the place down. Cori on the street was the City's problem, not the Centre's."

"A week later I walked into his office and found him holding her hand. He had given her a job. Her name was Cori Davis. He was Peyton Davis. He told me later that her name had to mean something in his life, but he was not sure, yet, what that was. In his world, names were symbols of something. Their same last name? That had to mean something."

"He eventually told me that those midnight movies were his operation, not the company's that owned the theatre. The main office was in Dallas, and the owners left him alone because they trusted him. He had gotten his bosses to lease the Centre to a local head shop called the Oklahoma Starship. The company got a flat five hundred a week and the Starship paid all the operating expenses: film, labor, cleaning, and advertising. The company was primarily interested in the Centre as a real estate investment and was using it as a tax write-off until Urban Renewal gave them a thousand percent return on their original investment. In the meantime, it got a hassle-free five hundred a week. Starship got any profit or absorbed any loss. But there was seldom a loss, and the profit usually averaged almost a thousand dollars for a four-hour operation."

"Oklahoma Starship existed only on paper; the head shop was in Peyton's head. The profit went straight to him. If the police had shut him down, Peyton would have lost almost fifty thousand tax free dollars a year. His manager's salary was only sixteen thousand. The money? Each employee got a regular check from the company, and then an envelope with cash from Peyton."

"As he told me about the Centre's past and future, I knew that Peyton was a crazy. Cori was the only sane one, but sanity was not enough to save us."

He has never used that word before, to describe Peyton. Crazy. Interesting, a minor deviation from his story. Perhaps because you are in the audience, the only living person to ever hear it? Do the living deserve the truth more than the dead? Harry, Dwight is the crazy one, for sure. Don't become him. That is what he wants, for you to become him.

A man wearing a cowboy hat was sitting next to Houdini. Next to him was a man dressed like a clown.

I whispered, "Who are the guys next to you?"

He looked to his right and then back at me. *I have no idea who the clown is. Probably part of an act that never made it big, but he is always here. The guy in the hat? Harry, I am disappointed in you. Were you not born and raised in this territory? Have you never taken a passenger to your airport? Have you never met a man you did not like?*

I looked again. The man in the cowboy hat leaned forward and winked at me, mouthing the words *talk to you later*. I was looking at Will Rogers.

"Cori had lousy judgment about men. She had come here that night to get her boyfriend, and she found him in the girls' restroom trading hash for sex in the corner stall. According to her, the next thing she remembered was waking up in the emergency room. That was the trait she shared with Peyton: self-delusion, altering the past to live in the present."

He says they were deluded, self-deluded. His failure to include himself is telling. And the bigger problem? We all knew Peyton. He was a lot of things, but far from deluded. Dwight? He has never wondered why he never saw us until Peyton arrived. As for Peyton talking to himself, that's another mystery, because he never talked to us.

"She lived at the downtown YWCA and was the happiest person I had ever known, but I never thought she was justified. It didn't take her long at the Centre to realize that if she wanted Peyton then she had to adopt me. I was his ghost and his shadow. I knew they were seeing each other away from the theatre. He got her enrolled at OU and helped her with her courses. I knew all this, but nobody else on the staff believed me. At work, they were almost too professional. Peyton's formality did not surprise me, but she acted too unnatural around him, too much yessir and nossir. It wasn't like her at all, but it fooled most everybody else. So, life with Peyton and Cori began, and I started seeing scenes and hearing music, wondering if I could ever be in love like them."

I was thinking about Sue. I was thinking about all the times she and I had gone to the outskirts of the Will Rogers Airport, parked my car, spread a blanket on the ground, and lay there watching the planes take off and land, talking about our future, kissing, touching, floating. It's the floating part that comes back to me when I swim at the Y. I close my eyes and float in the water, and I think of Sue, about the night she and I had first had sex, how awkward and unsatisfying it must have been for her. After all that time we had waited. But I also remembered what she said. "Well, at least we got that out of the way." Within a few months, we were doing it almost every night.

More people were sitting around us. Dozens, but, in the dark, it was impossible to know who they were. I glanced back at the man next to Houdini. Will Rogers was still there.

"Why couldn't it last? After Peyton died, I had an explanation, but Cori said I was 'over-explaining' and trying to turn them into a fairy tale. But I was right, I knew it. They should have never left the Centre. They had been going together for almost two years when Peyton asked her to move in with us, to move out of the YWCA and into the Centre. I was there when he made his proposal. I was there at the beginning of the end. I was the only one who saw it coming.'

"Cori did not want to live at the Centre; she wanted a home of her own. By then I had figured out what both of them actually wanted. The sticks and stones of a house were not the home that Cori wanted. She wanted to be her mother, and she wanted Peyton to be her father. Her parents had been the ideal couple. Even I truly believed they were exceptional, and Cori had grown up to her seventeenth birthday in a world as safe as a mother's womb. On that birthday, both her parents died in a car crash. When Peyton hired her, she was pushing thirty. She wanted to get married; Peyton was her chance to go back to the past."

"Cori turned down his proposal to move into the Centre, and I could see that he was surprised. Then she told him about a house they could rent only twelve blocks away. Peyton looked at me, and I could see his mind trying to imagine consequences, trying to control the future."

"Cori couldn't see the change at first, but I could. When she saw it, it was too late. He spent more and more time away from the theatre, sometimes letting me manage the midnight movies by myself. I joked about me being his 'cruise control,' but he didn't laugh. Cori was not the type to nag, or demand his attention, but she wanted him to relax and slow down."

"She was convinced that if they had each other, then everything else would just naturally fall into place. But Peyton had grown up with a rigid version of the future. Someone like Cori would come along, he had told me even before he met her, and that girl would be the culmination of a life. It had always been his vision that everything else would be in place before he met a Cori Davis. In its most basic form, I guess Cori looked at Peyton as a means to an end; Peyton looked at her as an end. Two rational people could have worked out that distinction. Sometimes he would show up late at night and we would go over the books or watch some tv, and Cori's name would never be mentioned. Other times, he would say the strangest things, wondering if Cori really loved him."

"For the nine months they lived together, Peyton lost more weight. So did I, but I did it intentionally. I had kept telling myself that I was tired of being everyone's favorite fat troll. The day Peyton died, I weighed 210 pounds. He weighed 140."

A common mistake, Harry, he thinks that life is a series of train cars. He thinks that we can merely detach a car from our past, lighten the load, leave it behind, and keep moving forward. My lesson to you, young man, is simple. Add a stronger engine to your train. The weight is always there, more as you get older, so you need to grow stronger as well. As for you, pay attention and note the difference between the facts that he seems to present, versus the subtle interpretation of those facts. If the facts cannot be verified, then all interpretations should be set aside.

"Peyton and I both had the same respect for Fate; that was the subject of our earliest conversations. How I happened to be standing behind him that smoky night with Mac and the Indians. How Cori happened to show up hot and bleeding. In the beginning, we disagreed about how life would eventually turn out. Peyton was convinced that adversity was merely a series of hoops to jump through before you finally, inevitably, through self-determination, achieved that nebulous something that life always had in store for you anyway. Peyton thought he and Fate were partners."

"I want you to think about Fate because how could anything but the cruelest of Fates explain why Cori got pregnant. She did not plan it, even Peyton admitted that. She had been taking birth control pills for years. She told me first, and I knew it was the end."

"A few hours before he died, Peyton asked me what I thought of him and Cori. I had thought about it plenty, a long time, and had known how I felt for years. So, I was serious when I told him. I told him it was like watching a movie, standing next to his blue Camaro as he was about to leave. Every scene blocked out and acted like they had already picked up their Oscars. I even hear the music. Not a line wasted. A great script and every scene a surprise even though it was inevitable. His last words to me? 'A movie. I like that. Get me a copy of the script, will you. I might demand a rewrite.'

"Then he drove off. Drove down a country road toward a bridge that had been closed for years because it had no center section. According to the newspaper accounts, vandals had evidently removed the barriers that had been blocking the road as well as all the warning signs. Peyton Davis, age twenty-five, was the innocent victim of a misguided and malicious prank. It was late, it was dark, he was probably driving too fast to see the gaping hole in front of him. The blue Camaro fell a hundred feet into a red clay ravine."

"Being a thorough and well-organized individual, Peyton had a hundred-thousand-dollar life insurance policy. Because it was obviously an accident, Prudential honored the double indemnity clause. Cori Davis was the only beneficiary. I knew that Peyton had committed suicide. I knew because, the night before he died, he and I had stood on that bridge and talked about Cori. We had dropped rocks over the side and timed how long it took to them to hit bottom. He didn't tell me what he was planning, but it made perfect sense when I heard the news. Prudential would not pay for a suicide; Cori didn't even get a good-bye. I knew it was supposed to be a secret between him and me. But, once again, I was wrong. At her baby's christening, Cori laughed and shook her head when I said it was too bad about the accident and how Peyton would have liked to be there. Peyton didn't want to be there, she said, or else he wouldn't have killed himself. He knew that bridge was cracked open. The first time they had ever had sex was when they parked on that bridge. It was one of their private jokes, and they went back there lots of times."

"I kept looking at the baby, looking for signs of Peyton. Then she showed me how much more she understood him than I did. She told me how she felt after I told her that Peyton was dead. She hated him. She forgave him. And she loved him. And then she tried to imagine what was going through his mind for those last few minutes. He would have been very methodical, we both knew, probably even wipe his own fingerprints off the signs. Then he would have walked out to the center of that bridge and looked down and stared. Then he would have leaned on the railing and he would have tried to imagine how she and I would react when we heard the news. That part we could imagine. But the part that would always be his secret, she told me, was that two or three seconds he was in the car, headlights shooting out looking for something, that three seconds he was falling to earth."

Dwight stopped. I thought he was through, but then it hit me that he was having some sort of flashback. He was trying to hold on to that moment with Cori.

"Cori went to school again, and she eventually married one of her teachers. I stayed here. I saw her for the last time years ago, right before she moved with her husband to his new job in California. Her son is surely grown now, and I would love to see him and her again, but I understand why she stays away from this place now. Too many ghosts."

"Too many ghosts" was ironic at least, and even possibly funny, although I knew that Dwight wasn't a man who told jokes intentionally.

Houdini was oddly quiet. He had said he had heard the story many times, he had mocked it to me, but, when Dwight finished, I could have sworn that I heard Houdini whisper, *Encore, encore.* Dwight left the stage, and his small audience got smaller. I looked up at the ceiling, all those tiny stars still shining.

The sad part, my young friend? It was all avoidable. Assuming that Dwight is telling the truth, just for the sake of debate here, then science would have saved Peyton. Although we were not familiar with the exact problem in my time, in my travels and research after my death, I now know how debilitating it can be to suffer from acute depression. Peyton was ill. He needed help. Doctors would have diagnosed him immediately. Medication could have saved him. Cori can be excused. She was not intelligent enough to recognize the problem. It was Dwight who failed him. Dwight should have seen the problem. For all of his posturing, Dwight is an intelligent man. The science was out there. Dwight will not admit it, but he was complicit in his friend's death. Of course, this is only my interpretation. But I would urge you to consider the obvious flaw in his version of history.

"Which is?"

It will hit you soon enough, Harry. I hope. Soon enough for you to go away and save yourself. The difference between fact and fiction. Dwight is a storyteller. If he is your only source of information about this place, you must tread slowly. All his stories about Peyton were from a time when the Centre was still showing movies. Myself and my ghost companions were seldom here, and, when we were, Peyton ignored us, as if there were greater mysteries than us to behold. All the stories from Dwight about Peyton, the time with Cori . . . he is the only witness. Then, after Peyton was gone, Dwight decided to make up all the rules.

Houdini was himself again. Me, I wanted to go find Dwight and ask him what movie was showing when he saw Sue and me. The stage was almost completely dark when I heard cats running down the aisles and then up the side steps to the stage, their paws thumping like little drums as they hit the wooden stage. Houdini huffed.

Only one show a night, Harry. If you're free, tomorrow might be interesting. I won't be here. The cats are a sign that Sam is getting closer. I hate cats.

THE SOONER SAGE

On a good day, I used to say, I didn't think about Sue. I didn't have a lot of good days. Going back to the Centre changed all that. Thinking about her was good again. Every night there, I thought about her, so every night at the Centre was a good night. I wished she could have gone with me. If for no other reason, she would be thrilled to meet the ghosts of famous people who appeared and disappeared. I'm pretty sure she wouldn't like Houdini, but Will Rogers would have charmed her.

Harry Mason, come up here and let's talk.

I had seen films of him many times. Old black-and-white movies and archived newsreels. I had seen old film of Houdini too, but his ghost and his film history were consistent. Rogers's ghost was a surprise to me. As he twirled his rope onstage, he actually seemed alive. Something about the motion of his arms, the easy flick of a wrist, all done while he was talking, it was all much more alive and natural than on film. He was twirling a rope over his head and then let it fly offstage. He had lassoed a straight-back wooden chair and dragged it on stage at the same time he doffed his hat and waved at me. Like he had done it a thousand times.

Don't make me rope you up here. I can do it if I have to. As you recall, that's how I got my start in the business. I was at a rodeo and a bull sorta went crazy and jumped in the stands. I roped him. I'm betting that you'd be a lot easier than a crazy bull.

I didn't recall anything like that. I read a book of his quotes once. I liked those, especially about politics, but the only thing that I recalled vividly about him was how he died. Remember, I was going to be a pilot. I was justifiably obsessed with famous plane crashes. The first time Sue and I had gone to the Will Rogers Airport, I told her the story of his death. "You're shitting me," she said. "You think that naming an airport after him might not be the most appropriate tribute?" I had laughed, and said, "I'll ask him what he thinks the next time I see him."

As I sat in the chair on the stage, I remembered that time with her, but somehow it didn't seem like a good question at that particular moment. In the past week, I had gotten past skepticism. I was in a world of dead people. No big deal. This particular dead man had an airport, a turnpike, and hundreds of other places named after him. I doubted that my name would show up anywhere except a tombstone, if I was lucky. I wondered how many places or things had been named after Houdini. How is anybody remembered? It dawned on me that a dead Houdini was the type to actually keep track of his legacies. I had a lot of questions for Will Rogers, but where to begin? He was now twirling two ropes at the same time, performing from his past.

So, I'm asked if I'll do a joint debate with my opponents in this here campaign. You know me. I'm running for president as the bunkless candidate of the Anti-Bunk Party. A joint debate with me and the Iowa icon Hoover and Governor Smith from the Empire State? Sure, any joint you can name. Can I appeal to the common man of America? Heck, you can't get any commoner than I can. Farmers, the salt of the American earth farmers? Those commoners? They need a punch in the jaw if they believe either of the parties cares a damn about them after the election. And you wanna know what really stumps me? Hoover is from the corn capital of the world, but I am supposed to be the cornpone candidate?

Hoover and Smith? I was trying to remember the year.

That line about every election expressing the will of the people, how they have 'spoken.' Hookum. Of all the bunk handed out during a campaign the biggest one of all is to try and compliment the knowledge of the voter.

He lassoed another chair from offstage and pulled it close to mine. He turned it around, the straight back facing me, straddled the seat, looked at me, took his forefinger and pushed the brim of his hat up, and then, with a flourish, he pulled a wad of gum out of his mouth and planted it on the top of his chair.

Now, partner, what's on your mind?

I had a list. I had a list for everyone I had already met and was to meet. Strange, how meeting ghosts will focus your mind. I should have stuck to my list, but out of the damn blue I blurted out, "How does it feel to be dead?"

An unseen audience erupted in boos and hoots and whistles. Shouts of *You'll find out soon enough* and *Go to hell* and *Who invited you?* and *Go away*. And then feet stomping, or at least I thought it was feet stomping. Paper cups and popcorn boxes came flying out of the dark and landed all around me on stage. Rogers had not moved. He just kept smiling at me as we both heard the sound of one person clapping, one voice shouting *Encore, encore*. Houdini had lied to me about skipping tonight. He was in the audience.

Rogers kept smiling. *Tough crowd, partner. You might want to polish your material.* With that, he started twirling again. *When I die, I want to die like my grandfather who died peacefully in his sleep. Not screaming like all the passengers in his car. Then again, the only difference between death and taxes is that death doesn't get worse every time Congress meets.*

Houdini shouted from the dark, *Tell him about the dogs.*

Rogers stopped smiling at me. He dropped his lasso and turned toward the dark auditorium. *If there are no dogs in heaven, then, when I die, I want to go where they went. That what you mean, Harry? But you keep making the same mistake, my trickster friend. This ain't heaven. It's an old theatre full of old ghosts. Heaven? We'll know it when we get there. Til then, if you got a problem with all the cats, take it up with Sam, and butt outta my act.*

The dead audience erupted in applause and cheers as he finished. At that exact moment a herd of cats lumbered across the stage, entering stage left and exiting stage right. More cheers from the crowd. Rogers waved toward the dark, motioning for everyone to be quiet. Then he turned back toward me, his smile slowly disappearing, replaced by an expression on his face that might have been curiosity, might have been sadness. I wasn't sure.

The cats don't bother me. Sam loves cats. Sam was here before me or Houdini or Mae or all the people nobody remembers, before Lenny or that singer with your name. Fact is, he was the very first one here. He was the opening act. In life and in death. When this place opened in 1904, he was here that night. He must have been lonely in the beginning, until others started dying and showing up. But he had the cats. Real cats, not ghost cats. But those cats died, and now we have live cats and ghost cats. Running all over the place. No, the cats don't bother me. They're a comfort for Sam. Why should we begrudge that?

He was talking very softly, as if the audience had disappeared, as if it was just him and me on stage.

You asked how it feels to be dead, right?

I nodded.

It took a while, but I'm fine now. You see, partner, there are two kinds of dead people. Those who were prepared for it, and those who are surprised, like I was. You live long enough, your body turns to a withered turnip over time, your bones ache, you don't sleep at night, and maybe you get sick and know the end is close. You're prepared for the inevitability. Sometimes you wish it would happen sooner. Know what I mean? You close your eyes, you wake up dead. After that it's all negotiation.

"And you . . ."

Been negotiating a long time. You gotta remember. I was fifty-five when I died. I felt terrific, assumed I had another twenty years of fun to go. Roping and riding and meeting Popes and Kings and Presidents. And then I had ten seconds to go from alive to dead. I was a bit confused, you might say. There was trouble right after we took off, but Wiley said he had everything under control. He was wrong. My heart was pounding, but I just figured I'd have a great story to tell when we landed. You remember what Cori said about Peyton, the thing she couldn't imagine?

I blinked, trying to remember.

Something about him having 'two or three seconds he was in the car, headlights shooting out looking for something, that two seconds he was falling to earth.' Me, I sorta think those were Dwight's words, put in her mouth by his memory, not always reliable, as you know or will learn, but I'm glad he did. I've heard the story lots of times. That's my favorite part. Peyton had three seconds. I had ten. Peyton was lucky. He wanted to die. When it hit me, the absolute certainty that I was about to die? I was screaming like a baby, no time for profound last words, and then everything went black. It was August 15th, 1935. I woke up here on September 22. Dwight's rules, or so he said. I had to be here on the anniversary of my last appearance on the Centre stage. I was here in 1928, September 22. When Dwight started making rules, after Peyton died, I was supposed to come back on that date every year, but I come back more and more because, despite Houdini, I like a lot of people who are here with me. Yep, I know, I said that I never met a man I didn't like. But then I met Houdini. Stick around, partner, you might meet a lot of people you like.

He was smiling again. Then he unstuck the wad of gum off the top of his chair and put it back in his mouth. I had only asked one question. I had more, but then I remembered Sue and me on a blanket at the airport.

"How do you feel about having the Oklahoma City airport named after you?"

There's an airport named after me? Seriously?

"Yep, and another named after Wiley Post."

He took in a deep ghost breath, paused to chew his gum, and exhaled.

I loved flying. Used to catch rides on mail planes all the time. It was great fun, looking down at Earth from a couple of thousand feet in the air. An airport named after me? I'm actually sort of honored, especially since it's here in my home state. Wiley would be thrilled. Damn shame about some of Dwight's rules. Unless you appeared on this stage, you can't return. Wiley was never here. I'd like to see him again, if for no other reason to ask him what the hell went wrong in Alaska. An airport named after me? I'll be damned.

"My girlfriend thought it was too much irony."

Sure, right? Bring her with you some night. I'd like to meet her.

I thought about her on stage with me at the Centre, meeting Rogers and the others. It was a good thought. But she and I were a million miles apart.

Give it some thought. Lemme know ahead of time. I'll make sure that everyone is on their best behavior, if that is ever possible. Regardless, you just make sure you are here in two weeks, June 1st. That's the big night of the year for us. Almost everyone will be here.

"The big night?"

Just be here, Harry Mason. I promise, you won't forget it.

HARRY FLOATS AS HARRY TALKS

You know how many times they thought I was going to drown?

I was floating at the Y. Houdini was standing near the edge of the pool, wearing some sort of old-fashioned man's swimsuit, a one-piece that included a sleeveless top. The thing I noticed immediately? Houdini was a mass of muscles, buff shoulders and biceps, and thighs that projected power. I wasn't really surprised to see him, but I was confused by his outfit.

"I thought you told me that, when you came back, all of you had to wear what you wearing at the Centre. You weren't wearing a swimsuit before."

Harry, you must pay attention. I said we must wear what we wore the last time we were on a particular stage. I wore a formal suit at the Centre, but I wore a swim suit many times on other stages. I also told you that Dwight does not make the rules for me. I can wear what I wish anywhere, as long as I wore it sometime on stage in my past. And, to remind you, I can go anywhere I wish, unlike the others.

"You coming in for a swim tonight?"

No, young Harry, I am here to clarify a few things for you, since you evidently are not going to heed my advice to avoid Dwight and his puppet show. I listened to your conversation with Will and realized that he was a good example of the flaw in Dwight's production.

I was floating on my back, the water and me almost motionless.

You must understand that all of his puppets are trapped in their past lives. Their memories and knowledge ceased at their deaths. Sam was the first, so he knows the least about all the others who followed him. When they met at the Centre, they were strangers to him, but they all knew who he was. Your new friend Will does not know anybody who performed on that stage after his death. Your singer friend, named Harry like you, was one of the last to appear on that stage, so he knows more about the others than they know of him. Indeed, he might seem to be an alien to them. And then . . .

"My singer friend named Harry? None of my friends are singers."

Later, Harry, later. He'll be there soon enough. Now, please do not interrupt me. And, for the record, from my research about you, I am not sure you have any friends, Harry's or not. Now . . . as . . . I . . . was . . . saying. All the people at the Centre only know what they lived. But I have been visiting long enough to see a distinct pattern. A community is evolving. With so many people who never heard of each other now intermittently meeting at the Centre, they, as strangers do, start to talk about their own lives, and thus they are no longer strangers. You see the obvious problem, of course, correct? It is human nature to lie about one's self. Myself, I know more about everybody else than they do about me. I am not under Dwight's spell. I can study history beyond my own life as I travel from place to place and time to time. But, this evolving community has only itself. Friendships are formed, and for some reason they often choose to come back here even on dates other than when they appeared.

"Will said something about being there on June 1st. It was a big night. What did he mean?"

Houdini, who had been orating at the edge of the pool of as if he was on a stage, jerked his head around and looked down at me in the water, staring, but he ignored my question.

Friendships are important, Harry. Perhaps they grow from a mutual experience? You live in a boardinghouse. So did I, as a child back on East 79th in New York City. You have had a great true love from your youth, as did I. I married Wilhelmina Beatrice Rahner when I was twenty. Bess was but eighteen. We were married until I died. Perhaps we could be friends, Harry, having both experienced true young love? By any standard, Will and I ought to be friends. We both performed on stage. We were both in films. Most importantly, we both loved flying. Did you know that I was the first man to pilot an airplane in

Australia? I was also in a plane crash. I survived, but I experienced the fear of death then as I never experienced it in my performances. I understand Will's terror. I was there, but I lived. Will and I should be friends now, but he shuns me and bonds with his nemesis, the cat man.

Houdini was raising his voice again. I let my ears slip just below the water line as I floated on my back, my eyes closed. Floating in silence, seeing nothing, I was thinking about cats and Will and June the First. But then I was thinking about nothing at all, as if I had gone to sleep. When I opened my eyes, I looked up to see Houdini again, wrapped in a straitjacket, blindfolded and gagged. He took two steps forward, fell into the pool, and disappeared.

Houdini was wrong about me not having friends. The radio Harry was drunk. The taxi Harry was stoned. We had to be the same person, our own best friend.

I've listened to Ducharme every Monday through Friday night since April of 1995. I wished I had not pissed him off with a certain phone call a year ago. I asked him about a song, wondering if he had ever heard it, and he hung up on me. I still wanted to be friends with him. I assume we would reconcile, as good friends do. Besides, I wanted to tell him about the Centre and its ghosts. He might be, I was sure, the only person who wouldn't think I was crazy.

THE CHANGEOVER

Dwight met me in the lobby, waving as I came through the door.

"Harry, I have some exciting news. I have a parking place for you."

He lived in a theatre of ghosts and *that* was exciting news to him? He walked past me, motioning for me to follow him, through the front door, and then he hopped in the front seat of my taxi. He *was* excited. He told me to drive around to the other side of the Centre. As soon as we got there, I was confused again. I saw a door with a window on each side. Did he mean that I could park in front of it, but still on the street, a street that had signs saying "No Parking Anytime"? I parked, leaving my flashers on, and he opened the door and waved me in. I was still confused. It was a large, empty space. Dwight should have been a real estate agent.

"Plenty of space here. Used to be a clothes-cleaning shop in the Thirties. Did a lot of work for us in the old days. We can put some shelves along those walls and you can store taxi stuff on them. And the best thing is that this door," pointing to his left. "It leads back into the theatre, so you can park and come inside."

"Dwight, I drive a taxi, not a toy taxi. You going to shrink it every time I want to get through the front door and park here?"

"Harry, I'm not a magician. Shrinking cars is magic. No, I'm a building manager. If you like this space, I can get contractors to knock out the front wall and install a sliding garage door. Might take a week, but it's not a problem. You just tell me when you want to move in."

"Move into a garage?"

"No, no, move into the Centre. I have lots of rooms I could fix up for you. In fact, I was going to show you one of them when I give you a tour of the upstairs. But you will still need a safe space to park your taxi."

"Dwight, I'm not moving into the Centre. The place I live in now might be a dump, but it is close to the Y and I like to swim every day."

I could tell he was surprised that I turned him down. He was also concentrating.

"A swimming pool." Murmuring to himself. "A swimming pool."

But then he perked up.

"Okay, my offer still stands. I'm going to have the garage door installed regardless. You just think about my offer, and I will think about a swimming pool."

"See that spot over there? I was beat up there when I tried to quiet some teenagers down. Peyton told me to ignore them, but I ignored him."

We were on the second-level mezzanine. More red carpet, more gold trim on the walls, but only one big mirror. There was also a small concession stand. I remembered it. Sold only popcorn and drinks, no candy. Two sets of doors led into the first balcony, where Sue and I always sat, up in the top row of seats, with nobody behind us, so we could make-out anytime we wished, which was always.

"But here is what I wanted to show you. This used to be my own private office, but I've cleared it out for you. The best thing? It has a window. You can see the street, the park, the Civic Center, the County Attorney's office. You can even see the jail. I remember how on some nights you could even hear the prisoners yelling through the barred windows. Peyton even hired a few of them after they were released. They turned out to be good people."

The door to the old office was thick translucent glass framed in metal. I was surprised. The office space was actually two rooms, separated by a sliding door.

"Lots of space, Harry. I'm thinking that I can convert this side room into your own private bathroom. You would have your own shower. Sorry, no kitchen, but lots of places to eat within walking distance."

"Dwight, . . ."

"Just think about it, Harry. Give it some thought. Rent-free, private garage and private bathroom. Just think about it."

I was thinking about Houdini warning me about Dwight, but I was also thinking about how Houdini seemed less and less reliable. And that private shower was tempting.

"Now, let's go to the top of the Centre."

He led me to a curtain at the other end of the mezzanine. I thought it covered a window, but Dwight pulled it aside to reveal a door. He unlocked it, opened it, waved me in, and then locked it before we ascended a dark stairway to another door that also had to be unlocked to enter.

We were in the projection room. We were not alone.

"Harry, meet Mac Duncan. He's in charge here. He's the guy who keeps the picture on the screen. I'm not sure if this room is the heart or the brain of the Centre, but Mac runs the show."

Mac was short and surly. In the dim room, it was hard to tell much else about him.

"You my replacement?" he snorted out. "You a scab? Well, fuck you. I know that Ferb has been trying to get rid of me for years, but I got a contract. The union will make your life miserable, you filthy scab. This booth is my territory, and Ferb knows that I've planted bugs in all this equipment. You push me out, it will take a year for scabs like you to get it running again."

I looked at Dwight, who just shrugged.

"You want this job, sonny scab boy. You might want to consider that Ferb is gonna make you carry the goddam film cans upstairs. I got a union contract. I don't carry cans. You know how much those fuckers weight? You consider a lifetime of carrying them from the front door, up all those stairs, and then back down again when the run is over. I got a contract. I do not carry cans. You want this job, you better get in shape. Carrying film cans will bust your balls."

I had an obvious question as I introduced myself. I had stepped closer, close enough to see that Mac Duncan was a very very old man, old without a wrinkle.

"Hello, Mr. Duncan, I'm Harry Mason. I'm just a taxi driver. Dwight is giving me a tour of the building. I absolutely swear that I'm not going to replace you. I used to come here every week when I was younger. Seeing the movies was magic. What you do here is magic. I can't replace you, but I am wondering . . . are you a ghost?"

"That's a good question, Harry boy. I wish I knew the answer. All I know for sure is that I'm gonna have to be stinking dead before Ferb gets rid of me. I got a union contract."

Another good question. The Centre was full of good questions. I looked at Duncan again. He was almost in a crouch, his fists clenched, like he was about to start throwing punches. My next question was evidently the key to Mac's heart.

"Would you show me how you do it?

Duncan unclenched his fists.

"Do what?"

"How do you put the movie on the screen?"

He blinked, and then he closed one eye and studied me, as if I was trying to trick him, as if I was, indeed, a scab who was asking him to train his replacement. A few seconds, and then his expression changed to that of a man who was just asked if he wanted his million-dollar lottery winnings in cash or a check. I looked around for Dwight, but he was gone.

"Step aside, taxi boy, and watch a master."

All that magic I had experienced when I was in the audience? Mac showed me the craft.

"First thing, you and your girlfriend are in a seat, probably smooching each other . . . I'm all for that . . . and you've been listening to that organ . . . and I've been rewinding old reels or splicing some clips here and there . . . I'm always working, taxi boy . . . and I go over to those cases over here . . ."

I was astonished. Mac was actually going to start a movie right in front of me.

"You gotta make sure that the reel is in the right case . . . young guys get sloppy and mis-file a reel . . . hell to pay from Peyton . . ." hefting a reel over to the top reel spindle, "This is a Simplex E-7, top of the line in its day . . ." opening a box under the spindle. "See all these gears and sprockets in here? You have to thread the film through all of them with just the right amount of slack or tension between the sprockets . . . too tight and you snap the film . . . too loose and the film starts jamming up . . . it's all loops until you get to this part . . . where the light hits it . . . that is straight up and down . . . and then down we go, through another loop . . . and then down to the empty reel on the bottom spindle . . . loop the end of the film on it so that the top reel feeds into the bottom empty reel . . . there, you see that, how it all has to be connected top and bottom but at the right tension . . . I could do it in my sleep now."

Film threaded, he opened the heavy black side-flap of the projector.

"See the curved mirror here . . . not your household mirror . . . that bastard is polished to hell and back and tough enough to withstand a thousand degrees if it had to . . . and this here is the carbon arc . . . that black beauty . . . as soon as I spark it . . . burns as bright as the sun . . . and that burning arc of light fills the projector and hits that mirror which then shoots it through this tiny aperture here . . . pay attention, right here . . . and that is the light that goes through the film and sends the image on to that goddam giant screen down there . . . but I still gotta do some other things before that happens . . . so, you come stand behind me and look out this window here, but pay attention to me, taxi boy, you only see this once . . . see this switch over me on the wall . . . that operates the curtain . . . organ is winding down, I start raising the curtain . . ." I heard a crackle of electricity. He had lit the carbon arc. He had one hand on a projector lever, the other was hitting switches. I was caught between looking at him work and wanting to see the curtains rise too. "This other switch here dims the stage lights and the side lights, and turns up the ceiling star lights just a little . . ." It was all happening as he spoke. "First curtain up, you see that?" Absolutely, I whispered, enthralled. "As soon as it is almost up and the second curtain starts splitting, I pull this lever, letting the light hit the film just as the sound track begins, and . . . ," I heard a lion roar. "Voila! It is showtime. Welcome to Hollywood, Harry."

"Is this what I think it is, the movie?"

"Yessir. Gone with the Fucking Wind. One of my favorites. Played here at the Centre for six weeks a long time ago. I got a bootleg print. Sometimes I watch it for myself after we close. Ferb is never happy when I do it, but, taxi boy, frankly, I don't give a damn."

"Mac, you really are amazing," I said, and I was sincere. "But as I recall, this movie is about three hours long and I . . ."

"I know, I know, Ferb is giving a tour, and I know that he has the stage reserved for more of his visitors tonight, but you are gonna watch this first reel with me because I still have to show you the most important part of my job. Twenty minutes."

So, I watched the first twenty minutes of *Gone with the Wind*.

"Here's the deal. Each reel is twenty minutes. The other projector over there has reel two threaded up. You are about to witness what we call the changeover."

He moved to stand between the two machines, looking through a small window toward the screen. He had his right hand on the lever of one machine, his left on a lever on the other.

"Pay attention. Look at the upper right corner of the screen. Do NOT take your eyes off that corner. Look for a dot." I focused on the screen, and then I heard a bell. "That's to keep me on my toes. Bell rings when it is almost time . . ." I saw the first dot. Mac had already started the carbon arc in the second machine and its top spindle was starting to feed film through the loops. "Three, two, one . . ." I saw the second dot, but I could not turn to watch Mac as he shut down the first machine and opened the aperture of the second all in one fluid motion. A seamless transition from one reel to another, the changeover.

"It's all synched. But if I miss those dots by only a second or two, the customers down there will get a jolt. The spell will be broken. The dream interrupted. I was called in one night on short notice when Peyton had gotten pissed at a young guy who missed two changeovers in a row. Told my steward something along the lines of if he's paying union wages, he better get union work. Peyton could be sonuvabitch sometimes. But I knew where he was coming from. I'm a union man."

"Mac, thank you for showing me all this. Serious thanks. And, trust me, I am not going to be your replacement."

"My pleasure, taxi boy. Truth is, I don't get a lot of visitors up here."

Dwight appeared again and tapped me on the shoulder. Duncan turned away and started to unload the reel from the first machine. "Gotta get back to work, taxi boy. Say hello to Harry for me."

HARRY MEETS ANOTHER HARRY

"I told someone about you, and he's very excited to meet you."

Dwight and I were in the lobby. He had a manila folder in his hand.

"One of the ghosts?"

I had stopped trying to find another word for them. Visitors? Guests? Residents? They were ghosts. Dwight was alive, or so he said. I was alive. I was in a theatre of ghosts. To me, Dwight was the theatre manager, although he had another title for himself.

"If you wish, a ghost. But I told him about you and he seemed very interested that you were a taxi driver."

"Dwight, I have a question for you, and please don't just say *that's a good question*."

I could hear somebody singing in the auditorium. I wasn't sure about the voice. Then I heard another voice singing, a female voice. They were both familiar, but I still couldn't pin them down.

"You already asked me if I could tell you all the people who came to visit me here over the years? Who performed here and came back?"

I was flummoxed. It sounded like a question I would ask, but I didn't remember asking it. Dwight handed me the manila folder.

"They're all in here. Alphabetically, and also chronologically."

"Alphabetically *and* chronologically?"

"What can I say? I'm a bookkeeper."

"Okay, I'll look at these later, but I do have a more important question for you."

He nodded.

"Do you remember what movie was playing when you saw me and Sue here?"

"That's a good question . . ." I was about to get angry, but then I realized he was looking down and smiling. Dwight Ferber was actually almost funny for the first time. "Of course, I remember, Harry. It was *Some Like It Hot*."

I looked around the lobby, trying to not let Dwight see my expression. I did not remember that title.

"Marilyn Monroe, Jack Lemmon, Tony Curtis," he offered. "Two men dress as women and join an all-women band."

It all came back to me. I had forgotten the title, but the movie came back immediately after Dwight simply told me the stars. How Sue and I laughed through it. The last time we laughed together. I looked around the lobby again. I wanted to see us, her and me, standing over there at the concession stand talking to Dwight. I wanted to see us when we were in love.

"Harry?"

I had my eyes shut, listening to Sue laugh.

"Harry?"

Dwight was being very patient with me. But then I figured, it wasn't as if he had anything else to do or any other place to be, just like me. Just like always.

"I'm sorry, Dwight. Just tripping down memory lane for a second. So, somebody wants to meet me? A ghost from my past?"

"Not somebody you ever met, but you know his music. So now he wants to meet you. I told him that you drove a taxi."

"Dwight . . ."

"Open the folder in your hand. Look at the April 4, 1976, date."

I looked. I looked twice. And then I said a really dumb thing.

"But he's dead, Dwight. He's dead."

I actually made Dwight laugh.

"Harry, that sort of seems to be the point of all this, doesn't it? He has to be dead for you to meet him."

The auditorium was dark, but I could see a dozen or so people sitting near the front. Well, not people. Ghosts, right? The clown that didn't have a name was there, and Will Rogers too. Others I had yet to meet. On stage, a man and woman were casually talking, as if they had just met at a bar and hit it off immediately. The woman was dressed in a sequined western shirt and her hair was piled thick on top of her head. The man was wearing jeans and a loose checkered shirt. He had more hair than the woman. Both were sitting on stools, their guitars resting in their laps.

Dwight was having to nudge me forward. Meeting Houdini and Will Rogers was a walk in the park. I was about to meet one of my true heroes. I was afraid he would be disappointed.

The man on the stage saw us walking down the aisle. He leaned over and whispered something to the woman, who nodded and then whispered something to him. Both laughed.

Harry, come on up. I want you to meet Patsy Cline.

Just as I was almost ready to meet him, he throws a curve ball at me. I hadn't paid much attention to the woman, but as soon as her name was mentioned I recognized her. I wish Sue was there. She wouldn't be impressed by meeting my hero, but she had loved Patsy Cline. I was in more of a daze as I ascended the steps up to the stage. As I approached them the man stood up and extended his right hand.

Hi, I'm Harry Chapin. I've heard all about you from Dwight.

I was shaking hands with Harry Chapin. Probably not a big deal for most people. Just another singer. Dead almost twenty years. But, back in a dinghy boardinghouse room, I had almost every album he ever released. My clothes and my records, lots of his, were my worldly possessions. All LPs, but not a record player to my name. I knew most of his songs by heart. I first heard him years after Sue and I split. I wished . . . hell, I wished for a lot of things and they all seemed to revolve around Sue being part of the wish . . . I wondered if she had ever heard of him.

Chapin motioned to Cline.

Patsy, come here and meet Harry Mason. He's an old friend of mine.

I was?

She slid off the stool, guitar still strapped around her neck, and seemed to bounce over to me.

My pleasure, Mister Mason. I'm gonna call you Mister because I'll get confused by all the Harrys in this place. I like this Harry a lot, but I do my best to dodge that magician fellow. And now you. One more Harry and one of you boys is gonna have to change his name. All the time I was at the Opry, I can't remember anybody named Harry. And now I'm surrounded by a covey of 'em.

I didn't know how to respond to that. She winked at Chapin and then looked back at me.

Relax, Harry. I'm joking. I can handle a lot more of you guys. And if I know anything about this place, I know that, after awhile, nobody gets confused. If I'm talking to you, you'll know it. Same with Harry here with me. Right, Harry?

Chapin grinned and nodded as she continued.

You take my stool. Harry and you got a lot of catching up to do. I'm headed out to Nashville, but I'll be back for the big party next week. Harry and I are going to do a duet. 'Spect you'll be here, right? Should be a full house.

I had heard him sing a thousand times, but I had never heard him talk. No, wait, a couple of albums he would have a brief story to tell, about his grandfather, or about a lesson that children needed to learn about helping other people. A New York accent, but not like you hear on tv? More Northern than New York? He talked fast for sure. And raspy? But who was I to comment about accents? I was born and raised in Oklahoma. I must have sounded like some actor was told to talk like a mutant combination of Texas and Arkansas. In high school, I had told Sue that I was thinking about going out for choir. I didn't tell her that it was only because she was in choir, a star in choir, and it was just an excuse for me to be around her more. Her jaw dropped. "Harry Mason, you will *not* go out for choir, and I sure as hell do not want to hear about you trying to sing in church. Nobody deserves that." And then she kissed me in the school hallway.

How was I supposed to talk to Harry Chapin? I began in the present, not the past.

"You and Patsy are doing a duet?"

Yeh, isn't that great? I just met her a few years ago, but we seldom show up here at the same time, so it is hard to plan things. Of course, the party is an annual event, so we should have started practicing sooner. Thing is, we can't agree on a song. You've heard her. How do I sing with that voice? I'm not winning awards for my voice, for sure. She's very patient with me, especially considering that she had never heard of me when we first met. I knew all about her, but I think she was a little skeptical that I was a singer after she heard me a few times. You got any suggestions?

Harry Chapin was asking me, Harry Mason, for a song suggestion? A song that he and Patsy Cline could sing together? I tried to remember if I was stoned. I looked down at the small crowd in the front row, clowns and cowboys. I looked up toward the top balcony, looking for the small window in the projection booth, wondering if Mac Duncan was watching all this. I looked around for Dwight. Chapin waited.

"That's a tough one, Harry. But I think you're right about your voices. Night and day. How about you each sing one of the other's songs. A solo of you doing her, and then her doing you."

He seemed skeptical.

Different strokes, Harry. I tell stories. She is more . . .

"I know, I know. But there is one song of yours that I think she would love, and her singing it would be gold."

Hit me.

"'Remember When the Music,' Harry. That's a song for her."

Chapin shook his head. I thought he was offended. But then I thought he was merely trying to clear his head of something. Cobwebs or booze or dope or a bad memory?

Came in wooden boxes . . . I love that song. Strung with silver wire . . . Allie had just died. My heart was broken, Harry. I wrote that when I was heartbroken and shit was happening all over the country. But, for Patsy? It's much too political. I'm not sure that's her style.

"Harry, you just said why the song is perfect for her. Your heart was broken. Heartbreak is something she understands for sure. You sing her that song. You tell her about your heart being broken as you wrote it. I'm telling you, she can sing that heartbreak."

Where did that come from? Out of nowhere, I had made Harry Chapin cry. I had made a ghost weep. He opened his mouth and just looked at me for a minute before he spoke.

Dwight told me that I needed to meet you. He wouldn't tell me why, just said that you and I would be friends for a long time. I think he's right.

Chapin died when he was thirty-eight. He would be thirty-eight forever. I was pushing sixty. I would always be older than him. Neither one of us spoke. We just sat on our stools. Then he started plucking the strings of his guitar, just notes.

Okay, Harry, we have a song for her. How about one for me?

"That's your call. I just know her hits, and somehow, I don't see you singing 'Leavin' On Your Mind.'"

I'll let her pick one as soon as she gets back. We'll pull it together. I think she's going to like your idea.

I had been postponing the one question I wanted to ask him, remembering how the ghosts had reacted when I had asked Will Rogers.

"Harry, what's it like to be dead?"

I didn't turn around, but I knew that the auditorium suddenly had a lot more dead people.

I was angry, Harry. I was mad as hell. I was on the Long Island Expressway, on my way to a concert. People were waiting for me. I was young. I had work to do. I thought I was finally becoming a good man. Not any straight lines in my life. All my roads had bends, no clear-cut beginnings, no dead-ends, but

I knew I was headed in the right direction. And then I saw that truck in my rearview mirror and then everything speeded up. Then it stopped. Will told me about having ten seconds. That's what I had too. Ten seconds, but he knew he was going to die. I just thought I was about to be in a stupid accident. I had ten seconds of frustration and anger, but I never thought I would die. That would be a horrible feeling. Same with Patsy, in her plane crash. I asked her, and she told me the same. She had ten seconds of terror. No life passing before her eyes. She told me, and Will was with us. The two of them were holding hands as they described their last ten seconds to each other, the same last ten seconds. In my final ten seconds I was still thinking about tomorrow. Another concert, another radio interview, more people to feed, money to raise, another song to write. I was too busy to die.

And then I woke up here. I was standing on this stage alone. So, maybe the accident was a dream, and that was part of the dream too, right? But I would wake up, I thought. I walked around this stage, but I didn't remember that I had performed here five years earlier. I wasn't wearing the same clothes I was when that damn truck jumped over me. It was all a new world for me. And I was alone. I went back to sleep. I woke up again, who knows how long had passed. You forget about time in this place. I heard a voice. "Hello, Harry. It's good to see you again." A man's voice without a body. Just a voice. The oddest thing was that I immediately knew he was right. I was dead. And that is when the terror began. My ten seconds.

But that passed. It only happens once. The worst part is only ten seconds. The seconds passed and then Dwight was onstage with me. His voice was different than the one I had heard earlier. He told me the Rules. You're not dead, Harry Mason, so you don't need to worry about them. For us, it's always do not touch the screen. Do not try to enter Peyton's Library. Do not try to make yourself known to any living person. No rattling dishes or shaking tables like at a séance. So, you see, you being here tonight, Harry, is a big deal. You can come and go and eat and drink and feel pain and pleasure both.

I interrupted. "You have no feelings, so senses? That's not existence.

That is . . . death."

We have memories, Harry. It is all inside whatever we are. Every moment of our lives. Love? Hate? Sex? Food? The touch of my kids, Sandy's smile. I have the memory of it all. But I don't have them. That was the worst part of being here and the other stages. I thought I would never see them again. But Dwight made it clear. Me and the others had to be here on the date we were here before, but we could go to any other stage on the dates when we were there. Always on stage, that was us until further notice. A lot of the other fellows didn't perform as much as I did, so they have more free time. They can go to the old places more than once, and a lot of them spend their free days back here. The year before I died, I did two hundred shows. Dwight has these books he keeps. Never shows them to anybody, but he says I was the busiest man of anybody who ever performed here. He said he didn't make the rules, about having to go back to all the stages on specific dates, but I think he was using that as a cop-out. The big party here is always on June 1, but I had done two shows on June 1 in different years, so I had to be at some college campus in Illinois or in Memphis. He said he would see if I could be exempt from the rules, an exception just for me, so that I would not miss the big party. Then I figured it out. Nobody misses the big party. It is the only night when we are all here. Everybody has that night free.

I hadn't been to a party in twenty years, big or small. Next week was shaping up to be an "event" for sure. I just wish I knew what the hell was the occasion.

"What's the big deal, Harry? Why is this so important?"

Chapin beamed.

Right, right, I forgot. Nobody knows about the party until it happens. I didn't know. I was just like you. Told something was coming but nobody told me what. Your first big party, the June 1 party, is when you are finally in the club here. The party is your frat initiation, Harry. You'll be one of us.

"But I'm not dead."

Go ask Dwight. He's got the Rule Book. Thing is, Harry, there are a lot of folks who are anxious to meet you. Dwight told them all about you. Yep, you're alive, and that, my man, is a big deal for us.

Chapin was getting antsy, I could tell. For a dead man, he had a lot of energy.

Gotta go, Harry. Making a trip to the Bottom Line in New York. Going to see my daughter.

"But, but . . . I thought one of the rules was . . ."

He looked around the stage, then walked to the edge and peered into the dark auditorium before turning back to me.

Just checking to make sure that Houdini wasn't here with us tonight. He's a wet blanket, thinks he knows all the answers, but I have a secret. I'm the luckiest guy here. For years, I was the most miserable. I lost my family when I died. I had been trying to spend more time with them. I knew I was working too hard. Gone too much. I was going to cut back. But the LIE got me. And then I was doing the ghost circuit, round and round. I always sang about circles, but this one was not what I had in mind. I had a gig at Bottom Line years ago, back in January of 81, so there I was in 1995, invisible. Same old, same old. But, Harry, I discovered the loophole in Dwight's rule. My daughter Jen had grown up and become a singer too. She was singing at the Bottom Line on the anniversary of me being there years earlier. She's amazing, a much better singer than I ever was. I was a damn blubbering ghost for sure, a tangled up puppet. She was right . . . there. But I couldn't touch her or hold her, or apologize to her for being gone so much. And then it hit me. She was on a stage I had been on. So, I knew that Tom and Steve, my brothers, were probably doing gigs at our old venues too. Took me a few months, of going to old stages and sneaking around . . . easy for a ghost to do . . . and finding schedules for their upcoming events. It was all there, with me playing by the rules. I could go back on the dates they were at a place I had been, on a date when I had been there, and for a few hours I could see them again. They never knew I was there, even when I was telling Tom or Steve that they were missing a beat or a note, or make a joke about how old they were looking. Harry, Harry, Harry . . . one night I was on stage with Jen and she asked her mother to come up to be introduced. And I got to see Sandy again, and Josh was with her. My heart was breaking, Harry, and I was the happiest ghost in the world. Josh is so big now, but still my dancing boy, and Sandy was still so beautiful. I stood right next to them, listening to them talk with each other. I was never mentioned. I didn't care. I was the past. They all had a future. I was a ghost. I loved them all. The first time it happened, I came back here and Dwight asked me why I was so sad again. I told him the story, about the loophole in his rules. He's a good guy, Harry, mostly, but he's not as sharp as he used to be. All he said was, "Let me check my books." Next thing I know he comes back and shows me the updated tour schedules for Jen and Tom and Steve. And he says I would have those dates free to travel to those stages, even if I had never been there before. June 1, however, was booked for the Centre only. He made me swear to never tell anybody else, especially Houdini. But you're alive, Harry. You're safe. If you were a ghost, I couldn't tell you. Dwight also told me a secret, even though I don't think he knew he was doing it, He said, "The rules? You and the others think that I make the rules. Not hardly. I'm the bookkeeper. I had to ask permission to get the rules changed for you. But I was told in no uncertain terms. No more exceptions." So now I get to sing with Patsy Cline and swap stories with Sam and Will. And I know people I would never have met before, with stories of their own. I always used to say that I was afraid that I'd be sixty-five and start saying that I should have done this or that, but I wanted to face old age and know that I had at least tried all I wanted to try. I would make mistakes, sure, but a mistake for a good cause is better than doing nothing. Harry, I wanted the fact that I existed to mean something. I thought I still had time, but I never made it to sixty-five. Hell, I didn't make it to forty, didn't even get to have a midlife crisis. I'm never bored here. But, dammit, I know enough about the other world, your world, to know that there is so much more I could do if I was alive.

Chapin had been lightly tapping on his guitar as he talked, the tapping slowly becoming more rhythmic. I wanted to tell him that his life had mattered. I wanted to tell him that I had sent the Harry Chapin Foundation a hundred dollars every year since 1982. He had always said, "When in doubt, do something." I hoped he wouldn't say it tonight. I was always in doubt. I did nothing. A hundred bucks a year was nothing.

"Harry, there's a story here. You as a ghost. A story for a song. Do you still write songs?"

The tapping stopped. He looked down and plucked a few strings, then he looked back at me.

Dwight chose you for a reason, Harry. I'm beginning to understand why.

I was flustered again.

Dwight also tells me that you have a girlfriend named Sue. Will I get to meet her?

Flustered was now an understatement.

"I doubt it, Harry. I haven't seen her in over thirty years. She's married, in a big house. Our paths don't cross."

Never say never, Harry. You just gotta make it happen. Okay, I am on the road again, but I'll be back to get with Patsy about that song.

I suddenly had one more question for him.

"Harry, you ever heard of a radio guy named Harry Ducharme?"

Chapin shook his head.

"I listen to him every night, used to call in, but he stopped taking calls after I asked him about you."

Chapin got off his stool and took the guitar from around his neck.

And?

"I called in one night and asked him if he would play your song 'WOLD.'"

And?

"He hung up on me."

Chapin stopped dead in his tracks.

You ask about my dj song, and he hung up on you?

"He even stopped taking calls from anybody. You got any idea why he would do that?"

A good question, Harry. But I got no good answer.

I wanted to listen to Chapin sing again, but I had a problem. All my albums were old LP vinyls. I needed a record player. One in the morning was not a good time to shop. My taxi had a cassette player, but I had no cassettes. I knew a few radio stations that played oldies, but I never heard Chapin on any of them. Then it occurred to me that I had not heard him sing in a couple of years, not since Harry Ducharme had played "Sniper" on his show, all ten minutes of it. That was the night I called him and asked about "WOLD." He was playing a Chapin song, so it should have been okay to ask him about another Chapin song, right? Wrong.

Ducharme had been agitated, that was obvious. After "Sniper" ended, I could hear him pounding on a table.

"This is one of his most brilliant songs but critics hated it and stations hated how long it was. But this is a dead-on song for sure. Whitman in that Tower. Whitman with that gun. What's more American than a psycho with a gun? Pop Pop Pop. Bang Bang Bang. Chitty Pop Bang Bang. Harry nails it. Harry knew Whitman, had to know him, like the good story-tellers, you have to know your people, your characters. You have to be your characters. I'm betting that Chapin knows the madness down deep in all of us, the goodness, the badness, the madness."

I thought Ducharme was hearing something in Chapin that I had never heard.

"That Tower. How perfect. We all live in the line of fire, folks. Somebody with a gun is always up there somewhere."

I could hear phones ringing in the background. Ducharme's voice disappeared. Just the phones ringing. But then I heard the trademark Ducharme sound. He would make a big deal of holding his mic close to a glass as he filled it with something liquid. He always said it was water, but I knew better.

"The pause that refreshes, folks. So where was I? August 1, 1966. He had a Remington 700 ADL, six mm. JFK was dead, King and Bobby were ahead. I was a kid. But Chapin was there. He saw it all. He saw America. Chapin tried to make it better, but he died too."

Ducharme had played a lot of other Chapin songs before this. That was one of the reasons I liked to listen to Ducharme. He played the music I liked. But he had never played what I thought would have been the obvious Chapin song for him. That night, as he ranted about violence in America being as American as apple pie, I thought it was time to call him for the first time. I had to pull into an all-night gas station that still had a pay phone. I thought I was doing him a favor, getting his mind off all the gun stuff. The line was busy. I called four times. He answered on the fifth.

"You rang?"

"Harry, big fan of yours . . ."

"Oh, please."

"No, no, for real. I heard your very first show, back in 95. You were reading a Dylan Thomas poem."

"You just saved yourself, friend. My only true fans love poetry. So, does this mean that you have a poem you want me to read? Hell, I'll even put you on-air if you have a poem of your own that you want to read. Voice unheard, I'll take my chances that you are a true poet, but no damn limericks."

"No sir, I'm not a poet. I just called to ask you to play another Chapin song."

"Your wish is my command."

"You've heard of "WOLD," right? It seems like a natural for . . ."

He hung up.

I tried to call him again, assuming that we had simply been disconnected. No answer, not even a busy signal. I called again. Just ringing, no answer. I went back to my taxi and turned on his show. He was back in his own world again, but no phones were ringing in the background. They never rang again after that night. I was his last call from the outside world.

I woke up. I was in my room. I was lying on my bed, still dressed. I stared at the ceiling. I listened for sounds in the hallway. Not even a mouse stirring. I looked at the clock. Four in the afternoon. Summer in Oklahoma.

Five more hours until it was dark. I couldn't go to the Centre until it was dark. Was that one of Dwight's rules, or did I just assume that? I suppose that was a good question too.

Five hours to kill. A swim would take an hour. I'd go to Denny's for an hour. My usual meal was breakfast. Not a lot of vegetables in my life. Coffee refills were free. But that left three hours. Bette Davis? "What a dump." Something like that? I had lived here ten years. The landlord liked to call me his *senior* tenant. That seniority had led me up from sharing a room with a guy who worked day shifts when I slept, to a private room, and then to a private room with a toilet. But, three hours in that room? Three conscious hours? I don't think I've ever done that. I just kept staring.

You ever have one of those feelings that you can't explain? A feeling that something bad has happened or is about to happen? That was me, looking at that ceiling. I sat up and looked around the room. Something was missing. The damn room wasn't that big. Whatever was gone should have been obvious. I got up and looked in the small closet. I looked under the sink. I went through all three drawers of the dresser. I stood in the center of the room. I looked at my bed. The bad feeling got worse. Everything else I owned, the material proof that I existed, was in that box under that bed. I dropped to my knees and crawled over to the bed. The box was gone. All the letters from Sue, all my Chapin albums, three Carpenters albums, and the one Patsy Cline album that Sue had sent me as a gift long after we split. Other stuff from my past. Gone. I no longer existed.

Houdini was behind me.

I warned you, Harry. But you wouldn't listen to me.

HARRY MEETS THE CAT MAN

Ducharme announced the end of the world that night as I drove to the Centre.

"I have been saying for years that the computer is going to kill us all. All that information overload. Soon enough, hear me, *mis*-information overload. Lazy information. Everything run by computers. Everything is easier, right? This email trend will kill us. Hell, we'll actually forget how to write a letter with our whole hand. We'll just peck at a keyboard with our fingers. We'll simply stop thinking. Computers will do it for us. More free time for us, right? I used to think that the problem was that we'd all be so dependent on the damn computer that we'll simply be its slaves. Stop it! You know I am right. Stanley Kubrick was right. It's too late to disconnect the HAL in our lives. HAL is going to pull the plug on all of us. But now I'm reading about a bigger problem, something even HAL can't fix. A couple of years is all we have, folks. Y2K is coming. We were so damn smart, we created HAL and his minions, but we didn't see the future. We left a poison pill in the universe. Stroke of midnight, the first second of the New Year, the New Millennium, HAL is going to blow its fuses and self-destruct. Everything shuts down. We're back to the Stone Age, paper and pencil, postage stamps, slide rulers, and actual conversations. We're all going to die."

I didn't own a computer, or a tv, but I did read the newspaper, if I could find a free copy at the Y or left in the backseat by a fare. Evidently, I was not Ducharme's target audience tonight.

I was trying to figure out how to kill a ghost who claimed he wasn't a ghost. Being stoned all the time hadn't killed all my nerve endings. I still had one that was burning to punch Harry Houdini.

I had gone to the Y for a swim, thinking he might show up there and lecture me some more. But there was an obvious problem, I realized as I floated with my eyes closed. You could kill a vampire with a wooden stake. You could kill a witch with water. But I had never seen a movie that showed how to kill a ghost. I swam for an hour, but Houdini never appeared. I still had hours to kill before it was dark. I got in my taxi and went to work.

"Work" is probably the wrong word for what I do. I never thought that driving a taxi was work. It was how I filled up my life, my conscious life. Thirty years? Close to thirty for sure. How many fares? Ten a day, minimum? Six days a week, minimum? Sixty a week? Two hundred and forty a month? Two thousand eight hundred and eighty a year? Eighty-six thousand and four hundred in thirty years? All those fares had faces, and stories I never knew. Natalie Kimmel's daughter had a story that I remember, but I cannot remember her name.

The only other important measurement of my life? Swimming laps. No consistent number a day. Hard to guess, but I'd bet a hundred or so thousand in thirty years. Great cardiovascular exercise, right? I'll live to be a hundred.

Ducharme was still fixated on the Murrah Building, the chaos of his first night on the radio in Oklahoma City.

"Have you seen them, folks, the five finalists for the memorial? I can tell you which one they'll pick. There's only one that matters. Six hundred-plus entries, from all fifty states, twenty-three countries, but only one is the one. You know the irony? It's the Germans who will win. The German chairs will win. Fair is fair. Art is art. Art is memory. Memory is life. If you have no memories, have you lived? I love those chairs."

I knew what I had to do before I went to the Centre tonight. I had to go back to the Murrah block. If ghosts lived at the Centre, where they had performed, ghosts surely lived at the Murrah site, where they had died.

Natalie's daughter was surely there. Close to ten o'clock, when it was finally dark, I went to find her. I jimmied a gate lock and walked in, but she wasn't there. Nothing was there. Just open unfilled space. I walked over the empty ground, listening in the dark for any sound of life, any whisper of a ghost. Nothing. In time, I thought, the chairs would arrive. I would come back.

"Harry, I am so very glad you came back. Tonight is special. Sam will be here."

Dwight had a clipboard in one hand. He had his ever-present flashlight in the other, even though the lobby was lit up like an opening night. Dozens of ghosts were milling around. See how easy that is to say . . . dozens of ghosts were milling around . . . as if it were true. I had seen them all before, even talked to a few. More than show business, the Centre had also been the stage for lectures and political debates. In the lobby tonight, Harry Truman was holding forth with William Jennings Bryan. A woman I had never heard of until Dwight introduced us, Dorothy Parker, was smoking in the corner, looking around at the others as if they were exhibits in a zoo. Next to her were two men dressed in red vests, bow ties, white shirts with puffy sleeves, with straw boater hats on their heads, half of a barbershop quartet, Harv Sprafka and Bob Leonard. Guys from a small town in Iowa, Harv a former mayor and police chief, Bob a reporter. Both good guys. A lobby of the famous and the obscure. I was no longer surprised by anybody or anything at the Centre. It was, simply, what it was. Houdini be damned.

I'll be honest. I'm having trouble telling time. I'm not sure how many times I was here before. How long ago did Dwight get in my taxi? Did I meet Harry Chapin last night, or last month? A month ago, I didn't believe in ghosts. Tonight, I'm surrounded by them. Hell, I'm talking to them. Nothing to see here, right? Move along.

Dwight thought he had outsmarted me. He had given me the list of names and dates about all the ghosts at the Centre, but he had left June 1st blank. Said everybody had to be surprised the first time. It was, after all, The Big Party. He and the others had also teased me about tonight, but Dwight forgot and left it on the lists. I knew who was coming. I was prepared. That Cat Man was coming. Sam was the Cat Man. Sam was Samuel Clemens. Samuel Clemens was Mark Twain. Mark Twain was the original Centre performer. May 26th, 1904. Twain? I had read a ton of his books when I was young, high school and my short college career. After meeting Rogers and Houdini and the others, I was ready for Twain. But I had to act surprised because it seemed to mean so much to Dwight. Twain was, indeed, a big deal. But then I wondered . . . Twain might be a big deal, but tonight was *not* The Big Party?

Flashlight in hand, Dwight led me down the aisle to the stage steps, and I tried to joke with him.

"No blindfold? No letting me see anything until the last second?"

He didn't miss a beat.

"No, that is for next week."

Will Rogers was waiting for us up on stage. Dwight turned me over to him and disappeared.

Howdy, Harry. We're gonna have fun tonight. You stand here with me and keep looking over to the other side of the stage. It's dark now, so pay attention.

I was also paying attention to the auditorium audience. The biggest crowd I had seen so far. A thousand? Stars I had met, but also backup singers and second-stringers. Harry Chapin and Patsy Cline, Harv Sprafka and Bob Leonard from Iowa. But I didn't see Houdini, and he was the ghost I wanted to see most of all. He and I had some business to settle. Rogers read my mind. I wondered if all ghosts could read minds.

Houdini is full of cowpatties, Harry. Me and Sam are friends. I mean, seriously, how could we not be friends? Now, look over there and listen up.

For some reason, I expected music. But the first thing I heard was a steamboat whistle. Fair enough, that made sense. But that was just to quiet the excited crowd. Lights dimmed in the auditorium. Then came a loud knocking, a heavy cudgel hitting the wooden stage floor? A heavy thud, silence, another thud, silence, another thud, as if Order was being called in some cosmic court.

Pay attention, Harry.

I stared across the stage. Out of the darkness at the other end came a puff of smoke. And then another thud. Another puff of smoke. I squinted and stared harder. I could see the glowing tip of a cigar, getting brighter as it was inhaled, then dimming, a few seconds, a thud, and another puff of smoke. Thunder and smoke and a tiny pulsating dot of red, all coming out of the dark side of the stage. I wasn't going to be surprised, remember? But I was.

The auditorium and stage became totally dark, making the smoke invisible. But the floor pounding continued its slow steady beat. The ghost audience was absolutely mute. I couldn't even see Rogers next to me. He was so quiet that I thought he was holding his breath, but then I wondered if ghosts actually breathed. You know, me thinking big thoughts, trying to figure out the rules of ghostdom. The floor pounding started to get closer . . . along with heavy footsteps, as if the walker were stomping each foot on the stage as he walked. A few seconds as the sounds approached, and then silence again. Was this how Twain always made his entrance? And then, a lightning spotlight beam shot down from the projection booth, encircling a man in a white shirt and white pants standing at front center stage.

I was looking at an old and stooped black man, with solid white hair and a scraggly white beard. His white shirt and pants were soiled. He held a staff of biblical proportions in his right hand. Breathing? I had wondered if ghosts breathed. Was I? I held my breath as he raised his right hand and slammed the staff back down on the stage, and I was sure that, somewhere in the world of ghosts, the ghost of the Red Sea was parting as thunder pealed. He never said a word as he raised his left hand and pointed to the dark side of the stage, from where the smoke had come. The spotlight kept shining on him for a few more seconds, motionless in that gesture. Then, poof, he was gone and the spotlight beam was shining a circle on the edge of the stage. Into that circle of light, smoke slowly drifted in, and then a hand holding a cigar, and then Mark Twain stepped into the light. Smoke, cigar, man.

I was still holding my breath, acutely aware that the audience was still completely quiet. I would have expected applause or cheering. It was a terrific entrance. But nada from the crowd. Twain stood at the edge of the stage and took a few more puffs, gazing up as if he were floating down the Mississippi on a raft, pondering a starry summer night, alone in his thoughts. Then he walked to the center of the stage, the spotlight escorting him. I felt Rogers nudge me in the side as Twain began to speak.

I am here to tell you that reports of my death have been greatly exaggerated.

A thousand ghosts went crazy. I exhaled. Then, just as the audience calmed down and Twain was about to speak again, the cats arrived. Dozens of them, padding across the stage as if they had reserved seats and could arrive late to any party. The ghost audience erupted again, chanting.

Meow meow meow meow meow meow meow meow.

Will Rogers was leading the chant beside me, clapping his hands. He leaned over toward me. *We started this years ago, and when we found out how much it upset Houdini, we made it a tradition.*

Who would have thought that being dead could be so much fun?

How many times have you heard me quoted thusly? But, of course, I never said it. I can understand perfectly how the report of my illness got about in 1897. I had heard on good authority that I was dead. I was talking to a reporter about James Ross Clemens, a cousin of mine, who was seriously ill two or three weeks in London, but got well. I told him that the report of my illness grew out of my cousin's illness. The report of my death was an exaggeration.

The misunderstanding could have died with me, but then Albert Bigelow Paine wrote my biography after I actually died . . . I credit him for his patience in waiting until after my demise . . . Albert was a bit of a fabulist, embellishing my words to the effect of 'Just say that the report of my death has been grossly exaggerated.' That misquote has itself been misquoted over time, and my renown for wit benefitted. As you all remember, since I have reminded you every year for almost a century, the difference between the right word and the almost right word is the difference between lightning and the lightning bug. In this case, I was the lightning bug, Paine the lightning. Then again, any biography is but the clothes and buttons of the man. To know me, you must read my autobiography. But, beware. Do you trust any man to tell the truth about himself? Still, an autobiography is the truest of all books; for while it inevitably consists mainly of extinctions of the truth, shirkings of the truth, partial revealments of the truth, with hardly an instance of plain straight truth, the remorseless truth is there, between the lines, where the author-cat is raking dust upon it which hides from the disinterested spectator neither it nor its smell--the result being that the reader knows the author in spite of his wily diligences. Now, consider our present circumstances. In lieu of reader, substitute listener, and you come to the Centre of things, with all us fine folks here, telling our lives, listening to others. Why dwell so much on these nits of storytelling? Every life is a story. We are all stories. But, my bosom companions, among us is the worst of any audience . . . the literalist. In his world, we must present facts, cross t's and dot i's. You know of whom I speak.

Ghosts in the audience were mumbling in agreement.

He insists on facts and reality, insists that he sees through the deceptions of others. You see the obvious problem here, friends. We are the others. In the literalist's world, we do not exist.

More mumbling and grumbling from the audience.

But, of course, we do.

As the audience applauded, Twain pulled a pocket watch out of his vest, flipped the lid, pondered time, puffed on his cigar. I thought he was about to continue, but he just stood there in the spotlight, motionless and silent. I wanted to ask Will Rogers if this was all part of Twain's usual performance, but Rogers was gone. Then came the heavy thump of the old black man's staff. From the other side of the stage, three thumps, and then Twain looked up again, toward the audience, and then he turned his head toward me. He looked down. A Persian cat was stroking itself up against his leg.

My good friend John reminds me to not enjoy listening to myself talk so much. I am here for other purposes. It is my understanding that we have a visitor tonight, and our host has asked me to avail this visitor with some of my time. But, for the rest of you, a special once-in-a-lifetime treat. Well, more of a gift from my friend Edison. Tonight, a motion picture. An entertainment concept about which I am reserving judgment. But our host . . . pointing up to the projection booth . . . and his laboring elves have prepared a diversion for you. A motion picture based on one of my books, starring my very good friend Will Rogers.

Rogers was standing next to me again, sheets of paper in his hands.

If my experience with this version of my story is any indication of how other writers have reacted to such adaptations of their work, all I can tell you is that you should never judge a book by its movie. Will and I have discussed this many times.

Rogers whispered to me. *He's just upset that Myrna Loy never performed on this stage. He really wants to meet her.*

Twain must have had terrific dead ears. He obviously heard Rogers. He turned, and I first thought he was glowering at us, but that was quickly replaced by a grin and arched bushy eyebrows, and then he put his finger across his lips, as if to remind Rogers that his interest in Myrna Loy was to be their secret only, but a secret now shared with me. Then he turned back to the audience.

And now, ladies and gentlemen, I present to you A Connecticut Yankee in King Arthur's Court.

Rogers walked to the center of the stage as Twain walked toward me. Just out of the spotlight, the old black man was walking across the stage toward me too. Twain, the old black man, and lots of cats.

Harry, let me introduce my dear friend John T. Lewis.

The old black man stepped out of the shadows. I extended my hand but he stopped a few feet away from me and simply nodded. Then he stepped back into the shadows.

A better person to spend eternity with, I doubt exists.

Out of the spotlight, Twain seemed older, almost frail. His white suit was frayed at the elbows, his moustache had noticeable tobacco stains, and his teeth, in the rare moments when you could see them, were yellow. His voice when not performing? He was from Missouri, a state which had never decided if it was midwestern bland or southwestern twangy, with an accent to match that schizophrenia. Twain's voice was more marked by a recurring cough, as if trying to rid itself of some sort of pestering phlegm. Tobacco killed him was what I always thought.

While Twain and I talked, Will Rogers was on the stage and screen at that same time.

Will explained to me how movies are made, how the actors just play the script they are given. I must say that whoever wrote this script had no idea what my story was about. But I suppose I should expect nothing more. Americans prefer all the rough edges of life to be smoothed out.

How could I ask him what I had asked the others? At that moment, he seemed to be the saddest man I had ever met. He forced the issue.

Will and the others tell me that you seem to be too concerned about what it is like to be dead. They worry about you. Me, I was dead a million years before I was born, and it never inconvenienced me one bit, so death is not that important, Harry.

"But you have to admit, somebody who falls into a theatre of ghosts might wonder about how they all got here."

No, no, my young friend, death is a blessing. We never become really and genuinely our entire and honest selves until we are dead. And not then until we have been dead years and years. People ought to start dead and then they would be honest so much earlier.

You ever meet somebody and realize that they are less than you expected? Twain was still treating me like I was in an audience with everybody else, paying to hear him wax witty and ironic. If not to make us laugh, at least to make us smile?

"Mr. Twain, I was hoping you could help me."

My formality was intentional. To his credit, he understood my change of tone. His cigar was a dead stub. He looked at it, as if contemplating whether to relight it or pull out another.

He did neither. He took a deep breath, which seemed to pain him, and he talked to me as if we were alone.

I was glad to die, Harry. The end of my life was misery. I was more and more alone. My gem Olivia was gone, how was I to live without her? When I was a young man, I watched a master kill a slave, murdered in front of me, without a second thought. My father died when I was twelve. I became a steamboat pilot and got my brother Henry a job on one of the river steamers. A boiler explosion maimed him. He took a week to die, and I was with him at the painful end. I was the cause of his death. Next came the divine War of the States. Our own punishment for the sins of our fathers. My own abortive service for the Confederacy was a mockery, of course, turned into a story to make people laugh. But death was everywhere, even finding old Abe, younger at his death than you or I now. The great cosmic joke? He was shot in a theatre, playing a role as profound as his assassin's was farce. But I met Olivia and I was saved from death. She managed my money and my heart and even my life. But she died shortly before I stepped on this stage for the first time. Before her, our young son died of diphtheria. Then my daughter, then another daughter, each death more grievous than the one before. I wrote books, I gave talks, I traveled, I made money and lost most of it, I was a legend in my own time, President Taft wept when I died. Was no one paying attention to me as I strode to the great oblivion? How my writing darkened as my lungs carbonized? But I am remembered for children's books? And my great love of America? A nation convinced that her imperialistic sins were different than the Old World's? That she was exceptional? Did she not see the blood she wasted? I once called God a malign thug. I might have been too kind. How often did we invoke God in our cause? How much death has come from a love of God, who thusly justifies all our sins to thank us for that love? Our special God. America the Christian. Bible-thumping America, inspired by a book of divine poetry in parts, but also the most damnatory biography that exists in print anywhere. It makes Nero an angel of light by contrast. If Christ were here now . . .

John Lewis appeared and gently touched Twain's arm.

. . . there is one thing he would not be . . . a Christian. Yes, yes, John, I know. We have a long time ahead of us. So, Harry, you wanted to know about death? Did I mention that I was glad to die? I often commented about my entrance and exit being coordinate with the return of Halley's Comet. And, so it was. As they say, all comedy requires good timing. My only regret at the end? Teddy Roosevelt outlived me. I looked forward to his demise. I would not have attended the funeral, but I would have been glad to send a letter saying that I approved of it.

The ghost audience was applauding, but not for Twain. The movie was over and Will Rogers was motioning for Twain to come back on stage and take a bow with him. Twain waved back at him and then looked around for John Lewis. Seeing the old black man approach us, Twain turned to me.

Sorry for the stemwinder, Harry. But I do want to say that I am glad to meet you. I certainly hope you will be with us next week for the Big Party. And I want to hear more about your friend named Sue. I had a daughter named Olivia Susan, but we called her Susy. I adored her, as did her mother. So, please tell me all about your Sue when we talk again.

With that, he turned to face Rogers at center stage. His back to me, I watched him straighten up, rotate his shoulders as if working out century-old kinks, clear his throat, light a new cigar, and walk toward the spotlight. John Lewis walked parallel to him, but stayed in the dark. The cats stayed with me

THE RED DOG

I had a week until the Big Party. I was still waiting for Houdini to show up again. I swam in the mornings, went to the Centre at midnight. I was starting to think that me and Dwight were the only living people in my world. Mac Duncan was still iffy. I still drove my taxi, still had fares that were supposedly alive, but I didn't remember them at the end of my shift, as if they never existed.

The dead were real. Dwight's list was numbered, a total of two thousand one hundred and fifty-seven. I had probably been introduced to less than a hundred. Quick hellos and talk-to-you-later encounters. More unknown than known to me. Dwight reminded me that every star required a back-up crew. So, in addition to the lead performers in Centre history, my new world had lots of musicians and dancers, dressed as they were when they last appeared onstage. A century of changing styles.

I was probably less impressed than I should have been. The famous dead often didn't interest me as much as they should have. After all, wasn't I wasting an opportunity that nobody else had? I could stand next to Harry Truman or Huey Long and would be at a loss for words. William Jennings Bryan? I kept looking for Fredric March. Aimee Semple McPherson, I had never heard of, but Dwight told me all about her evangelism and claims of faith healing. I had looked at her and wondered how Twain felt about her. But then, one night, I saw them standing together, with ever-present John Lewis off to the side, and the two of them were laughing together, his cynicism and her zealotry set aside. I asked him later about what they had been laughing about, and he had a quick one-word answer: *Houdini.*

Much more white than black, my new ghost world. How to interpret? The Centre had obviously been a white world, but the black world was always there even if white Oklahoma City ignored it. I grew up here but didn't know about the Deep Deuce district until I was almost fifty. A few blocks from the Centre, the Aldridge Theatre had featured bigger names in black performers, and the Deuce clubs had greats like Jimmy Rushing and Charlie Christian and Ma Rainey. Hell, Ralph Ellison had his first job in the Deuce. But that's mostly gone now. Somebody might bring it back, who knows?

The Centre could not match the Deep Deuce in black ghosts, but it had more than I expected. I had never heard of the Whitman Sisters or Pat Chappelle and his Rabbit's Foot Show, but it was Twain himself who introduced me to them. Along with them came their bands and singers and dancers. Twain also introduced me to Ella Fitzgerald, who had only been a ghost for about a year. She was still meeting her Centre companions. I knew who she was, had seen her on television a long time ago, but she seemed even bigger as a ghost than she had been in life. Literally, bigger. *So, you are the famous Harry everybody has been telling me about*, she had gushed as she pulled me into a warm hug. *You gonna be here for the party, right? This joint will be jumping.* I assured her that I was, indeed, on the invitation list.

I told Dwight my biggest disappointment about the Centre's ghosts. He didn't seem sympathetic.

"Rules are rules, Harry. To be here now, you have to have performed on this stage. In person, flesh and blood, alive."

"I know, Dwight, but this is a movie theatre. I would have thought that stars in the movies shown here would be invited back."

"I don't make the rules. And remember . . . nobody is *invited* back."

"You don't make the rules, but you do enforce them, right?"

"Yes."

"Then who the hell does make the rules?"

Dwight paused, looking around the stage, then up at the projection booth, and finally back at me. He knew I wouldn't like his answer.

"That's a good question."

I didn't, but I had lost that fight a long time ago, the fight for answers.

"I was just thinking that I'd like to meet the stars of the movies I have seen here. The movies that Sue and I saw here."

"Harry, I hate to disappoint you, but most movie stars are very boring people. They would be boring ghosts too. So, do you really want to meet those stars, or the characters you and Sue saw on the screen?"

I couldn't resist.

"That's a good question."

"Fair enough. All I can tell you for now is make sure you're here for the Big Party. You'll either have all the answers you want, or be more confused."

I was in my taxi, listening to Harry Ducharme, wondering what he looked like in real life.

"The bastard is guilty. Verdict just in this afternoon. Timothy McVeigh is guilty. I started this gig when he drove a van up to the Murrah Building. Sic Semper Tyrannis, kiss my anus, Timbo. You ever see a face that was looking for a fist? I should be more Christian, right? Forgive and forget. I guess I answered my own question. I'm not a Christian. I do sorta like the Old Testament. But McVeigh hasn't got enough eyes to pay back what he owes us. And there are more of him out there, folks, more to come. The creepy underbelly of America, perhaps the true heart. No, no, I have it. I have it because I read a poem that I cannot remember, so come back again tomorrow. I will find it and read to you. Something about rough beasts and passionate intensity."

Houdini was in the backseat, wearing a tuxedo. I had just dropped off two drunks at the Red Dog Saloon on Northwest Tenth, an old stripper haunt of mine before I switched from booze to weed. I was happy, but not in a good happy kind of way, to see him again.

"You coming or going?" I asked him.

He was looking at the front door of the Red Dog. A black-shirted bouncer outside, the two drunks fumbling in their wallets, a stripper looking my way. I could tell that she wanted a ride. I had a lot to say to Houdini, but the girl, probably still a teenager, looked like she was exhausted. I had been there too many times in my distant past. Sometimes, you never forget a look.

I made eye contact with Houdini in the back. "Stick around if you want, but I'm taking this girl home."

The look on his face? Indifference? Boredom? Curiosity? Whatever, he just shrugged.

You're the driver, Harry. You and I have plenty of time.

I expected him to disappear, but he merely slid over to the far side of the backseat, almost pressing himself into the door, as if afraid the girl would give him some sort of bug if she got within a foot of him.

"Thanks, Mister. You saved me tonight," she said as she settled in next to Houdini, invisible to her, who kept staring out the window next to him. It was starting to rain.

"Where to?"

"You know where the YWCA is, downtown?"

Of course, I knew. It was a block away from the Centre.

"I'll get you there in fifteen minutes."

"No hurry. Trust me, no hurry."

We drove in silence for a few minutes. Three people in a taxi, in the rain, and none of us in a hurry to be anywhere. I was seeing a pattern in my so-called life. Then Houdini did a really shitty thing. He talked to me. He talked, knowing that I could not talk back to him.

You remember Dwight's story, Harry. About Peyton and Cori. Remember where Cori lived? Why don't you ask this ... person ... if her name is Cori. Would that not be apropos? And you and Dwight could ponder the significance? You tell him that you met a ... person ... named Cori tonight, who lives at the Young Women's Christian Association. And we can both then watch him fall to pieces.

It was too much. The way he said *person*, the disdain in his voice, too much. I blurted out, "I'm beginning to understand why nobody likes you."

The girl had been looking out her own window, probably lost in a world where it never rained and she wasn't a stripper. Hearing me, she jerked her head around and locked on my eyes in the rearview mirror.

"Uh, I'm sorry? What?"

Houdini looked at her, then me, and then out his window, mission accomplished.

"No, no, I'm sorry. I was having an imaginary conversation with my boss. You know, something I wanted to say to him, but I guess I don't have the courage. He's an asshole for sure, but I gotta keep quiet about it. I can't afford to lose this job. So, sorry. I should have kept it to myself."

I was improvising like crazy, but she smiled and turned back to her window.

"Asshole boss, eh? I'll trade you. Mine for yours, sight unseen. Your boss might fire you. Mine would do worse to me."

How does a person hear that and not have his heart broken? Me, I was going to be sixty in six months. I was not her father. Hell, I was almost old enough to be her grandfather. But at that moment I wanted to kick a ghost out of my taxi and then drive a teenage stripper back home, wherever it was, even a thousand miles away, drive her back a year, and let her start over. I wanted my taxi to be some sort of magic carpet ride. But we all ended up a block away from the Centre.

As soon as I pulled up to the front of the Y, she pulled out her purse and started rummaging for the four-dollar fare. Houdini and I waited. She kept rummaging and then she looked up at me, her eyes wet and wild and lost. She was about to lose control, I could tell.

"It's all gone, everything I made tonight. They took it." Her shoulders began to shake. "I'm sorry, mister, I'm sorry, I'm sorry. I don't have any money to pay you."

I did what you would have done.

"Hey, no problem. This ride's on the house. You just get inside out of the rain. Get some sleep. You can pay me anytime. Okay?"

She kept looking at me. I mean, seriously four dollars is next to nothing, right. She had nothing. But she kept looking at me, then past me, just a blank look in her eyes, as if she didn't want to get out of the taxi. Houdini was looking at me, rubbing his nose with a forefinger.

"Hey, Miss, it's no problem, seriously."

She just kept looking past me.

"Say, how much are you missing? How much did you make tonight?"

She blinked.

"A good night, it was a good night for a Monday. Maybe sixty dollars, but I had to give the manager twenty."

I reached under my seat, where I kept my fare money in a zippered bank bag, pulled out three twenties, turned back and handed the cash to her.

"You take this. You get yourself a good breakfast in the morning. You put some in a safe place. You take care of yourself, okay? You need a cab any time, you call and ask the dispatcher for Harry Mason. I'm almost always on duty, especially late at night. Next time, you pay and you give me a big tip, okay? Now, get outta here."

She held the money in both her hands, sniffled, and wiped her nose with her sleeve. She put the money in her purse. Then she leaned forward and softly kissed me on my forehead.

"Thank you, Harry. Thank you for the ride. You have been an angel tonight. If you're around the club and have some free time, ask the doorman if Sue is working. I owe you a dance for sure."

A minute later, Houdini and I were alone and speechless in my taxi. The rain had stopped.

Harry, I will admit. Even I didn't see that one coming.

Parked in front of the Centre, I told Houdini to wait until the Harry Ducharme show was over. Actually, I needed some time to reorganize my mind. I thought he would object, tell me that I couldn't tell him what to do, but he just leaned back in his seat and closed his eyes.

I had two questions for him.

"So, do you realize that you have no friends here? At least, none that I have met yet."

He was not offended, not even defensive. He spoke as if he were delivering his own eulogy.

Harry, do you think that people die and become different people? Better people? No, they are the same. Magnanimous or petty, the same. Wise or foolish, the same. And it has been my experience that of all the things that people refuse to give up, the chief one is their delusion that they will not die, that death is merely a door to another life. I have few friends here because everyone here cannot accept the Truth. They are dead. They do not exist. Dead people hate that truth.

"Who are you then? Right here with me right now? What are you?"

What would Dwight say?

My blood pressure probably shot up thirty points and I was about to yell at him. Instead, I yanked open the driver's door and moved to get out of my taxi and tell Houdini to go to hell at the same time, but that made no sense either. Hell? Where was that? I lived in a world of ghosts who, for the most part, seemed to be having a great time.

I am not here to give you answers to those kinds of questions, Harry. You asked why am I disliked. I answered, but you did not accept that answer. There is also another answer. These people do not really know me. I invented a hundred devices that aided me in my escapes, but I never patented any of them because that would have required me to reveal my secrets. During the Great War, even as a Hungarian, I was a patriot. I canceled my tours and often held classes with American soldiers and sailors, showing them how to escape handcuffs or any other restraints if they were captured by the Germans. I was a good man, Harry. I loved life, but I hated lies and superstition. I suppose the great irony of my life, and death, is that that I swore to my adored wife Bess that I would contact her from beyond death, that I would send her a message from the other world. I contradicted everything I believed in, telling her to listen for a secret code that would be sent to her, a code that would spell out "Rosabelle, believe." For ten years after I was gone, she held her own seances, but I did not make contact with her. I loved Bess, as much as you loved your Sue, or Sam loved his Livy. As much as the singer Harry loved his Sandy. Bess is dead now. You will die eventually. As much as you want to believe that you will not die, you will, and you will be gone. All of this is but a dream, Harry. When you wake up, you will be gone. As long as I am here in the Centre, I am a reminder of that truth to everyone else. How can they not hate the proof of their nothingness?

"Harry, every time I think I'm getting used to all this, you confuse me. You cannot be right. And, besides, sometimes you can be a bit of a jerk to everyone else."

He nodded.

Remember me telling you that people are not different after they die. Our emotions do not die with us. I am angry, Harry. Angry that I am dead. Angry that I will never see Bess again. Angry that I cannot seem to escape all this yet. But I will. I can escape anything.

Houdini was a hot mess of contradictions for sure. He had no friends at the Centre, no friends in death. But at that moment, as I looked at a talking dead man who refused to acknowledge being a ghost, he was something I recognized. He was still human. He was angry. And anger is something I understood. For the first time, I actually cared about him.

But I still had a second question.

"Were you angry when you stole all my stuff back in my room?"

I stole nothing from you.

"You did, you did. You admitted it to me."

No, Harry, I just said that I had warned you but you had not listened to me. I did not steal anything from you. If you want your life back, you have to look inside the Centre.

He was talking in circles again.

Tomorrow would be a good time to start asking the right questions, after the Big Party. The right questions. I assume you'll be here. It is actually the highlight of my own year, as for most of the rest of the souls who let themselves be imprisoned by Dwight. One more thing, Harry. That list of names and dates that Dwight gave you, pay more attention than you obviously have so far. You have missed someone. Dwight's own filing system. He alphabetizes by first name, not last. Go find my name. I assume that you are not so blind as to not see who is next to me.

An hour later, I was staring at names on a list. Houdini was right. I had been oblivious. Right between Harry Chapin and Harry Houdini was . . . Harry Ducharme.

THE BIG PARTY

Perhaps Houdini had been right. I wasn't asking the right questions. Asking good questions was not the same as asking the right questions.

I drove to the Centre at ten o'clock. Ducharme's program started at ten.

"Here we are folks. Tuesday, under the sign of Gemini, and the end of the world has been revealed in today's number one hit, some piece of bubble gum titled 'MMMbop' by Hanson. I know, I know, Hanson is local, if you really count Tulsa as local. Support the troops, especially local troops. Boomer Sooner. But, seriously, this is what the kids are buying? I'd play it for you, but that would mean I'd have to shoot myself right here on air. End of the world? Am I being too pessimistic? All I know is that the twenty-first century is getting closer, and if that damn Y2K doesn't obliterate us, pop music will. If not pop music, then it will be Jerry Falwell. If not that fat fudger, then it'll be something or somebody else. All I know is that we've only got maybe two and a half more years and then we'll all be ghosts, if we're lucky. Now, I need to refresh my glass of water, so you listen to some real music for a few minutes while I am gone."

The first notes of "Hey Jude" came through my radio and I was trying to put pieces together. He used the word "ghosts" and he talked about the end of the world and then he plays . . . the Beatles? And all this on the night of some sort of mythical Big Party? Was he even in that studio? Was it all pre-recorded? Questions, but not even good questions. But I knew one question I was going to ask Dwight for sure. Good or right, who the hell knew, but I wanted to know why Harry Ducharme was on his list.

For the first time since I had picked up Dwight on that rainy night in April, I could see the Centre from a mile off, as if Urban Renewal had leveled the entire block around it, leaving the theatre alone. Alone, but utterly majestic. Every bulb in the usually dark marquee was lit. Spotlights on flatbed trucks were shooting beams into the air, crisscrossing back and forth. The streets were packed with cars and limos, each glistening as if newly waxed and polished, none of them newer than 1957. The closer I got, the more I could see that the lobby was packed with ghosts, some I knew, most I did not. Evening gowns and tuxedos, blacks and whites, shoulder to shoulder, champagne glasses and cigarettes galore.

Mark Twain and Will Rogers were waiting for me at the curb, motioning for me to pull into a space reserved right in front of the box-office. As I pulled up, I realized that I was dressed like I always did, like an old taxi driver in Oklahoma City, Oklahoma. In other words, I was about to be totally embarrassed. I parked, but I was frozen behind the wheel, not wanting to get out. Rogers came around to my window and motioned for me to roll it down.

Harry, showtime in fifteen minutes but we can't start without you. Hurry up, partner.

"I can't, Will. I just don't. . . fit in . . . or something. I look like a bum."

Rogers shouted to Twain, who seemed a bit peeved at the delay.

Sam, I told you he might act like a fish out of water.

Turning back to me.

Harry, see that young man over there, in the red vest, looks sorta like James Dean, but only sorta. He is about to come get your keys and go park this taxi in the garage downstairs. He's your personal valet tonight. So, you are going to get out of this cab right now and hand me the keys.

I got out. I handed him the keys. The young man approached. Rogers held up a finger, pausing him, and then he went to the trunk of my cab, unlocked it, and then tossed the keys to my valet. From out of the trunk, Rogers pulled a new wardrobe for me. Not really new. It was the best suit I had ever owned in my life, but it looked like the day I bought it. Sue and I were members of a friend's wedding while we were still in high school. I was the best man, she the maid of honor. The bride was pregnant. Sue had taken me to J.C. Penney's and picked it out. Forty-plus years ago? I had kept it since then, from lodging to lodging, sealed in a bag I was eventually afraid to open, in fear that moths and memories would fly out. *Moths and memories?* An odd phrase, even for me.

Twain had joined Rogers, each with his arms crossed, as if they were parents inspecting their child about to go out on a first date. Rogers handed me my old/new suit.

Get dressed, Harry. We're late for a very important date.

"Here? Right here?"

Both just stared at me.

In front of a theatre full of ghosts, in the middle of Couch Drive in downtown Oklahoma City, I stripped down to my shorts and undershirt and put on my old/new clothes. All I needed was a tie, which Twain pulled out of his pocket, frowning as he handed it to me. After I put it on, he finally smiled.

And that puffer Houdini thinks he is the only magician in town.

Rogers was nodding and laughing. Then each man took one of my arms and escorted me into the lobby.

It was not just opening night for an event. It was opening night for the Centre itself back in 1904. The plush red carpets were spotless. The mirrors and chandeliers were burnished and blazing in lights and reflections. If I had ever thought that ghosts had no reflection, I was wrong. Many of them were preening in front of the glass. Red and gold and blue and black and white and silver and yellow clothing, formal coats and gowns and surroundings all blurring together.

The crowd turned and looked directly at me as Twain spoke.

Fair Ladies and Gents, our guest of honor, Mister Harry Mason, the well-known Baron of Public Transportation, about whom you have heard much, some of it true.

Applause erupted, some cheers rang out, hands raised champagne glasses in a communal toast. On the stairway at the far end of the lobby, Houdini stood alone, but he too had his glass raised in my honor as he acknowledged my entrance, seemingly happy to see me even if accompanied by his self-proclaimed adversaries. From a distance, I could see that he was talking to me, but I heard nothing, nor could I read his lips.

Twain motioned for the crowd to quiet down. Me, I wondered where the cats were. Then the crowd parted and Dwight Ferber stepped out. He was in a tux, but it was at least three sizes too big for him. In his right hand was a black strip of cloth.

"Welcome, Harry. I hope you enjoy the evening. But, as you know, the rules require you to enter blindfolded."

On the distant stairs, Houdini was rolling his eyes. This time, I could read his lips.

I warned you.

"Dwight, wait a minute. I have a question for you."

He kept walking toward me.

"Your list of names."

He kept walking. Twain and Rogers stepped away from me as he got closer.

"Harry Ducharme is on that list. Why is he on that list?"

Dwight stopped in mid-step. The crowd went mute. I looked for Houdini, but he was gone.

"Harry, we have plenty of time for that answer. All you have to know is that he is not here tonight."

"I'm not going anywhere until I get an answer."

"Harry, all I can say to you at this moment, this precise and not to be offered again moment, is that you refusing to put on this blindfold and refusing to go into that auditorium . . . that would be the biggest mistake of your life."

I felt a soft hand take my hand and hold it, and then a woman's voice.

It's okay, Harry, I will lead you down the aisle.

I turned to my right to see a sadly beautiful young woman with a gaunt face, long brunette hair, and wide eyes. I knew her, I had seen her face on dozens of albums, but I could not remember her name. Then another voice, to my left, Harry Chapin, taking my left hand in his.

It's okay, Harry. I'll be right with you on stage when we remove the blindfold.

I nodded, taking one last look around the lobby. Ella and Patsy, Bob and Harv from Iowa, Twain and Rogers, Truman and Bryan, Mae West, Al Jolson, Enrico Caruso, Fatty Arbuckle, Fred Astaire, and dozens more, all of them softly clapping to encourage me. Dwight handed Chapin the blindfold. He stepped around in front of me, his back to Dwight, and as he tied the cloth around my head he whispered, as if not wanting Dwight to hear.

Showtime, Harry. Just remember that you're the guest of honor, but you're not the star. Even if you cannot see, pay close attention to what you hear. A hundred years of music, all played by ghosts. Also, most important, the star of the show is going to ask you a question about your name. Tell her the truth. Understand?

I didn't, but nodded anyway. I was in the dark, literally.

Good deal. Now relax, this is going to be a great night for you. Karen and I will hold your hands and lead you to the stage, put you in the chair of honor, and then I'll stand behind you until it is time to remove the blindfold. After that, you're on your own.

Drums, and then more drums. Kettledrums? As the doors to the auditorium opened, I could hear a soft slow pounding of a hundred drums. Then I heard somebody in the audience shout *Harry's here* and the crowd started cheering and chanting my name over and over, *Harry Harry Harry,* and then the drums kicked up the volume and the beat. I was running for student body president again. Thundering. Just as quickly as it started, a minute later the chanting stopped. It didn't die out. It simply stopped. The applause continued, a lot of whistling, but no more *Harry.*

Then the snare drums, the opening to a Twentieth-Century Fox movie. I could still feel the hands of Harry Chapin and the woman named Karen guiding me down the aisle. The carpet beneath me seemed to be vibrating with the drums. And then the horns. Trumpets announcing the arrival of . . . Harry Mason? Tubas belching? Brass and percussion swelling but then fading as a choir began singing "When the Saints Go Marching In." That was too much. It was all a joke. I was the object of a joke. Is this what Houdini was warning me about, that I was simply a joke to a room of ghosts who were obviously bored with their own lives, their afterlives? I no longer believed in any of them. I wanted my own life back. I tried to raise my hands to take off the blindfold, but Harry and Karen held me tight. I was surprised at how strong she was. Harry talked to me, almost having to shout over the din.

Relax. We're almost there, but we're going to stop here for a few seconds.

This was not what he had promised when he told me to pay close attention to everything I was going to hear. This was insanity. But I stood still, as directed by a ghost, and then, as choir voices faded, there was nothing but silence. No music, no voices in the crowd, utter silence, until I heard the trill of a single clarinet, and then strings and horns, the opening to "Rhapsody in Blue." A symphony orchestra of ghosts and Gershwin. A time-machine.

"Harry, I love you."

Sue and I were in that auditorium when we were seventeen, our first "classical" concert. Neither of us had ever heard Gershwin. How was that possible, I wondered later, to live that long and to have never heard. . . this? Sue had wrapped her arm around mine as we sat there in the Centre, her head leaning against my shoulder, and she was crying, but it was what she called her *happy* cry, when life was so perfect that she would weep.

"Harry, I will always remember this moment. Forever. With you."

I was blindfolded, but I could see Sue.

Gershwin's rhapsody became the bridge threading through a medley of movie music. *Gone With the Wind*, Gershwin, *The Way We Were*, Gershwin, "Somewhere Over the Rainbow," Gershwin, "As Times Goes By," Gershwin, "Moon River" . . . and Gershwin.

I was standing still in the aisle, in the dark, swimming . . . no, floating . . . in my past. I no longer felt my arms constrained. I could have taken the blindfold off, but I just . . . floated.

I heard Chapin's voice.

I'm up here, Harry, onstage, waiting for you. Straight ahead.

I started walking, a blind man among ghosts. Chapin began singing a song about life being a circle. As I got to the steps leading up to the stage, other voices joined Chapin. Love lost a thousand times, and then found again, a children's game.

Give me your hand.

Chapin helped me up the steps and led me to a chair, guiding me into it.

All that was for you. But there's more.

He took off my blindfold just as Ella Fitzgerald started singing "Someone to Watch Over Me." I was on stage, blinded by a spotlight shining directly in my face. I blinked, then I could see. I could see the auditorium packed with ghosts rising to give me a standing ovation. Ghosts of the known and the unknown. Ghosts of clowns and cowboys and jugglers and tap dancers and ballerinas. I could see all the ghosts who had been in the lobby now onstage. I could see a symphony orchestra in the pit in front of the stage. I could see cats running down the aisles, all of them headed for the stage. A hallucination? Nope, I had stopped believing in hallucinations weeks ago. Everything around me finally made perfect sense.

But then I saw the stairway. Gold railings, red carpet sparkling as if diamonds had been woven into it, the stairway started at the top balcony and curved down over the main floor to the other side of the stage from me. An utterly transparent stairway. I could see right through it. I was back to my first night at the Centre, mesmerized but totally confused.

Fitzgerald stopped singing, walked to center stage and pointed to the balcony.

Ladies and gentlemen, it is my pleasure to welcome my dear friend.

I followed the line of her raised hand. All I could see was a glowing dot at the top of the stairs. Motionless, but flickering brightly. And then the dot started to fly around the auditorium, like a flitting lightning bug, and then back to the top of the transparent stairway. Every eye in the theatre was following it. Every hand held together as if in prayer.

The flitting dot turned into . . . Tinker Bell? Right out of *Peter Pan*, a tiny fairy with a magic wand which she waved like a conductor's baton, spreading diamonds as dust in the air. She flew in a wide circle around the auditorium, sometimes just hovering in midair, arms akimbo, looking down at the still silent, still enthralled, audience. Then she flew directly at me, still tiny, no bigger than she seemed when she was a hundred feet away, hovering a few feet from my face, letting me finally see her face up close as I heard a breathy soft voice.

You must be Harry.

And then she was a dot of light again, back at the top of the stairway. A pulsating dot of light that turned into . . . Marilyn Monroe.

The audience released itself in some sort of orgasmic happiness. You would have thought they were alive.

I recognized the dress immediately, the ivory-colored cocktail dress with a pleated skirt, the one she was wearing in *The Seven Year Itch* as she stood over the subway grate, hot air blowing up to expose her legs, the dress of a thousand photos, the dress that ended her marriage to Joe DiMaggio. I didn't know much Hollywood history, but I knew that dress.

She began walking slowly down the transparent stairway, holding what seemed to be a covered birdcage in her left hand, waving with her right hand. The applause was deafening. On stage, the lobby ghosts began to form a line in front of the curtain. Twain's cats were there too, but perfectly still in a circle around him, their own cat eyes focused on Monroe. I kept staring at her descent. As the audience got more frenetic, she walked slower, almost in slow motion. Almost to the stage, she turned in my direction and locked eyes with me. The ghost of Marilyn Monroe was more beautiful than any picture of her, any movie of her, and she was looking at me as if I were a puzzle.

She set the birdcage down on the stage and then, without losing eye contact with me, raised her right hand over her head, forefinger straight up, and slowly spun that finger around. Everyone in that theatre stopped in mid-motion, frozen as if in a still photograph. Locked in place, a tableau. Except for me. She began walking toward me and was changing with every step. The dress disappeared and she was wearing a white terry-cloth bath robe. Her hair was pinned back in a ponytail. Her makeup was gone. She kept walking toward me. She was not the same, but she was still beautiful. Every spirit in the theatre was still looking toward the spot where she had been before. She and I did not exist in their line of vision. We might as well have been alone in the Centre.

She stopped a few feet in front of me and it was then that I understood her look. She was looking at me as if I did not exist, that I was the ghost, not her, that I was not real. She stepped closer and spoke in that soft breathy, almost child-like voice I had always heard in her movies.

I have heard about you.

I did not know how to respond to that.

I have a few questions for you.

Chapin had warned me.

Is your real name Harry Mason?

I nodded.

Have you ever been an actor?

I shook my head.

Have you ever met Harry Cohn?

My confusion was obvious. I had never heard of Harry Cohn.

That's good enough.

I knew I was going to have to ask somebody about who Harry Cohn was.

Have you ever lied?

I nodded.

Have you ever hit a woman?

I shook my head and shuddered at the same time. Evidently, the right answer and reaction.

Have you ever hurt someone?

I was going to shake my head. I had hit a man once, but I didn't hurt him. I had never hurt anybody. But I immediately knew that wasn't the truth. I had hurt the only person I ever loved.

I nodded.

It occurred to me that that was the trick question, the one she already knew the truthful answer to. If all this was a test, I thought she seemed pleased that I had passed.

Are you a good man?

No, this must have been the trick question.

"I have no idea. I really don't," was all I could say.

If her expression meant anything, I had finally become less of a puzzle to her. But, her to me? I was frozen in place as something miraculous happened. Her voice changed. Gone was the breathy child-like Monroe voice of her movies. The Monroe in front of me now spoke like a woman.

Well, Harry Mason, we are going to work on that. Me and you and some of my friends.

"Can I ask you a question?"

She tilted her head but still nodded.

"How did you do all this . . . this stopping life … or death, whatever it is we are in? I've seen strange things in the past month, but nothing like this. This suspension of everything and everybody else. How can you do this?

And your voice, why is it different?"

She smiled and then licked her lips. She rubbed a finger across those wet lips and then used it to smooth out an unruly eyebrow. She then gestured to the scene around us, sweeping her hand around.

All . . . that . . . is Marilyn Monroe. I created her. I can make her appear, or disappear. If Marilyn Monroe is a star, the people made her a star. But I made Marilyn Monroe. You and I are here by ourselves, Harry. You get my personal voice, not my public voice, for now. I can turn it on and off when I want. I have to go back to being the public Marilyn soon enough. I have a party to host. My public will want my public voice. But you and I need to talk again, and I think I know the perfect place for some privacy.

"Here?"

Just over there offstage, in Peyton's Library.

"Wait, wait, nobody goes in there. That was Dwight's second rule. Not even him."

She rolled her eyes, put her thumb and middle finger together, and reached over to pop me on the nose.

Harry, have you been listening? I am Marilyn Monroe.

"You know, at least for one time I would like to understand this rule business. There are, or are not, rules. Dwight makes the rules, or he does not. All of you are ghosts, but Houdini says that ghosts do not exist."

It takes time, Harry. You're new. You're not even dead, so I can tell you one secret. The rules, if they exist, only apply to dead people. Not to you. Dwight won't tell you that because Dwight wants to believe he is in charge of the Centre. But . . . I will tell you one rule that we all obey. None of us get near that damn screen.

"I asked Dwight if I would meet any movie stars, but he said that only stage performers were brought back. When did you perform on the stage here?"

I was on tour for The Seven Year Itch back in 1957. Thirty minutes of press and radio people interviewing me on this very spot. It was June 3rd, and Dwight tried to tell me that I could only appear on that date. But, Harry, I told him it was June 1st or not at all. You see, today is my birthday. And I like parties.

"But..."

Harry, it was a performance. I was on this stage. I was acting. The date is irrelevant.

I was racking my brain. How did I not know about her being in town that night? Of course, of course, Sue and I had gone to Tulsa to see her dying grandmother. A two-hour drive and she never spoke.

I had one more question, a stupid question, but stupidity had never stopped me before.

"Tinker Bell?"

Oh, Harry, that's all part of the myth. I was supposedly the model for the Disney animators. It's not true but, when I saw the movie, I could see a resemblance. I always thought those guys were a little bit pervy anyway. But it was fun, Harry, fun for me to think that people might see me as Tinker Bell. Fun for me to imagine myself as a fairy with a magic wand. Life is not always fun, especially for a myth, so I fly around as Tinker Bell when I come here. If you ever become a myth... and a ghost... you'll want to have fun too.

Monroe stepped back, her hair flowing around her re-made-up face. She was wearing the dress again and I stared as she walked back to the other end of the stage, her hips swaying. Once there, she turned back to wave at me, raised her arm, twirled her hand, and the motionless dead came back to be living ghosts. From frozen silence to party pandemonium.

She turned back to the audience and spoke in her breathy public voice.

Hello boys and girls. Am I late?

Just then she spotted Ella Fitzgerald. The two women ran toward each other and started hugging and shrieking. Friendship with Fitzgerald re-established, she started walking down the line of ghosts assembled onstage, shaking hands or hugging as the spirit moved her. When she got to Houdini, he did a half-bow and she extended her hand for him to kiss. For a cynic, he seemed as smitten with her as everyone else obviously was. As he bent his head down to honor her, she did a quick side glance to me and rolled her eyes. But I could see her then speak softly to him as he raised his head. His face was beaming with pleasure at her acknowledgment.

Twain was last in line, still surrounded by his cats. Monroe was obviously happy to see him. She ignored his extended hand and reached up to pull his mustached face toward her, kissing him on both cheeks.

Her court having paid homage, Monroe was offered a throne. A real throne, from where I had no idea, but there it was back at the start of the line. She walked toward it, but stopped to whisper to Houdini, who nodded enthusiastically and stepped out of line to disappear offstage. Within seconds he returned, like magic, leading four men wearing blue blazers and white derby hats. They were carrying another throne and set it beside the one for Monroe. She gestured a *thank you* toward Houdini, who bowed and seemed to be the happiest person on stage. Monroe then pulled Ella Fitzgerald out of the receiving line and offered her the second throne. Fitzgerald did not hesitate. While that was happening, the tuxedoed orchestra started playing symphonic disco. I had been through an acid phase years ago. This was better.

The Queens seated, the show began.

Acrobats first, the Bouncing Bullards, a young man named Paul and his four sisters: Emily, Carrie, Tess, and Sarah. They were all wearing navy-blue and white leotards with *BB* embossed across the front. The advantage of being a dead acrobat? Every flip can be done in slow motion and then the entire body suspended in air longer than humanly possible; that is, impossible for a live human. The closing flourish? Four Bullard girls stacked on top of their brother as he spun around.

Next up was a quartet. Harv and Bob from Iowa had found two new partners, but compromises had to be made. The new partners were a nun and a priest, Sister Jeannine and Father Bill, who insisted that Bob and Harv join them in singing "Dominique" in French. The second song was

Iowa's revenge, sort of. Bob and Harv started "Marian the Librarian" from *The Music Man*. Sister Jeannine and Father Bill did their best to go along.

I was listening to the music but watching Monroe. She was thoroughly enjoying herself, as was the audience. For the entire show, I had never seen anybody having as much fun as she was. Thing is, so were all the performers. Bob and Harv and Bill and Jeannine were almost unable to finish singing because they were also trying not to laugh.

Comedy acts followed. A stripper wearing nothing but a giant bubble. Lines of high-kicking dancers. Black musicians, white musicians. Singers singing songs that kept everyone silent as they closed their eyes and remembered their earlier lives.

Harry Chapin and Patsy Cline stood together and exchanged solos. She sang his "Remember When the Music," almost making him weep. He sang her "Sweet Dreams." Her voice was better on his song than his on hers. It made no difference to either of them, or to Marilyn and the audience.

And so it went for another hour, an all-star revue, complete with a finale of Monroe leading a conga line of the lobby ghosts around the stage, bongo drums pounding and trumpets blasting, her in front with Twain behind her, his hands holding on to her bouncing hips. But, as the music faded and the dancing slowed, she had one more surprise.

She turned back to the auditorium and announced, *I have a special gift for Sam tonight.* With that she went to retrieve the covered birdcage. Nobody was prepared, especially Twain.

Maestro, a drumroll, please. Let me introduce Josefa.

Her wish was a command. Drums sounded again. She quickly lifted the cage cover and before anybody had time to realize what was happening, she pulled a yipping Chihuahua out of the cage and put it at Twain's feet.

He went bug-eyed as his cat entourage scattered in panic, racing all over the stage, around the other ghosts, sometimes between their legs, chased by a five-pound Chihuahua named Josefa. Two thousand ghosts were in comedy heaven. Even Twain himself was soon roaring with laughter. Houdini? Houdini had the look of a man in love with the woman who had vanquished Sam's cats.

Dwight and Houdini and Chapin, the others, had all been right. They had promised a big, a great, party. They had undersold themselves. I loved everybody in that auditorium right then, that world, loved them all, and almost envied them.

Monroe started motioning for the crowd to settle down. Almost in sync, the sound and light both waned at the same time. She twirled her hand again and then she and I were alone in the Centre. She was right. She was Marilyn Monroe.

She motioned from across the stage for me to come to her, pointing to the now-empty throne next to her. As I got nearer, the thrones became old wooden-backed theatre chairs with red cushioned seats. She stood and met me at center stage, inside a single blue beam from an overhead spotlight. She spoke like a woman again.

This is for you, Harry, this, and a story.

She kissed me.

Soft at first, then firmer, her arms encircling my waist. I was in the Centre of the universe, kissing Marilyn Monroe.

She stepped back, and all I could do was look at her face, her eyes, her still-wet lips.

Do you remember that kiss?

I almost stuttered, "Marilyn, I will never forget this moment, ever."

You weren't kissing me, Harry. Not this kiss . . . that other kiss.

I blinked.

I'm a ghost. I'm real, but I'm not flesh and blood. When we kissed, two things happened to you. The two most important possessions you have, any living person has. Your imagination and your memory. You imagined what kissing me must be like, kissing the one and only . . . me. She smiled and paused. *That was the beginning. But you were remembering a kiss from someone else. You thought you were kissing me, but you were actually kissing . . . Sue. That is what you felt, the memory of Sue. Her lips, not mine.*

"But . . . you . . ."

You know the saddest thing about being a ghost, Harry. All we have are memories.

Chapin had told me the same thing. Ghosts only had memories.

Kissing you, I felt nothing, except your pleasure. And your pleasure was itself a pleasure for me. But it was not desire. That's sad, Harry. I wish I had known you when I was alive. We might have had some really good times, but somebody somewhere made the worst rule of all for a ghost. We can only desire, only feel love and sex, with another ghost.

"Why are you doing this, saying all this to me. It seems so . . ."

Cruel?

"Yes."

Would you rather that I did not kiss you? Rather that you never felt what it was like to kiss her again?

"That's the cruel part. Feeling again, and still not having. I thought you were a good person, Marilyn. I was having a wonderful time tonight. I was happy."

She pulled me toward her and kissed me again.

I am a ghost and I am a star and every star is a fantasy to someone. Harry, you and I are just starting. When I come back next week, you and I are going to Peyton's Library and you are going to tell me all about Sue. Everything. If you ever want to be with her again, I am the only person who can make that happen.

"Is that another rule around here?" I was teetering between anger and despair. "Everything to be explained later, not now, the future only. You people have all the answers and I have all the questions?"

I have to go, Harry, but I do have one question for you.

"Do I get to say 'that's a good question'?"

She kissed me again.

Tell me a song that reminds you of Sue. The song that always breaks your heart, but you always listen again, over and over. What is it?

MUSIC AND MEMORIES

I woke up. I was still wearing the same clothes I had worn at the Centre's Big Party. But that was days earlier. I wanted to get up, but I just lay there. It was still dark outside. I went back to sleep.

I woke up. Something was different. My heart was pounding. I jerked myself up and put my feet on the cold floor. It was June. It was not supposed to be cold. It was still dark. I reached for the cigarette lighter I always kept on the table next to the bed.

It had been a gift from Sue to me when we were still in high school. She had bought it at a pawnshop for a dollar. Some GI had taken it from a German POW in WWII and hocked it in Oklahoma City. She was a smoker and I had started the habit so we could smoke together, a ritual that required we get somebody else to buy the cigarettes for us.

"Too young to smoke, but not too young for sex, Harry. Go figure."

We had started both vices within months of each other, but the smoking was a phase we soon left behind. She had a coughing fit during a rehearsal for a play, and that night we shredded every cigarette we had. But she made me promise to keep the cigarette lighter.

"A reminder, Harry, a reminder of the dumbest thing we ever did. And just for you, a reminder of me. And if you make a joke about me being the dumbest thing you ever did, I will kill you."

I fumbled in the dark, knocking the unlit lamp off the table. I was about to start cursing Houdini when I heard something metal being tapped against the wood tabletop. I swept my hand over the table and found the lighter. I clinched it in my hand and lay back down on my side, my hand shoved up into my armpit, safe from anybody or anything. I went back to sleep.

I was driving to the Centre, sorting out titles. Monroe had asked me about a song, a song about Sue, but somebody had stolen all my albums. The problem was that too many songs reminded me of Sue, so I couldn't give Marilyn a specific answer. The great irony is that none of the songs were ones that Sue and I had shared. None of them reminded me about specific times we had together. They were songs that I heard years after we split. Songs I wish I had heard with Sue beside me. Songs I wondered if she would have heard on her own, in her post-Harry life, songs that might make her think of me. Would a song be the knot that tied our thread back together again? Jesus, listen to me. Knots and threads and songs and it's all just words. The worst of purple prose. I'm not a writer. I'm a taxi driver.

Monroe was in the backseat with Houdini, each seemingly oblivious to the other. I looked again. Harry Chapin and Karen were together, studying what looked like sheet music. Houdini was gone. If Dwight had made rules about where and when his ghosts could appear, there was obviously some sort of rebellion in the works. With Chapin and Karen in the back seat, Monroe had moved to sit beside me in the front.

"What happened to Houdini?"

The three of them ignored me. It started to rain. I started to reach for the radio button but Monroe reached over and stopped me.

Harry, you know the first rule of being a trial lawyer?

The rain was coming down harder, so I had to keep my eyes on the road.

Never ask a question that you don't already know the answer to.

"About Houdini? You think I already know what happened to him?"

No, sweetheart, I'm talking about my question to you.

She released my hand and disappeared. I punched the radio button and waited for Harry Ducharme to explain all this for me.

"News, news, news for the three of my listeners who have actually read a book. Before you switch me off, mea culpa, I joke of course. My listeners are the elite of American culture. Interpret that as you will. You are all bright stars, or this country is in deep feces. I am, of course, the Edward R. Murrow of talk radio. The voice that launched a thousand shits . . . ships . . . across the Oklahoma prairie. I'm not from Oklahoma, not steeped in the lore. Imagine my surprise to discover that your state was not created by Rodgers and Hammerstein. No, you Sooners are the offspring of land-grabbing homesteaders. Boomer ba-da-boom Sooners. Known for stealing land from Indians, for oil, and for football. But, seriously, you get rid of my man Barry Switzer and now have some nonentity named John Blake? I give him one more year."

Ducharme had a habit, more often seen lately, of losing the thread of his own monologue. I slowed my taxi down, letting him rescue himself. The sound of a spoon tapping on the rim of a glass was usually a good sign.

"But all that avails not. Pigskins avail not. Tonight, I bring you news from New York City, a city with 7,342,636 souls. Do I need to remind you that this entire state only has 3,372,917 souls? New York City has Broadway. Oklahoma has John Blake. I, obviously, am in the wrong studio. Wait, wait, I forgot, I used to have a show in Gotham City. I used to have shows in a lot of places."

A very audible gulp, and then his voice changed, lower and slower.

"But the real news is from the Kennedy Center in New York. Not official yet, but in the pipeline for sure. Drum roll. You heard it here first. Coming soon: The Mark Twain Award for Humor. I know the country as a whole deserves this award. A joke. But the effetes and elites and hall-monitors of culture are actually going to recognize individual comedians. And here I quote from the first draft of the announcement: 'It is to be presented to individuals who have had an impact on American society in ways similar to Twain. The JFK Center chose Twain due to his status as a controversial social commentator and his uncompromising perspective of social injustice and personal folly.' Anybody ever see a comedian in a buffet line? Anybody see a comedian at an open bar? Anybody see how comedians have the sharpest elbows in the room? Actors might be insecure. Comedians are one heckle away from being institutionalized or homocidal. All I hope is that these things do not turn into a snobby version of the Golden Globe Awards. But if they want social commentary they better dis-inter Lenny Bruce and posthumously give him the first award. And George Carlin ain't going to live forever. Hell, why not go back and tell Will Rogers to keep his feet on the ground for sixty more years."

I had an odd feeling that Houdini was not going to be happy to hear the news. I looked in my rearview mirror, but the backseat was empty.

"Okay, enough news that nobody cares about. Time for a song. A total change of pace. A request from a stranger. I get to work and there's a note that isn't supposed to be there. This studio is my fortress, not to be breached. You know that I don't do requests anymore. I ask the manager. He is clueless. Said he never saw anybody in the studio. Folks, I am the music czar of my show, but right here in front of me tonight as I sit down is a pink envelope with a handwritten note inside, signed with the initials NJB, and I can tell you that it was the smell that got me first, some sort of perfume that sent me back to high school and my first kiss. How could I say no, right? So, for NJB, here you go."

Never ask a question that you don't already know the answer to.

It was *the* song.

Dwight was in the lobby, wearing an apron, pushing a vacuum cleaner. He saw me and waved.

"We need to talk," I said.

He pointed to his ear and shook his head. I walked over and unplugged the vacuum.

"We need to talk about Harry Ducharme."

"Ah, your radio friend."

"Dwight, I never met the guy, but I want to know why he's on your list."

"Harry, why is anybody on the list? Seriously, if anybody performed onstage here, they are on the list. I have no control over who's on the list.

History is history."

"Is he dead?" For me, *that* was a good question, an important question.

"I suppose I should have explained everything when I gave you the lists. Go look at the names again. Look for check marks next to them. One check, dead. Two checks, has come back here as a ghost. Ducharme, you will see, has no checks next to his name."

"You don't think I stared at all those names. Right at them. There were no check marks next to any of the names."

Dwight seemed puzzled.

"Right, right. Perhaps those marks are on my copy only."

"Dwight, are you jerking me around? I was warned about you."

That got his attention. His confused face morphed into a squinting angry face, but that face morphed into a bemused face. He looked around the lobby, then up to the mezzanine, as if he suspected that we were not alone. I knew who he was looking for.

"Harry, I'm just an old man who has been here a long time. I like to say that I'm the bookkeeper, but I'm also the janitor. I have learned how to repair the plumbing and paint a wall when it is peeling. Peyton taught me all these skills, the basic maintenance skills, and . . ."

"I'm not interested in Peyton. I want to know about Harry Ducharme."

"Ah, your radio friend. As you like. Ducharme was the host dj that I hired for a midnight show a week after he arrived in Oklahoma. We had teen bands on the stage, and he was the 'host' if you please, although he wasn't very hospitable. He was inebriated and evidently did not care much for teenagers. The feeling was soon mutual and I had to ask him to leave. He demanded I pay him in cash. We had contracted for a two-hour show. He was on stage less than thirty minutes, but he wanted all his money. I paid. A lesson I learned from Peyton. Sometimes, paying off a problem was better than negotiating with it. I paid him off, and then a week later I got the word from the owners that they were closing the Centre down, as of that date, and so the movies stopped, leaving me and Mac to ourselves.

I guess you could say that your radio friend was the last person to perform on the stage. His behavior that night, and us closing a week later, I sometimes think there is a connection. Some significance, but, then again, probably not."

"Stop it, Dwight. Stop this bullshit. I have listened to his show every night since he began in 1995. Midnight, he has never broadcast from this theatre."

"Harry, it was a Saturday night, and he was not broadcasting."

Of course, of course, Ducharme was a weeknight show only.

"So, he is alive, and you have met him, right?"

Dwight nodded.

"He performed on the same stage you were on a few days ago."

"He's alive? He's really alive?"

"Harry, this seems very important to you. Yes, he is alive. But he will die. I have no control over that. But he is on my list. Then again, so are all those teenagers in the bands that night. Eventually, he will return here as a ghost, and then decades later, he will have to deal with those teenagers again. I tend to think that he will consider himself in hell then. And I will admit, I did not like him."

"You talked to him before. You can contact him again, right? You can ask him if he would let me meet him. Hell, ask him if I can simply call him."

"No, Harry, I won't do that."

Houdini was in the rearview mirror in my head as I stood face to face with Dwight.

I warned you, Harry. But, of course, nobody listens to me.

"Why not?"

"Nobody calls him, or so I hear."

I walked away. It dawned on me that the only reason I had come to the Centre tonight was to ask about Ducharme. I had my answer. As I opened the door to go back to my taxi, Dwight called to me.

"Harry, my offer still stands. You should move into the Centre. I've been getting that apartment ready for you upstairs. Some nice furnishings. I even got you a record player."

This is what I understood about Harry Ducharme, because I understood it about myself. I knew nothing about him in real life. His age, how he dressed, the lines in his face. But I did know that he had those lines. He had my face, I was sure. He lived in the past, hated the future. His face would show that. If we ever passed on the street, I would see my face coming at me.

Neither Sue nor I had a tv when we were growing up. I can say that to one of my young fares today and they give me that *You grew up in the Stone Ages?* look. Nor did we have a record player until almost our senior year in high school. Our friends did. We liked going to their parties. Sue was dirt poor. I was just poor. Buying a record player meant having to buy records. We couldn't do that. I was also . . . her description . . . I was *atonal.* A weird word that she had to explain to me. I thought she probably invented it. I suppose there might be some sort of clinical condition like that, the inability to absorb different tones. Maybe not. But she had a simpler explanation.

"Harry Mason, you have no taste in music. Worse, you don't seem to care. It's all just background noise to you. And you sure as hell can't sing."

Sue could sing, angelic alto, and she loved music. More importantly, she had a radio. And the radio provided the soundtrack to us. In my parents' car, as we were in the backseat on a date, the car radio was turned low. Our breathing was louder. While we would do our homework together at her house, me sitting at one end of their shabby couch, her lying with her feet in my lap, each of us reading a book, the radio on. The 1950s. I'd give you a list of all the songs we loved when we were together, but *the* song wouldn't be on that list. Those were all wonderful songs we heard over and over. Bobby Darin and Paul Anka and Elvis Presley and Pat Boone and Johnny Mathis (especially) and Nat King Cole, groups like The Platters and The Teddy Bears. All those and more. Sappy bubble-gum pop?

Sure. Dinosaurs now? Sure. But they sang about love, and we were in love. Sometimes we would stop studying, turn up the radio, and Sue would lip-synch the songs. She would sway when the music swayed, shake when it shook, holding an imaginary microphone in her hand, and I would applaud. Sometimes she would pull me up and make me join her, but I think she did it just to amuse herself. Remember, I was "atonal." I was also a very spastic dancer. After a while, I would stand by myself and perform for her. She always applauded, always sincerely happy. "A for effort, Harry, A for effort." And she would hug me, a hug that sometimes turned into a slow dance, regardless of the music.

So how come none of those songs, when I would hear them years later, none of those songs ever made me cry about the past? So how come I didn't immediately know who Karen was, helping Harry Chapin lead me to the stage for Monroe's party? I had a dozen of her albums. I had seen her face a thousand times.

Marilyn's question? Karen Carpenter was the answer.

Nineteen Seventy-One? Twenty-six years ago? I had stopped listening to music on the radio. I drove my taxi and smoked my dope and ferried the living from here to there in Oklahoma City, Oklahoma. I had not heard from Sue in almost a decade. Serendipity? Why turn on the radio that rainy Monday night? Flying in my taxi. I was thinking about her. I might have stopped listening to music, but I never stopped thinking about her. Yes, I was a sappy love song all by myself. Stoned and sappy and I turned on the radio. DJ chatter for a few seconds and then I thought I heard Sue singing.

Long ago . . .

Was that it? The voice? It only took a few chords, but I soon knew it was not her. But for those first few seconds I was hearing Sue. The music itself? The clarinet, the soft drumming, the short piano flourish right before I heard the voice? *Long ago.* The lyrics? How many times have I listened to them for these twenty-six years? Or was it simply the moment? The very first time I heard Karen Carpenter's voice, singing about long ago.

I've listened to all her songs since then, over and over. Many are heartbreaking. Perhaps if, that first time, I had heard a different song by her, would it be *the* song? A good question, but irrelevant.

"Superstar" is the song. Monroe knew it. Ducharme played it. I wondered if Sue had ever heard it . . . surely, she had, right? The never to be answered question: Did she think of me? That was the key distinction. When I heard "Superstar" for the first time, I didn't think about us, just her. Sure, listen to any love song enough times and eventually it is about two people, not one. I wasn't in "Superstar." And then, slowly over time, I was. But I wasn't the superstar.

It was on the radio. Three and a half minutes. And then it was over. And the present erased the past. It was midnight. I had to wait until nine in the morning to find a record store that was open. I bought the three albums in stock, and I bought a record player. Dozens followed over the years. My collection. And then I heard Chapin's "WOLD" and I collected him. I went through three record players. Vinyl LPs became scratched, but not replaced. I simply didn't hear the scratches. After a year in the boardinghouse, my record player died. But I didn't need it anymore. All I had to do was look at the album cover and I could hear the songs.

Then I was invited into a theatre of ghosts and somebody stole my albums. I had been warned, right?

PEYTON'S LIBRARY

I went to the Centre more and more, looking for Monroe and always hoping that Dwight would not be there so I could go touring all by myself. Even late at night, the front door was always unlocked. If the Rules didn't apply to me, I could do anything, right? I would park a block away and walk to the theatre. Peer through the front door glass into the dark lobby, on the lookout for Dwight. Slip in, but I was never alone. More and more of the ghosts introduced themselves to me and would tell me stories about their lives. Dozens. I told them that I was just visiting and they seemed disappointed. I told them that I was avoiding Dwight and they didn't act surprised. I asked them about the Rules. They all seemed to agree with what Dwight had told me about them. I didn't tell them that Monroe and Houdini and Chapin were able to ignore some rules and work around others. Except for Houdini, however, all of them adamantly agreed with Monroe . . . stay away from the damn screen.

One night, I was onstage with Trout, Mermaid, and Bubbles. Trout and Mermaid were a married couple. Bubbles was their trained seal. They had been famous for hauling a giant glass tank up onstage and doing tricks underwater. I had never heard of them. But, then again, I had never heard of most of the ghosts at the Centre. Trout and Mermaid were a happy couple, in and out of the water, obviously comfortably in love with each other. They even made fun of their own Trout and Mermaid costumes. When not doing their act, they were happiest when they mimicked other acts they had seen. They did a terrific version of a droll George Burns and ditzy Gracie Allen. I thought they should have been a comedy team. Bubbles was a happy seal too, as long as he got his ghostly sardines. It all made sense. If I could see ghosts, I could see all the parts of their prior lives. Water tanks, bicycles, swings, nets, trained animals, hoops, feathers, bowling pins, all the paraphernalia needed to amuse the millions.

Trout was tossing sardines to a clapping Bubbles. Whether intentional or not, he let slip something that I shouldn't have been surprised to learn, but I was. I was fooling myself to think that I was successfully avoiding Dwight on my visits.

Dwight told us you were coming, so we taught Bubbles some new tricks. You want to see them?

"He knew I would be here?"

He asked us to be here tonight to entertain you. Harold Arlen was supposed to be here, but his flight got postponed.

"Wait, wait, his flight got postponed? Ghosts don't fly."

Trout thought I was trying to be funny.

Harry, all we do is fly. Well, that and hang around here, just like you.

Mermaid started flipping her mermaid tail and Bubbles started clapping his seal flippers again, barking for another sardine. I gave up. All I knew for sure then was that even though I couldn't see him, Dwight was always watching me. Some sort of Centre Santa Claus, keeping lists, checking them twice. I decided to keep that comparison to myself. But then I wrote a mental joke for Marilyn Monroe, something about asking if she was on the naughty or nice list. I wanted her to laugh.

He says you might come live here. That would be great. I know that he is very tired. He needs somebody to take care of things so he can rest. We all like you, Harry. Come live with us.

Psst, over here, Harry.

I could hear Monroe, but I couldn't see her. I was onstage in the dark. Trout and Mermaid were gone. At the back of the auditorium, through the open doors, I saw the lobby lights flash on and off. I started slowly inching my way along the stage to get to the steps down to the main floor, assuming that she was in the lobby.

Harry!

It was a loud whisper.

Harry Mason, stop your skinny butt right now and wait for me.

I not only stopped. I froze. Then I felt her hand take mine and lead me to the corner of the stage. She was invisible, sort of. I could see some sort of hazy vapory version of her next to me.

"You do realize that Dwight knows I am here, that he surely knows you are here too."

A soft laugh, almost wicked. How else to describe it? But wicked in a good way, not evil.

You do realize that he is an old man and that I am Marilyn Monroe. Do I have to keep explaining that to you?

She squeezed my hand tighter, pulling me further off stage and the further we went into the darkness, the brighter she became. I could see a door in front of us, the door to Peyton's apartment, the room I had seen my first night.

Open the door.

I turned the knob. It did not budge. I tried again. Tighter than Dick's headband, something like that. Only Dwight had the keys.

Monroe kissed me. I was starting to get lost again. Then she softly tapped three times on the door.

Open the door.

I turned the knob. It opened easily.

Never fucking forget, Harry. I am Marilyn Monroe.

Inside was the same room I had seen that first night. Still immaculate, still arranged as if it was in a museum. The same pictures on the wall. The same lifelessness.

We're almost there.

I knew where we were going, but I didn't see the door that I expected. In fact, except for a closet door, there was no other door in the room. I pointed to where I thought the door was supposed to be.

"It was there, the door that Dwight said nobody was allowed to open."

Harry, look again. I'm beginning to see a pattern with you. You miss the obvious. The door is right in front of you.

And there it was. But something was different. There was no door handle. Just a door.

"I could have sworn . . ."

Open the door.

"There's no handle."

Open the door.

Monroe was exasperated.

I'm not opening that door. I'm not even touching that door. Open the damn door, Harry. Pay attention to me. Dwight cannot open that door. As much as he has tried, and I've seen him try for years, he can't enter that room. And it's killing him, knowing that Peyton is keeping a secret from him. Me, I don't need to use a door to enter a room, any room in the universe. But you do, Harry. You need to go through that door. You need to go through that door of your own free will, find a warm place to sit down next to me, and tell me about Sue.

I put my palm on the door.

You are such a tease, Harry.

I felt the air turn cold in Peyton's apartment. Almost chilly. Wintry?

Harry, I'm waiting.

I pushed the door. It softly and silently opened. Warm air washed over me, and then I saw the light. Monroe was waiting for me on the other side.

I stepped into Peyton's Library.

Books on shelves. Books as far as the eye could see. Books in a warm room larger than the Centre itself. A room larger than the universe. A room with no walls and no ceiling. A room of spiraling staircases leading to more levels and more shelves and more books. A million readers in a million years could not read all those books. Books with spines of every color, every language. A room of new book smells and musty book smells. A room of green carpets. A room lit by smokeless torches and candles. A room of shadows and silence.

The door shut behind me.

Straight ahead but far away, I could see Monroe sitting on a couch next to a circular stone fireplace, reading a book. She seemed oblivious to my presence. I walked toward her. As I got closer, she looked up and smiled at me. I had seen smiles like that before, stoner smiles of happiness, euphoria, slow-motion smiles.

I love books.

She went back to reading as I sat at the end of the couch. She was wearing her white bathrobe, her bare feet curled up under her bottom. Hair hanging wet, as if she had just gotten out of a shower. Two glasses of wine on the small table in front of us.

"Marilyn..."

She did not look at me. She just gestured for me to be quiet.

Neither one of us spoke for an hour. An hour? I don't know. A long time. I put my head back on the couch and closed my eyes. I had once read something about how our lives were never quiet, even when we think we are. We are always surrounded by the white noise of modern life. Electricity in the wiring... white noise. A house touched by wind... white noise. Walking across a carpet... white noise.

Peyton's Library was quiet. For a few minutes (hours?), with my eyes closed, I tried to imagine noises. I thought about the fireplace a few feet away from me and could see logs burning in my mind, feel the heat flowing around me in waves. I heard nothing. I went to sleep.

Wake up, Harry, wake up sleepyhead.

I blinked myself awake. Marilyn Monroe was still sitting across from me, painting her toenails. Her hair was wrapped in a towel. Her face was scrubbed and makeup-free. One of the wine glasses was empty. I was still speechless.

I love this room.

She talked without looking at me, concentrating on her toenails and then her fingernails.

I'll admit. I was a little leery of meeting another Harry. The name always brings back bad memories for me. I mean, how could I forget that wolf Harry Cohn. He wasn't the first one I met. When I started modeling, it was like part of the job. And if you didn't go along, there were twenty-five girls who would. After Johnny died, I had an agent named Harry . . . ha! another Harry, but he was okay . . . Harry Lipton. I'd tell him about all these high-powered executives at Hollywood parties who would offer me all sorts of gifts in exchange for sex. What can I say to wolves like that, I'd ask him. He told me that I would learn. And I did learn. There were plenty of them. I didn't take their money. If there is only one thing in my life that I am proud of, it's that I've never been a kept woman, but I kept riding in their limousines and sitting beside them in swanky places. There was always a chance a job, and not another wolf, might spot you. Then, in '47, I signed with Columbia. After I had my screen test, Harry Cohn calls me into his office and invites me to take a trip with him on his yacht. I'm not sure why that was some sort of tipping point for me, I sure wasn't a vestal virgin, I'd slept with producers. I'd be a liar if I said I didn't. But Harry Cohn hit up on me on a bad day, a bad day for him. I told him that I'd only ride his boat if his wife came along too. The sonuvabitch dropped my contract.

I used to say that dreaming about being an actress was more exciting than being one. I was wrong. Being in front of a camera was exciting, being an actress in Hollywood was hell. I was going to be an actress, Harry Mason, new friend of mine, going to be an actress whatever it took. I just had to learn how to deal with the Harry Cohns in Hollywood. Still, I never got over the name Harry. But Sam and Will and your singer friend Harry told me that you were okay, so now we can be friends.

In all that time, I just stared at her.

So here we are, Harry, snug as bugs in a rug.

I kept staring. She stared back, squinting her eyes, wrinkling her forehead, mocking my expression of wonder. She pointed to the full wine glass.

You gonna drink that?

I just shook my head, staring. Was I missing something in what she said? She reached over and picked up the glass, taking a big gulp.

I love this room. I wish it was real. I mean, I wish I had had some version of it a long time ago. I come here a lot. She paused and I could have sworn that what she said almost made herself laugh. *This is my favorite place to have sex.*

My expression did make her laugh.

I suppose it's a good thing you weren't drinking when I said that. Else we'd have wine spit all over the couch.

I found my voice.

"Marilyn, are you telling me . . ."

Harry, ghost sex is all I have. You think I was going to give that up after I died? I had a lot of sex when I was alive, a lot more good sex than bad. Sure, sometimes I had to close my eyes and imagine I was somewhere else with somebody else. Fucking for Hollywood was some of my best acting. But the good times, on my terms, I loved being a woman. But here I am now, in Ghost Town, Oklahoma, and the pickings are slim. Too bad you're not dead, Harry. You're sort of cute for an old guy.

Was I blushing? I was certainly stumbling for a witty comeback.

"But I thought you liked older men."

What had Sue told me, all the times I tried to tell her a joke, to be funny? "Harry, I wouldn't quit my day job if I was you." Monroe looked like she was reconsidering her newfound friendship with me.

Look, Milton Berle, in your case, I was joking.

Thing is, that hurt. Monroe saw right through me. She slid over to my side of the couch, with the wine glass still in her hand, and kissed me.

I'm sorry, Harry. I wasn't really joking. Sometimes, I do wish you were dead.

I hadn't been that complimented in thirty years. Marilyn Monroe wanted me dead. The problem? There wasn't a living soul I could tell.

"Marilyn, I've heard rumors that we all die eventually. If you're just a little patient . . ."

Well, you better die soon. I'm always going to be this age, my sexual prime. You die in your nineties, all promises are off. Right now, Sam is at the top of my age fetish. You at ninety are merely going to have to watch. Deal?

Did that mean what I thought it meant? I wanted to change the subject.

"You know what I'm still trying to figure out? Who's running this place? Who makes the rules? How come you and some others ignore the rules? Is Mac in the projection booth alive or dead? Where does Dwight fit into all this? And those are for starters."

Good questions, Harry.

She slid back to the other side of the couch.

Here's what I like about Dwight. His butt is usually wound up too tight, except when he talks about Peyton and Cori. He lets his hair down then. He misses them all the time. I have no idea if he is even telling the truth about them, but he seems to believe himself. Peyton is gone. Cori is probably still alive somewhere. But Dwight is stuck in the past, just like you and me and most everybody. The past makes him happy. Dwight in the past is somebody I can care about. Dwight the manager, bookkeeper, or whatever he calls himself, that Dwight is not to be trusted. The Hungarian is right about that. Except for the Screen Rule, Dwight made up all the other rules and he has 99.9 percent of everybody believing him.

"But not you?"

Nope. Me and Houdini and your singer friend Harry, maybe Sam and Will at times, we figured it out. The rule about not entering this room? He made that up because he can't get in it. He has to believe that since he can't, nobody can. Truth be told, the only people allowed in this room are people I invite. The rule about only appearing here if you performed here? Sam's friend John Lewis never appeared here, but one time Sam told me how he wished John were with him and I told Dwight, and Dwight said he would talk to his "boss" . . . as if a boss existed . . . and John was allowed to appear. Dwight will do almost anything I ask. The rule about having to appear on the date we last appeared here? Fake. About only appearing at venues where we performed before? Fake. Here's my favorite Dwight story. Harry Cohn, the dick wolf I told you about. He was in vaudeville before he was in Hollywood. He actually performed on this stage. He died before I did and so I show up one time and that bastard is waiting for me. He was bragging about how many people had turned out for his funeral. I had the divine pleasure of quoting my friend Red Skelton, who said, when asked about the crowd, 'It proves what Harry always said. Give the public what they want and they'll come out for it.' I then told Harry to go fuck himself and his yacht in hell. And while Harry watched, I went up to Dwight and said that I was never coming back to the Centre if Cohn was allowed to be here. It was him or me. Dwight gave me the old saw about asking his boss. All I know for sure, and everyone else has confirmed it, Harry Cohn has never been seen here again.

But here's something I have come to understand. Rules are important. Even ghosts need rules. There were rules in life, why not rules in death? Most people are hotwired to obey the rules. Me? If I had observed all the rules, I'd never have gotten anywhere. Harry, here's the sum of my wisdom. If you break the rules, being dead is not so bad.

"Is this when I get to ask you about being dead, how you died?"

Sam and Will told me about you and your death questions. Your singer friend Harry and Patsy, them too, you want to understand the end. The end reduced to that final ten seconds. Right?

I nodded. She took a few seconds to blow on her freshly painted fingernails and took the towel off her head, letting her hair free to fall around her scrubbed face. For a moment, I wished I was dead.

I grew up poor, worked on a line making airplanes in the War, made movies, married a baseball Hall-of-Famer and a Pulitzer Prize-winning writer, slept with a President and a hundred other handsome men, kissed a few beautiful women, had an up and down life . . . but you want to know about me dying? What are we going to do with you, me and my ghost family, what are we going to do with you? Harry, life is more important than death.

Will told me about the Ten Second thing, the . . . final ten seconds of life. I had that too, but not like him and Patsy and your singer friend. First thing, forget that crap about me killing myself. I could be depressed as hell, do some dumb self-destructive things to myself in my life, but I wanted to live. I actually had high hopes for my career. Sort of finding my niche. The thing with Jack? Me, my own little heartbreak hotel? I suppose, but even I knew that he was never leaving Jackie. Was I too pushy? Probably.

But I still had my ten seconds. I took my pills, as usual. I was just waiting for the sleep to come. I wish those pills were good at getting me high, but I guess they had one job to do . . . put me to sleep. They always worked. And then, as I was going under, I started to hear voices. Real voices. Not in my head. In the room. Familiar voices, men. I could hear them walking around. I thought I recognized the cologne of one of them, too strong, and I was going through my mind remembering all the men I had known like that. And if you are over there thinking I was hearing and smelling ghosts . . . stop it. Respectable ghosts don't wear that god-awful English Leather. I knew these men, but I was fading fast. I wasn't afraid. I was just curious. And then I heard the last words of my life. One of the men was talking to another, "Too bad, she's still fuckable." So, tell me, Harry, you tell me who was in that room. That's the question I want answered.

"You've come to the wrong person for answers, Marilyn. Very wrong."

I know, I know. We're all in the same boat, floating in an ocean of questions.

"That's a good line. And I know how you feel."

A good line? Yep, I'm a poet and don't know it, but my tits show it. They're long fellows. A good line? How about we're in a boat of questions, floating in an ocean of . . . nothing. Is that a good line too?

I sat there wondering. Who else could Norman Jean Baker have become if she had not become Marilyn Monroe? She was back to blowing on her fingernails, the two of us in a room without walls or a ceiling, surrounded by books. She looked up at me and smiled a sleepy smile, and then she went back to blowing on her nails, wiggling her fingers and then shaking her hands. She held both hands out in front of her and nodded in approval. Then she turned those hands toward me for my opinion.

Perfect, Harry, pretty damn perfect if I do say so. You agree?

She was absolutely right. I agreed.

So, now, Harry bear, tell me about Sue. Tell me something that you've never told anybody else. Maybe not even yourself.

I was talking to Monroe in a library without a ceiling, but I kept looking up anyway, searching. The bookshelves seemed to go forever upward, but at the very center of the space above me was a dark circle. Monroe nudged me.

A story about you and Sue?

"I'm sorry. I was just wondering about this room. Wondering about that darkness up there."

She looked up, then back at me.

Harry, what do you see when you look up at the auditorium ceiling? All the lights are down, and the movie hasn't hit the screen yet, what do you see there up in the dark?

A trick question, because the answer seemed too obvious?

"I see stars. Tiny twinkling stars."

She raised her hand and turned it in a circle. The candles in the room dimmed and then went out. The fireplace slowly disappeared. We were in total darkness. The only sound was her private voice.

You put your head back on the couch and look up, Harry. Tell me what you see.

I looked up.

"I see stars, tiny stars."

And there you go, an answer to one of your questions. Now, Sue.

We wanted to be together all the time. School was easy. The rest of our life took effort. Church was just a few hours a week. I would go to her house more than she went to mine. We both had part-time jobs, and that was a problem for a while, but then she made her first major accommodation for me. I had an early morning paper route, too early for her to get away from her house. I had swim practice three months a year every day after school. But then I got my first paycheck job as a fry cook at a hamburger place. Sue quit her job at a flower store and got a job at the Piggly-Wiggly across the street from my burger job. She had loved that flower shop job.

My boss was Marcus Horstmeyer. Old-school immigrant. He had worked his way up in America and owned two burger joints. *Mark's*. Not a fancy menu, the basics of burgers and fries. But the place I worked at was a good location. And Horstmeyer actually took pride in his food. The best fresh meat, and potatoes had to be cut on the premises and cooked to order, not precooked. "American food" he called it. The Pepsi-Cola rep offered him a cut-rate deal to switch from Coke to Pepsi. He laughed. I was there. "Coca-Cola is American. Only American drink."

He liked me a lot, thought I was super dependable, so he almost always left me in charge by myself while he spent more time at his other location. I suppose we were all blind back in those days. His other location had a McDonald's open up across the street my senior year.

Sue being at the Piggly-Wiggly meant she could spend break time with me, or come see me before and after her shift. Her favorite joke was to have one of her co-workers call my place and ask, "Does Harry work there?" and of course I would say yes and the caller would ask, "Do you sell burgers there?" and I would say yes and then the caller would say, "I'd like to order a dozen Harry burgers." How many times could that be funny? I knew the punchline after the first two calls, but I always played along because I could always hear Sue laughing hysterically in the background. Her coworkers always thought they were the first person to ever make that call.

The best thing about that arrangement? Sometimes she would bring food over from the Piggly-Wiggly, steaks or chops, fresh fish, whatever, and I would cook it on the grill at my place. We would have the best meals of our lives that way. I would tell her that all the world's great chefs were men. She would remind me that I was just seventeen.

I had long suspected that she didn't eat much at home because her family had to stretch their meal money further than a just God intended. I could never envision Sue ever being overweight in her life. So, she would stuff herself at *Mark's* and I would watch her spit food when I made her laugh. Eventually, it all crashed, sort of.

I saw her running across the street from the Piggly-Wiggly, almost tripping in the parking lot. My place was empty, lunch rush over, and I was just looking out the window, thinking about her. I just stared as she got closer. Something was obviously wrong. Just as she got to my place, she saw me looking at her through the window. She stopped dead in her tracks, eye to eye with me, as if she were having to decide whether to come in or go away. I didn't wait. I ran outside.

"Harry, I just got fired."

And then she was in my arms, arms wrapped around me as if I was the only thing keeping her from falling down, crying, coughing, tears down her face, snot dripping out of her nose, and then I could feel her hands beating on my back as she whispered, "Fuck, fuck, fuck."

"Sue, I don't understand."

What else could anybody say at that moment? She just kept crying. I was standing outside with her when I saw my boss driving up. He parked and got out, studying the scene. I didn't know what to say, but he just waved his hand as if to say *not to worry* and then he walked past us and went inside. Sue eventually took a deep breath and told me her story.

"They found out, Harry. They found out I was stealing from them. Every day, I took food home with me. I thought I was careful, and it was fine for a while, but I guess I got sloppy. Or somebody at the store tipped them off."

"But . . . you were stealing for your family, right?"

"Of course."

"Okay, okay, that was wrong. But we can get you another job. And you know that I would have helped you. I've been saving money for school, but I would have helped you."

How many times have you heard it . . . that girls mature sooner than boys? Sue was a hundred years older than me. As she leaned back to look into my face, she had that look of a parent looking at a child, hoping that child would stay as innocent as he was at that moment.

"Harry, all that food I brought over here for us . . . I stole it. That food that you and I deliver to my neighbors on Fridays, that food in Piggly-Wiggly bags, that I told you was a donation from the store . . . I stole it."

"Jesus, Sue, how much have you stolen?"

"Not enough, Harry, not enough."

Horstmeyer had been at the order window, listening to Sue confess to a felony.

"Young lady, you come here."

Sue and I whipped around, busted. Both of us expected something bad.

"Your family is hungry? You steal?"

She nodded, not looking up.

"Nobody should be hungry in America. You bring your family to here every Sunday afternoon. Everybody, but no pets. You eat a good Mark meal. All I can do. And you . . ." pointing to me, ". . .you cook that meal, but I not pay you. You understand?" I nodded. "But understand this, young Harry. You steal from me . . . I fire you."

She was a tough cookie, Harry. I would have loved her too.

The candles were lit again, the fireplace glowing, more embers than flames.

"Marilyn, how did you know about the song?"

A few years ago, I heard Karen sing for the first time here at the Centre. I'd been around singers a long time, Ella and a lot of other great singers, but I had never heard anybody like Karen. My favorite was the one about rainy days and Mondays. How many times had I felt that one? Too damn many. She is so sweet too, but sad. I think it's going to take a long time for her to be happy here.

"But, my song?"

Harry, I heard that song long before I knew about you. Sam and Will and I all talk about you. You are our project, figuring you out, you and Sue. You know who understands you best? Your singer friend named Harry. I think he knows things about you that you don't even know. Go figure. Thing is, Harry Mason, you are important to all of us, even to that cranky Hungarian Houdini. In the long run, you are going to . . .

"Marilyn, the song?"

She fluttered her eyelashes at me, and then she sighed.

Call it intuition, Harry, women's intuition. All us girls have it. I was going to have Karen sing it the night I arrived to meet you, up there on stage, all part of the show for you, but then I figured that you wouldn't be ready. You might have some sort of nervous breakdown in front of two thousand dead people. Old stoic Harry, flying in his taxi, his little world in order, and suddenly we start dropping memory bombs on you? No, you weren't ready. But, that song, and me knowing? Marilyn Monroe, Harry, Marilyn Monroe's intuition.

She wasn't telling me the truth. I was in a world of rules that weren't really rules, half-truths and hints. I had been told by one ghost not to trust another. I thought she was different. Then again, she *was* different, but different in ways I didn't understand.

Harry Mason, keep talking. Something about Sue that nobody knows except you.

There are moments like this for everyone, I suppose. You are racing through life, maybe simply cruising, but everything in the future looks right and bright, everything bad in the past behind you. But you get the ten-second warning. Sudden unexpected death in the family, you're fired, the missiles have been launched, ten seconds, but the outcome cannot be changed. Life stops. You become rubble.

Sue was on the phone, crying.

"I waited and waited, but it never came."

"Sue, I don't understand."

"My period, my period, my regular as clockwork period never came. Harry, I'm pregnant."

I defy any man in the same spot to be any more stupid than I was. We had been having sex for years, how did she not get pregnant before now?

"Are you sure?"

Never ask a pregnant woman if she is sure she is pregnant. I suppose I was lucky that we were on the phone, not across from each other. Only years later did I figure out why she had called me rather than telling me in person.

"I'm as serious as death, Harry Mason. I'm going to be a mother. You are going to be a father. I wish I was dead. That's how serious I am."

I had just gotten out of the Air Force. I was planning to go to college. Sue and I were going to get married in the future, year and date to be determined. She was going to be an actress first, wife second, mother third. Me, I was assistant manager at a Sheraton Hotel. That's where we met after the phone call, in the lobby of a hotel.

"Harry, what are we going to do?"

In all the years I had known Sue, I knew that the worst thing I could do was try to make a decision for her. In that lobby, I wanted to look at her without her seeing me look at her, to see if her face would tell me anything. Not her face for Harry, but her own private face for Sue. I wanted to know what she wanted. A couple of years earlier, we had just gotten out of bed with that glow that comes from good sex with somebody you love, the complete comfort with our own bodies, inhibitions cast off, desire temporarily satisfied, and the pleasure of knowing that the other person naked with you was the person you had wanted all your life.

Stop for a minute, Harry.

"Stop?"

I just want to think about what you said . . . the pleasure of knowing that the other person naked with you was the person you had wanted all your life . .

. that's a wonderful line. And it came from you knowing her at that moment? You know what I know about you, Harry? You talk different when you talk about her. You're almost a poet. Not quite there yet, but getting close.

"Marilyn, I'm not sure what I was feeling when it happened, the two of us after sex, but it's how I remembered it."

That's all that matters.

She had gotten out of bed before me and I had watched her walk naked around the room. I had seen pictures of naked women before. I was a guy, after all. Magazines shared among guy friends, magazines discovered at the homes of older male relatives who thought they had hidden everything, but who had forgotten how they were when they were young, how we all had some sort of radar for those kinds of pictures. Leave us alone long enough, we searched. Photo magazines, "model" magazines, "art" magazines. None of them were Sue. I watched her walk around and then she passed by a full-length mirror and . . . stopped. To look at herself. She forgot I existed. It was as if she was some sort of alien, discovering life on earth, seeing it for the first time, and she was mesmerized. How could something be so beautiful?

Harry, did you ever think that she was seeing herself through your eyes?

"Harry, come here. Stand by me."

How could I say no? And there we were, five minutes after we had been entwined, almost gasping for breath, and then standing side by side in front of a mirror, seeing ourselves together for the first time. I wasn't as impressed by my body as she was about hers, but that was okay because I wasn't really looking at our two bodies right then. I was looking at our two faces together. Her eyes were focused on the two bodies. I was focused on her face and mine, and at that moment I wondered what those two faces would look like if we combined them, if we ever had a child.

And then we were in a hotel lobby, me having a flashback to that moment in front of the mirror.

"Harry, what are we going to do?"

Did I really believe that it would all still work? That being in love was enough to be happy? That the future would not change, but merely be postponed?

"We could get married. You know I want to marry you."

"Harry, I love you, I really do, I adore you, but I'm a bit overwhelmed right now."

She knew it was not the answer I expected. My face always gave me away, all my life.

"My mother says I should go to the Gladney Home for Unwed Mothers and live there and then give the baby up for adoption. We can always get married after that, when the time is right."

She was looking down when she said it, not looking at me.

Marriage or adoption, those were the only two legal options we had. Abortion was not only illegal, it was dangerous. We both knew girls in high school who had tried that, or so the rumors said. They both dropped out of school afterwards. Marriage or adoption. I knew what I wanted. And then Sue seemed to offer me a lifeline.

"Would you really want to marry me now, be a father so soon? You know, I'll probably turn into a cow and you'll never want to touch me again."

I just shook my head, an imprecise response in that situation for sure.

"But you just said we could get married."

I shook my head again, much more adamantly.

"No, no, Sue. I meant that there would never be a time when I never wanted to touch you."

Were those happy tears, or sad tears? She looked around the lobby, as if trying to memorize every detail so we could remind each other of that moment fifty years in the future. At least, that's what I think she was doing. She looked back at me and smiled.

"What time do you get off? And you have keys to all the rooms in this place, right?"

I nodded.

"You get the best room the Sheraton has available, preferably the honeymoon suite. Mark it unavailable or to be cleaned or whatever you have to say to take it off the books. I want us to do it today, do it a lot before I turn into that cow. I sure as hell don't have to worry about getting pregnant, do I? You talk a big game about always wanting to touch me, Harry Mason, but I'm not taking any chances."

Three weeks? We planned a new future for three weeks. We had a lot of sex. We talked about baby names. We set a wedding date. We both agreed that it was to be a civil ceremony. No church hocus-pocus for us. We talked about how to make a living and have a baby and still let her do local theatre roles, adding lines on her resume. She finally started to laugh again. Three weeks.

"Harry, I'm not pregnant anymore."

I was at the front desk of the Sheraton. Sue swept into the lobby and waited patiently while I checked in a couple. I could see her shifting her weight from one foot to the other, looking around the lobby like she had done three weeks earlier, antsy as if she had had too much coffee. As soon as the couple got their key and walked off, she rushed the desk.

Three weeks. Future closed. Future opened. A baby to be born. A baby no longer existing. I was as prepared for the end of her pregnancy as I have been for its announcement. Not at all.

"It happened yesterday. A miscarriage. My doctor told me that it was fairly common in first-time pregnancies. Something about bodies not really being prepared. I was not to blame myself. It just happens. He gave me some pills for the pain and told me to rest for at least a week. But then I'll be fine."

"You're not pregnant anymore?" I was at sea again.

Her excitement disappeared. She was on stage.

"I'm sorry, Harry. I know that we were both looking forward to being the parents of a perfect child. This is really sad. But we'll be okay. We'll still get married. We'll still have kids. It's all going to be okay. Trust me. I'll make it happen for both of us."

Two more weeks. I came to the surface slowly. Sue was alternately happy, sometimes sad, but mostly happy. Two weeks, and then we went to the Centre to see a movie. It never crossed my mind that something other than a miscarriage had happened.

You okay, Harry?

I was trying to remember what that hotel lobby looked like, but it wouldn't come back.

"I'm fine. Just feeling odd. I haven't thought about that time in a long time. Those three weeks, and then the time after that. But everything is clear now."

Everything?

"Marilyn, why do I think that nothing I have told you is a surprise? That you didn't need to hear me talk about that time? You know about my songs, remember?"

Harry, you talking isn't for me to hear. It's for you to hear.

The light in Peyton's Library was getting dimmer. I was sleepy. I wanted to go back to my room.

Dwight told me about seeing you and Sue that night. You know, that was one of my best roles, even though I was a bitch on the set. I'm glad you liked it. Wait, wait, did you like it? I mean, considering how it is connected to Sue leaving. Are you and me okay, Harry?

I was surprised. Was my opinion of her that important? Or was she acting?

"We're okay, Marilyn, okay a lot. I'm just tired."

You know, I was pregnant three times. Only once was I happy that I miscar-

ried. I think I would have been a good mother.

"I think you would have been a wonderful mother." I was not acting.

And here we are at the Centre. I was a dot in your life a long time ago, like those little dot holes on the screen, and other dots, all eventually connected.

I almost laughed. "Marilyn, sometimes you try too hard to be profound."

She leaned over and flicked her finger on my forehead. I told myself that was a good sign.

Time for me to go, Harry, but you're welcome to spend the night here. I've slept on this couch a thousand times. Best bed in the world . . . or the otherworld. Lie down, close your eyes, go to sleep.

I did as commanded. As I was dozing off, my eyes closed, I had one final question for her.

"You seem to know all about me and everything. So, tell me, is Sue okay now?"

A kiss on my forehead.

Go to sleep, Harry. If you hear any voices, ignore them. For now.

JUNE 28, 1997

Harry Has a Birthday
Harry Sows Discord
Harry Gives a Tour
Harry Explains a Song

"Kiss me, it's my birthday. I'm fifty. I know, you're shocked. I don't look a day over thirty. My secret? I stay out of the sun. I spend most of my life in a studio like this one. I avoid human contact. Stress will age you. Contact with humanity will age you. What will save you? Potatoes will save you. Potatoes pulverized into a clear liquid. Yep, Harry Forster Ducharme arrived a half century ago. I'm halfway through my existential journey. My life will become a legend, a myth, a cautionary tale? Women want me, men want to be me, right? And how do I plan to celebrate tonight? I have comp tickets to the Tyson-Holyfield fight tonight, closed-circuit at the Myriad. I love Tyson. He's an animal. Probably an underrated philosopher too. Not in Ali's league. I mean, who could be? So, I'll go see Tyson pound Holyfield and then go cruise Second Street looking for a place to eat. I suppose I should already know all the best places to eat, been here a couple of years but, truth is, I don't get out much. Speaking of truth, here's a secret for you. Forget everything I just said about my birthday. The truth? I'm not sure this is my real birthday. My parents raised me and told me this was my birthday, but they adopted me when I was five. But there's no birth certificate for me. I got nothing, no memory of my life before that. I was found sitting on the bank of the Cedar River, near Ashfield, Iowa. Scooped up by a wandering Quaker, raised by Mary and Joseph Ducharme... don't laugh... yes, Mary and Joseph... and given the name Harry. I'm sure they told me who that Harry was, but I can't remember. How did this date become my official birthday? The simplest of reasons, and probably one of the reasons I loved my Quaker parents. It's the day I was found by the river. If you gotta have a birthday, they would laugh and tell me, why not the day you were found? Hell, I might not even be exactly fifty, but close enough. You figure it out. Me, I choose fifty. Okay, time for a birthday song. Before I do that, I'm taking a bathroom break. Wait, wait, I almost forgot, I just have one comment for the *Oklahomans for Children and Family* anti-porn crusaders. As I am emptying my bladder, I will be aiming for them. You know the latest, right? How they managed to get the public library in trouble...I mean, the public library...for having a video of *The Tin Drum* on the shelves, and then the holy-rolling County Attorney Bob Macy and his Gestapo start raiding video stores. They even went into somebody's private home without a search warrant and confiscated a copy. You want to bet that Macy and his brownshirts have their own private stash of porn? I was all set to have a monumental birthday, watching my own private videos, pondering my physical existence, and now I have to start looking over my shoulder as I wait for a knock on the door. But these guys probably don't even knock. Anti-porn crusaders...don't get me started. I was venting to my boss a few hours ago and he told me that I should've been here in the 70s when the FBI raided the Centre Theatre and hauled everybody in for showing something called *Deep Sleep*, some sort of *Deep Throat* knockoff. Thing is, porn is like death and taxes and prostitution...it ain't going away. Where was I? Right, right, the bathroom. When I get back, I'll tell you all about some sort of serendipity. Or stupidity? Since I'm a big-time radio star, I get all sorts of advance review copies of books. Guess what I got this week? A new kid book titled *Harry Potter and the Philosopher's Stone*. Some publishing publicist figured that Harry Ducharme would just love a book with a prepubescent character named Harry Potter, right? Harrys of the world...Unite! Harry Potter... a wizard. Harry Ducharme ... a whizzer. And that is where I am headed now, to the whizzer, as you folks enjoy Harry Chapin singing about bananas. Ya'll enjoy this while I figure out a way to make a porn movie of Harry Potter."

I was right. Harry is not his real name.

Houdini was in my rearview mirror, in a straitjacket again, blindfolded. Me, I wasn't concerned about Ducharme's name. I was thinking that his rope was getting shorter and shorter. Oklahoma wasn't New York or L.A.

"Harry, I haven't seen you in weeks."

I've been resting.

"Why would a ghost need to rest?" It was a serious question. All the ghosts at the Centre seemed to have some being-alive holdover habits. Rest, sleep, and judging from Marilyn, sex.

I'm not a ghost.

Obviously, a ghost who denied being a ghost was not going to be much help for me in understanding ghosts. I looked in the rearview mirror again. Houdini was in his swimsuit, waving his hands at me as if to say "ta-da . . . nothing can hold me prisoner."

And, besides, my young friend, my absence does not seem to have hindered your social life. You are fast becoming a favored guest, always in demand. I had hoped you would be my ally. Alas, I am destined to be your Cassandra. Warning you about the truth, but being ignored.

"Harry, you might warn me more clearly, less cryptically. Hell, you keep telling me that Sam and Will are enemies, but I see the opposite."

You lack a broad vision, Harry. You see yourself as only a small part of the universe, insignificant. Thus, you lack the power to understand the value of symbols.

"Harry, I understand friendship. You have no friends."

And you?

I shut up.

Young Harry, I apologize. I consider you to be my friend. I hope you will let me be your friend.

I looked in the rearview mirror again and shrugged an acceptance of his offer. He was wearing a tuxedo.

To the point at hand. I consider myself to be an American. But I make no pretense of representing America. I am not one whom other Americans, when asked by foreigners, would point to and say, "He is America." Your friends Sam and Will are such men. In their times, lionized as representing America. Ignore for now the fact that America itself is a ghost, something you can see, but when you try to grasp it . . . it is not there. That is another discussion. When Sam and Will died, America wept. They were icons. They were manifestations of the American psyche.

But who was the true American? Will was born in Indian Territory, not yet part of America. At a place named the Dog Iron Ranch. His blood is red in color and in genealogy. He is Indian, Oklahoman, and American. My favorite line of humor of him was him saying that his ancestors did not come to America on the Mayflower, but they met the boat. His father was a leader in the Cherokee Nation, but here is the fact that marks Will as truly American: His father also served in the Confederate army. Of course, so did Sam, albeit abortively.

Sam? Born in a locale known as Florida, Missouri. Hannibal was not his birthplace. A truly self-made man. Riverboat pilot, reporter, entrepreneur, social critic, as was Will. Of course, America chooses to set aside Sam's late-life fascination with young girls, his Angel Harem. A true reckoning would encompass everything, but America does not want its symbol to be so complicated. To be the greatest humorist in your history, he must remain unsullied.

"Harry, where are you going with all this?"

Presidents wept when they died. No one wept when I died, Harry. Nor will the country weep when you die. We are not extensions of some national self-image. But here is a secret I know about Sam and Will. They were human. They were aware of how they were perceived by others, their growing significance in the American heart. Will was on his way to supplanting Sam as the Great American Humorist. At a certain point in a public icon's mind, he starts to believe what others say about him. And that is a dangerous thing to do, Harry, to believe in your own mythology. Will and Sam will not admit it to you because they do not admit it to themselves. Each sees himself as "the" American.

Why should I be angry? Houdini was on a rant about two men he obviously did not know. He was talking in terms I did not understand. Still, I was angry?

Harry, here's what else I know. If each represents America, then America is a nation of irreconcilable psychoses. Sam hates America. Will is entertained by it. They cannot coexist for eternity.

There was only one way for me to resolve all this. I had to take Sam and Will for a ride in my taxi.

I asked Marilyn how to do it.

Harry, Dwight thinks he runs this show. You want something to change or happen, you ought to let him continue thinking that. You know what they say about attracting more flies with honey rather than vinegar. Will and Sam can go with you anytime you want, but you ought to ask Dwight first anyway. Trust me. Sweeten him up. Men love that, even cranky old Dwight.

When I walked into the lobby, I was surprised to see the projectionist Mac Duncan talking to Dwight. Mac was waving some papers in Dwight's face, muttering something about "it" being in the contract. Dwight stood there with his arms crossed as Mac stormed back up the stairs.

"Dwight, a bad time for you? I can come back."

He was not a happy camper.

"He got loose. How did that happen? Did you have anything to do with it?"

"No, I'm sorry. I don't understand. I just got here. Are you okay?"

He was not okay. He was more than unhappy. He was livid.

"Does everyone think this place runs itself?"

I thought he was about to hold his breath in some sort of weird tantrum, but his breathing got heavier and quicker instead. Mouth breathing only. His eyes were fixated on something a few feet in front of him, something I could not see. He was glaring. Seemed obvious to me that I was there at the wrong time.

And then he snapped out of it.

"I'm sorry, Harry. Didn't mean to go off on you. These things happen every so often, even before you showed up. So, so, here you are again. We have some new guests tonight you might want to meet. Bronco Billy Anderson and Clayton Bates. I guarantee, you have never seen an act like Clayton's."

"Sorta out of sorts tonight, Dwight, but I do have a favor to ask of you."

He scratched the side of his head, more suspicious than curious.

"What can I do for you?"

"You have a rule about everybody being restricted to appearing only at the Centre when they are in town. I'd be very grateful if you made a one-time exception for me."

Immediately even more suspicious. More scratching.

"It depends. And I would have to check with some others, but what do you want?"

"I'd like to take Sam and Will for a taxi ride tonight, show them some of the sites around town, places that mean a lot to me, might interest them too. I have one place in particular that I want to take Will to, but I want it to be a surprise."

I was expecting him to ask me about the "surprise" for Will, and I would have told him, but he simply started to negotiate.

"I might be able to help you, but I'm wondering if you've given my offer any more thought."

I was trapped, so I played dumb.

"Your offer?"

"To come live here. Make this your home."

My hesitation gave me away, but not fatally. He immediately had a counteroffer.

"You can decide later, I'm fine with that. But if you want me to break a rule for you, I'm going to require that you at least come upstairs and look at the apartment I've prepared for you. Take a look for me, and I'll arrange for Will and Sam to ride with you. Deal?"

"That's sounds fair. Let's do it."

"A deal is a deal, Harry. Remember, a deal is a deal."

We went up to the second-level mezzanine to the old office that he was reserving for me. The thick glass door had two locks on it. Dwight unlocked both and pushed the door open for me, stepping aside to let me go in first. What was once small empty two-room space was now a large luxury suite. Every piece of furniture looked like it had been stolen from some Gilded Age Vanderbilt or Astor estate. I had never been surrounded by such opulent beauty. I walked around touching everything. Dwight was pleased with my reaction.

"Remember, Harry, a deal is a deal."

I was standing in front of an armoire closet. I opened it and saw a rack of new clothes. And then I looked down at the bottom to see the box.

All my albums and letters. All my stuff.

I did not speak. I did not turn around. A deal was a deal.

He did that? He stole your stuff? Stole your life?

"I guess Houdini was right."

Let's not go that far. But Dwight is certainly showing a new wrinkle that I didn't expect.

I had left the Centre hours earlier, expecting to find Monroe in my taxi. I drove around, even getting some bar-closing fares, wondering if she would simply pop up in the backseat with a couple of drunks who were oblivious to being in the company of Marilyn Monroe. Instead, she showed up while I was doing my morning swim at the Y, wearing her white robe, dangling her feet in the water as I floated in front of her.

"I didn't say anything. I was doing what you said. Letting him think it was all in his control."

But you did not agree to move in, right?

I shook my head. Then I swam over to the edge of the pool and pulled myself up to sit beside her.

Okay, let me think about this for a while. The important thing now is that you got what you wanted, but if Dwight can make his so-called permission contingent on you going to see that apartment, I can make my own contract riders.

"Marilyn, what the hell are you talking about?"

If you are going to show Will and Sam the hot spots, I want to come along.

"As far as I can tell, you have the power to go anywhere you want, my taxi included, anytime you want. I can't stop you."

Harry, I should be more precise. I'm not demanding anything. I'm asking your permission.

"Marilyn, do men say 'no' to you a lot?"

The next thing I knew, she stood up next to me, dropped the robe, and jumped naked into the pool without making a splash. It happened too fast. Trust me, too fast. She disappeared under the water, surfacing in a few seconds, glistening, and answered my question.

Nope, not a lot.

I needed a bigger taxi.

Marilyn, Sam, and Will would have been a full house, but I had forgotten about Sam's friend John Lewis. Sam insisted that he be invited too. The five of us getting into a taxi became a circus clown act. All us men being gentlemen, we insisted that Marilyn sit up front with me instead of jammed in back. The problem? John Lewis was too wide to sit between Sam and Will. He also refused to relinquish his wooden staff. He held it across his lap, with one end out a side window, the other end perilously close to Will's crotch. I drove for less than a block when I looked in the rearview mirror and saw three unhappy men. Marilyn looked back and then poked me in the shoulder, speaking in her public breathy voice.

Pathetic, you men are such martyrs. John, you get up here and let me sit between Sam and Will. Harry, pull over, but do not look in that mirror of yours.

I'm about to be sandwiched between two comedians.

Sam and Will beamed. John didn't speak, but he did nod in agreement when I suggested that his staff go in the trunk. The tour began. I had planned a surprise for Will, but that was to be the last stop. He was familiar with some spots, like the State Capitol, but even he was interested in The National Cowboy & Western Heritage Museum over on 63rd Street. Surprisingly, Sam was not. As soon as we walked in and saw the giant "End of the Trail" sculpture, I knew that a cloud had formed over him. All of us stood under it for a few minutes and were about to move on, but Sam refused to budge.

The infinite sadness of it all. There are times when one would like to hang the whole human race and finish the farce. History? We sanitize it and then sanctify it. This work? All the downward angles and visions. The defeat. Put here, on this sunlit altar, a monument to what America did to the Indians, but also a monument to what America began to do to the world in 1898.

I was beginning to think that this tour was not a good idea, but Will tried to reestablish good cheer.

Sam, we're dead. We don't matter anymore. Our profound wisdom, compounded by experience, don't matter anymore either. Me, I don't plan on being depressed for the rest of eternity. You should lighten up. You'll live a lot longer, so to speak.

John began pounding his staff on the floor as if he was agreeing with Will, sort of a "Hear! Hear!" gesture. It was thunderous. Nobody else in the room heard it. Of course, nobody else in the room knew they were in the presence of ghosts either. I had to stay as mute as I could, or else I'd simply be the old guy talking to himself in a museum. I did not want to be that guy. I also had a flashback to my brother Frank, talking to himself. I probably should have been more generous toward him back then.

Marilyn offered a diversion, back to her personal voice.

Harry, take us to the . . . let me see if I can say this without laughing . . . take us to the Hall of Great Western Performers.

And off we went to see a room with hundreds of pictures and statues. An hour later, Will and Sam were enthralled by Marilyn's critique. John Lewis almost smiled.

Excuse me, they have Ronnie Reagan and Barbara Stanwyck but not me? And! . . . Dale Evans! How could they ignore my stardom in River of No Return? *And, double excuse me, they left you out too, Will? America's Cowboy Philosopher? But I was glad to see Audie Murphy included. He was such a sweet guy. And Harry Carey too. As for me, I think that we all ought to get together and do a movie with Harry Mason here, a western, so he can be immortalized here in his hometown. And while I am on a roll here, Harry, I need to remind you that we are not tourists. We're your friends. Anybody can show us places like this. We want to see the places that matter to you.*

Lewis pounded his staff again.

Thirty minutes later, we were parked next to the Murrah Building site. Giving them the history, I was reminded that ghosts are mostly oblivious about events after their death. An obvious point, right? Murrah was personal for me, but Will was struggling to understand how such an event could happen. Sam was not struggling at all. Marilyn? She disappeared and then reappeared, and then all of them, John Lewis too, disappeared as I waited outside the fence. She had taken them into the grounds. Thirty minutes later, they all reappeared, all visibly shaken except for Monroe.

Ghosts, Harry, a hundred and sixty-eight ghosts, all of them trapped there, waiting for some sort of memorial to set them free.

"Can I go inside and see them too?"

Monroe just shook her head.

I took them to the house in which I grew up, telling them stories about Frank and my parents. Took them to Grant High School, to every place I had ever worked if that place was still standing, telling them stories about what I did. The Sheraton was still there, but run by a different company. I took them to where Mr. Tubridy's dry-cleaners had been, then to where Sue's home had been. I hadn't done such a formal circuit in years, and was sad to see that a lot of the places in my past didn't exist anymore. I even drove by the Red Dog Saloon, resisting Marilyn when she started teasing me and the other men about escorting her inside. She even made clucking sounds, like we were chickens.

It was totally dark by the time we got to my last stop. It was where I wanted to ask Will and Sam about their friendship, if it was real, if Houdini was wrong. That was the reason I had told Marilyn ahead of time. But another reason was personal.

"Will, I need you to close your eyes for a few minutes. Okay? Promise me, okay?"

Rogers squinted at me.

I'm not sure. . .

Monroe interrupted him.

Will, close your eyes. Trust me, this is not a trick. Harry has a surprise for you. You can trust him too.

"Also, when we stop, keep your eyes closed. Marilyn will help you out of my taxi but you are NOT to open your eyes until I tell you."

In a couple of minutes, we were at the entrance to the Oklahoma City Airport. Rogers kept his promise, letting himself be guided out of my taxi to stand facing the large stone sign, illuminated by floodlights, announcing: WILL ROGERS WORLD AIRPORT

All our eyes were on Will as he opened his eyes. We were not disappointed. He blinked, then opened his eyes wider, looked around to find us, and then back at the sign. A kid at Christmas. The rest of us? Sam started clapping and we followed suit. Marilyn kissed Will on the cheek. Sam laughed and kissed him too.

I'll be damned.

"I told you. In a few minutes we'll go in the terminal. You'll see yourself plastered all over the place. Next time we're out, I'll take you to the Wiley Post Airport. Not as big as yours, but you'll have a story to tell him if you see him again."

I was leaning against my taxi as Sam and Will walked closer to the sign, stopping to stand and talk a few feet away from it. I could see both of them were having a good time. Soon enough, Sam put his arm across Will's shoulders and gave him a good shake, as if to say "Well done, old man."

Marilyn joined me to watch her friends.

This was a nice thing to do, Harry. I guess we all like to be remembered. In the big picture, your name on a wall isn't much, right? But tonight, you made Will feel good. Me, I'm just glad I didn't meet you in L.A. or you'd be taking me to my crypt to show me my name, and I sure as hell do not want to see that. So, what else is on your agenda for tonight?

"I want to ask them why Houdini says they are not really friends, that they are actually enemies even if they don't know it. Something about fame and symbols and ego, I'm not sure what Houdini's point is."

Harry, first of all, consider your source. I've had years of professional therapy, and I know enough to tell you that Houdini is more messed up than I am. He needs a good shrink for sure. You want to know if Will and Sam are truly friends? You look over there at them. You can't hear them, but you can watch them. Look close. Tell me what you see.

I studied the two men from a distance, their stances, their physical interaction with each other, the way they laughed, the way that Will was using his hands to seemingly describe the takeoff and landing of an airplane. How Sam tilted his head to listen more intently.

And?

"I see two men who are happy to be with each other right here and now."

That's enough, Harry. The here and now. You can start asking all sorts of questions, but sometimes the answer to a question is right in front of you.

The two of us stood there, willing to wait as long as Will and Sam wanted to talk by themselves. John Lewis had reappeared and was with them too, not talking, but obviously listening.

So, Harry, forget about the Hungarian trickster. You have more important questions to answer.

"Such as?"

Such as where you are going to be living in a few months.

"Marilyn, I'll figure that out later. Dwight said I had lots of time." She rolled her eyes. "But I do have one more question for you."

Such as?

"If you could go back in time and change one thing you did, one decision, what would it be?"

Another good one, Harry, and one I've been asking myself ever since I died. Problem is, I have too many possible answers. I'd ask the same question of you, but I already know the answer.

I kept looking at the three men in front of me.

If you went back in time, you would go with Sue to Hollywood. You would not hesitate. You wouldn't come up with some reason to not go with her. You think that if you went with her, you would still be with her today, that your life would be different. I'm not sure about that, but I'm sure about one thing. You going with her, or not, didn't make a difference to her dreams. You there or not, she was not going to be a star, or even an actress. In Hollywood a girl's virtue is much less important than her hairdo. You're judged by how you look, not by what you are. Hollywood's a place where they'll pay you a thousand dollars for kiss, and fifty cents for your soul. I know, because I turned down the first offer often enough and held out for the fifty. Harry, she went to Hollywood. Hollywood, goddam it. Me, I actually loved acting. Sometimes I was even good at it. Hell, sometimes my best acting was faking an orgasm. We're all actors, Harry. But Sue wanted to be a Hollywood actress. Different. Talent is irrelevant. You could have held her hand all you wanted. But she failed. She might go to her grave blaming herself. I know that feeling. And while I'm riding this pony, I will tell you right now, Harry Mason, Sue didn't fail. It wasn't her fault. Thing is, Hollywood is full of people who want you to fail. I'm betting that Sue met every one of them. And if you ever wonder why she cut off contact with you, and I know you do, it's because she thought she was a failure, to herself and to you, and she didn't want you to love a failure. It was all about how she felt about herself, not how she felt about you. Now, you and me have to go get the three musketeers over there and go back to the Centre. My couch offer to you still stands. You're a good man, Harry, but no good man could have saved Sue.

After midnight, alone in my taxi, almost back to my boardinghouse room, I turned on my radio.

"You tell me, folks. Did you see that coming? He bites off Holyfield's ear and spits it out? He bit him! I take back all my jokes about Mike being an animal. The good news? I put a hundred on Holyfield, on a lark. The bad news? I put two hundred on Tyson and I picked the round. So, you tell me. Does any of this make any sense anymore? Scully and Mulder might be right. The answer might be out there somewhere, but it's not in this studio tonight. How else to explain the latest round of inductions into the Songwriters Hall of Fame? Sure, Joni Mitchell and Phil Spector are shoo-ins. Harlan Howard? I doubt that most of my dozens of fans have ever heard of him, but any man who could write 'I Fall to Pieces' or 'I've Got a Tiger by the Tail' or 'Heartaches by the Number' has my vote too. Jimmy Kennedy? Okay, okay, 'Red Sails in the Sunset' or 'Harbor Lights' or 'South of the Border'…sure, why not. Ernesto Lecuona? Who? One song we sorta remember? 'Malaguena'? One sorta memorable song? Okay, more power to them all. It's nice to be in some hall of fame for something somewhere. We all know that I am headed to the Radio Hall of Fame. Wait, wait, I'm betting that none of you even know there is a Radio Hall of Fame. And a Marconi Award? Okay, here's my point. Why do we even have a Songwriters Hall of Fame if they ignore great songwriters like Harry Chapin? This is the fifth year in a row that Harry was eligible to be nominated…but it's as if he never existed. I mean, c'mon folks, Harry never bit off anybody's ear. If anybody can explain this to me, call the station, leave a message. And, please, do not, do not get me started about them ignoring Harry Nilsson too. Have they got some sort of grudge against guys named Harry?"

"Do you think I can just make all these people appear when I want? They have a schedule. I just keep track of the schedule. He's here less than the others. Of course, since you began coming here, he has appeared more often. But if you really want to see him soon, I can make some calls."

I had just asked Dwight if he knew when Harry Chapin was coming back.

"No hurry, Dwight. I just heard somebody talking about him a few weeks ago and I thought he might be interested to know about it."

"Who . . . who was talking about him?"

I thought that was an odd question, so I lied in my answer.

"Oh, nobody, really. Just some fare I had who asked me if I was a Chapin fan. Out of the blue, he just looked around my taxi and asked about Chapin. Said he wondered why he never heard him anymore. He was surprised when I told him that Chapin was dead. No big deal."

Dwight shrugged. He looked around the lobby, as if checking for burned-out lightbulbs.

"I'll see what I can do. Come back tomorrow night?"

"Sure."

And then we both heard singing, some sort of discordant chorus. Dwight walked over and opened the auditorium door. Chapin was on stage with the nun and priest, the couple who had sung with the guys from Iowa the night of the Big Party. Dwight turned back to me.

"Well, I guess you don't need me after all."

And then he walked off in a huff and went upstairs. When I turned back to the stage, a fourth ghost had joined Chapin and the Church. I started walking down the aisle when Chapin spotted me.

Harry, come on up. Marilyn told me that you were looking for me. Come meet my friends.

Up onstage, handshakes all around. First, the nun and priest.

This is Bill and Jeannine Ayres.

Then he motioned a tuxedoed black man over.

And this is Clayton "Peg Leg" Bates. You missed him a week ago. Best dancer in this joint.

That was Bates's cue. He started a show-stopping tap dance routine, ending with a spin and a bow, his taps hitting the wooden stage like a machine gun firing. He came over and shook my hand again, waved to an invisible crowd, and exited with a tapping strut. On stage, I was applauding along with Chapin and his two Catholic friends.

Not bad for a guy with one leg, eh?

"Excuse me?"

Peg Leg has one good leg, the other is a wooden crutch attached to his knee stump. I wish I had seen him when I was alive. He's a song waiting to be written.

The nun Jeannine spoke.

Harry, we have to be going. I need to help Bill on his memoir.

Chapin responded before I could.

Absolutely, no problem. The two of you get to work. Just remember to make me look good, okay? In the meantime, I will tell Harry here all about you and Bill being sinners.

The three exchanged hugs, and then Jeannine and Bill came over and hugged me too. A minute later, Chapin and I were alone onstage.

"Harry, you just introduced me to a one-legged tap dancer and a nun and a priest who are sinners. Any other surprises for me?"

I could see that he was about to use my question as a straight line for a joke, trying not to give himself away with a smile. Then he motioned for me to turn around and sit down. Two chairs had appeared, facing each other, with his guitar propped up against one. Next to each chair was a small table. On each table was a bottle of beer.

Bill and Jeannine are two of my dearest friends. I talk about somebody being a song waiting to be written. That's them for sure. A singing nun and a crusading priest meet, form a singing act, perform to raise money for charity, fall in love, and get married. In my world, I don't care if the Church cared or not.

I think that their God blessed them. And Bill is a big reason I got involved in the hunger movement. Harry, I'm telling you true. Bill and Jeannine are good people that did good work for God.

Chapin put the guitar across his lap and took another swig of his beer, tipping the bottle toward me. I took a sip of mine. I wanted to compliment him, but I was afraid that I would come across as a suck-up. Him? He was patting the guitar, looking down at it and then up at me, as if he had known me in another life but I was sitting across from him right then and I had forgotten that we already knew each other. Does that make sense? I was missing some connection we had. So, he sat there, drinking beer, looking up and down, waiting for me to say something, to make the connection.

"Harry, if you could go back and do something different, some specific something, what would . . ."

He stopped me with a quick palms-up, as if he had been told ahead of time that my question was coming.

Too many, Harry, too many. Did I do a lot of dumb bullshit stupid things? Sure. I was a member of a big club of fuck-ups. Tell me who ain't. Every damn soul in this place is in that club. I should have told Sandy I loved her more often. I should have hugged my kids more often. I should have done more of the small essential good things that a man needs to do. Was I late to the do-good party? Sure, but I got there. I thought you were a fan of mine, knew my songs. Remember me singing about all the times I've listened and all the melodies I've missed? And all the magic words, and all those potent voices, and all the choices I had back then, how I'd love to find that I had those kinds of choices again. But I don't, Harry. I'm dead. You . . . you still have choices to make ahead of you. Big choices. Don't miss the boat, Harry. Don't be dead and have somebody ask you the same question, and you immediately know the answer. Forget your past. Pay attention to the decisions you make in the future.

Our beer bottles were empty. How long had it been since I actually drank a beer? Weed can make you fly. Beer can make you crash. My taxi mantra. I had so much I wanted to ask Chapin, but I was sleepy, and the idea of that couch in Peyton's Library, only a few feet away behind magic doors, that idea was itself making me even sleepier.

"I was listening to Harry Ducharme a few days ago."

The radio guy who hates my radio song, right?

"The one, but he loves your other songs and he's upset that the Songwriters Hall of Fame never inducts you."

Chapin leaned back in his chair and started to lightly pluck the guitar.

Tell him to relax. Me getting into some sort of music Valhalla isn't going to feed a single hungry child. It's not going to make me alive again. I'll be a plaque on a wall. Sure, I'd like the recognition. I wouldn't have minded being number one with a bullet, but I'd still want to have made a difference in the real world. Thing is, I know a lot of people in that Hall of Fame, a lot of them ghosts I have met and ghosts you might. Most of them are good people. None of them ever said that getting a plaque was any part of their ambition. Well, a platinum record plaque maybe. So, tell your friend to relax. Besides, the fat lady hasn't sung yet. If I'm not there in twenty years, then my feelings might be hurt.

"I wish you could talk to him."

Who knows, shit happens, right? Me and you and him might be drinking beer together one day. Until then, would you give him a message from me? Tell him that song wasn't about him. I've known a few DJs who took it too personally, thought I was singing about a loser. If your friend thinks that, set him straight. That song is about all of us. We're all wounded warriors. We have dreams, we make mistakes, we hurt people, life goes on.

How long did we sit there? I wanted to go to sleep, but he seemed like he wanted to talk some more. How often would this chance come back to me? Any of this? What if this was all a dream? Not an original question.

Harry, you've got a lot of questions. Most everybody here worries about you. You're down on yourself too much. Marilyn cares about you a lot, and she is sort of the gold standard we use around here. She likes somebody, we give that person a chance too. She told me all about you and Sue. Me, I think I knew a Sue once, back in '72. Marilyn and me and a few others, we would like to meet your Sue one day. Harry, you've got potential, even for an old guy. Hell, you even seem to like Houdini, and that killjoy card shark has just about zero friends here. You? You're a lot more forgiving than you give yourself credit for. And in the big picture, forgiveness counts for a lot. You think I'm a big deal, with all the work I did for my causes, that all those things proved I was a good man. Thank you. But so are you. So, here's what you're going to do for me now. You are going to tell me a story. But you can't mention Sue at all. Tell me a story about something you did a long time ago that you are proud of, even if you didn't realize it at the time. Tell me a story, and I'll see if there's a song in there somewhere.

I saved the life of Chet McKinney's wife, or I ruined it. I never knew for sure.

Chet McKinney was a lounge singer at the hotel where I worked. A proverbial piano man. Never a big name, but he had a following, and his following brought friends along for Happy Hour and then Last Call. As part of the deal with the Sheraton, he was given a suite to call home. Two meals a day were comped, for him and his wife. The hotel also did his dry cleaning and laundry. Two dark suits, frilly shirts, and spit-polished shoes every night. Chet had a whiskey voice that had seen too much whiskey. But he could sing all the standards. And he could do a swell Dean Martin ad-lib as he took a break from playing the piano and walked around the lounge, glass in hand, telling jokes and flirting with the women. I was still in my shallow twenties, a newly unattached single male, and I thought that Chet McKinney was a giant dick.

After all these years, I can still remember his name, but not hers. We all knew she was miserable. Chet was not subtle. They were seldom seen together, but she was always wandering around the Sheraton at all hours of the day and night. How to explain the compromises anybody makes? Chet used to joke that she was a "mail-order bride." I suppose he was almost right. She was Asian, probably lovely when young and "introduced" to American men through a matrimony service. All perfectly legal. Chet chose her. The great mystery among the Sheraton staff was why he stayed married to her. He obviously did not love her. His lounge groupies were a steady source of entertainment for him. Some of them were married but still shopping for love and marriage. He would tell his wife to leave him alone for a few hours, and she would obey. She seldom spoke to any of us. We assumed she was an alcoholic. She walked in precise, slow and small steps, never making eye contact. But it was none of our business, right?

August in Oklahoma City, an inferno even at midnight. Friday, the weekly front desk audit. Back in the days when all the front desk machines still had a paper trail to be reconciled and cross-checked by hand, looking for irregularities. Very old-school bookkeeping. In our case, the hands belonged to Hector Salazar. He worked in the upstairs office during the week, but Fridays were his night to shine. He always requested that I be on duty at the front desk when he was working. Why me? A good question. Hector was a short man with very quick hands and bad eyes, forcing him to hold the tapes close to his face as he studied them. Sometimes he would lay the tapes on the counter and bend down close to hover above them, red pencil in hand. But he could do all that and still talk to me about his family back in Portugal. Well, his family and a hundred other topics. Hector was a talker. It was Hector who let me in on a secret. Chet's contract was not going to be renewed in the Fall. He had three months of Sheraton hospitality left, but he didn't know it yet.

Midnight, I got a call at the front desk for room service: two Western omelets, two glasses of orange juice, two Bloody Marys. A woman's voice. Room 444: Chet McKinney's suite. I tried to explain that Room Service was closed for the night, but the woman insisted that she was starving and that she be connected to the manager. I told Hector to pick up the phone. Instead of backing me up, he told the woman, intentionally exaggerating his accent, "I'm sorry, but the kitchen staff is gone for the night. But I can have my assistant go in the kitchen and see if anything is in the refrigerator that might be available."

Fifteen minutes later, I was standing in front of the suite door, carrying a tray of leftover shrimp cocktail that I had put in clean dishes, plus a plate of seemingly fresh vegetables. I even managed to find a couple of beers in the refrigerator.

I knocked, announced myself, and waited for a few seconds while somebody looked through the peephole in the door to verify that I wasn't a mass murderer. The door opened and there stood Chet in his Hugh Hefner robe.

"Put it on the coffee table, and this here is for you."

I set the tray down and turned around to see a dollar bill extended to me. I had been tipped less before. As I was leaving, I heard a woman's voice in the bedroom.

"Chet, honey, I am famished. Come feed me."

It was not his wife, that was obvious, but also not a surprise.

When I got back to the front desk, Hector had another assignment for me.

"Just got a call, something about a body in the swimming pool."

The Sheraton pool was at the center of a large enclosed patio. It was surrounded by folding lounge chairs and umbrella tables. One of the reasons I took the front desk job was that pool. I had unrestricted access to it when I wasn't working, any time of the day or night.

There was no body in the pool, just a floating lounge chair. There *was* a body on the edge of the pool, however. Chet's wife. She wasn't dead, I knew that right away. She wasn't even prone. She was sitting on the edge of the pool, her feet dangling in the water, her arms clutching herself, her upper body rocking slowly back and forth as if trying to put herself to sleep. The midnight humidity was almost as wet as the pool water. The pool patio area was in the middle of an open courtyard surrounded by four walls and five stories of rooms. The staff joke was that whoever laid out the plans for that pool obviously did not want anybody to get a tan. Maybe at noon, for an hour, you could get direct sunlight. But, at night, that pool area was a dream. The pool itself had an underwater floodlight. A few patio-light posts cast dim light, and the room windows above and around it offered intermittent starlight. That was how I wanted to describe it to Sue if I ever saw her again. (Sorry, that just slipped in.) The surface of the pool was always calm when it was empty. Wind never reached it. Why so many details? I was talking about saving a woman's life, right? But these details are coming back now, especially how the surface of the pool seemed to have a slow wave to it because Chet's wife was slowly kicking her feet in the water, and that disturbance set off a soft ripple, wavy motion originating with her small feet, the blue liner of the pool itself lit up by the underwater light, and those waves turned blue too. I stood there that night, already sweating through my dress shirt, thinking how beautiful the whole scene was. I wanted to go swimming, float on my back and look up at the walls and windows around me, listen to a storm roll in from the west, knowing that thunder and lightning were coming and it would be a spectacular show.

Chet's wife kept rocking back and forth. She did not belong there. Such human misery did not belong there.

"Mrs. McKinney," I called to her, but did not move toward her. "Are you okay?"

She stopped rocking and looked up at me. We had crossed paths many times, so she recognized me. Looking straight at me, she nodded slowly as she uncrossed her arms. I started walking toward her.

Slow-motion ripples in the water. Slow-motion life. She closed her eyes and leaned forward, falling softly into the pool. For the first few seconds I simply stared, watching her sink to the bottom of the illuminated blue water, expecting her to pop up. Five seconds, ten? Whatever, too long. I jumped in the pool and had her in my arms in an instant. We came up together and I just held on to her in the water. She was alive but lifeless. If I let go of her, I knew she would sink to the bottom again. So, we floated together in the deep end of the pool until I was able to carry her to the shallow end, where I could stand up and walk to the steps at that end. Up and then out of the pool, I carried her to a lounge chair and laid her down. Her breathing was okay. Her eyes were open. We were both soaked but the hot August air kept us warm. I heard the first rumble of thunder in the distance. Did I tell you? I was a shallow young man, but at that moment I understood how someone could kill another human being. I wanted to kill Chet McKinney. But all I could do at that murderous rage moment, as I was on my knees, was hold the hand of his crying wife, whispering to her that everything would be okay, lying to her.

An hour? Less? Enough time passed so that Hector got worried about me not coming back, so he called the police. I learned a lot that night, bad lessons. After I told the police what had happened, finding Chet's wife, rescuing her, waiting with her, the next thing I know Chet McKinney shows up and reclaims his wife. He apologizes to the police for their having to come out so late. His wife was not well. She often had these episodes. He would take care of her, Thank you, officers.

I punched him as hard as I could. Sucker-punched him right in the gut.

Next thing I knew, I was face down, handcuffed, and Chet McKinney was defending me.

"No, no, officers. I'm fine. No harm done. The young man has a bit of a temper, but he is still a hero, for saving . . .," and he said his wife's name, said it out loud and now I can't remember it. "I will certainly not press charges."

The next day, the Sheraton fired me.

Harry, that's a great story. And the old bastard was right. You were a hero.

"You didn't ask about when I thought I was a hero. You asked about something I did that made me proud. I will always be proud of punching that sonuvabitch. But, hero? Nope, I still failed her. I never went back to see how she was doing. I gave up."

He didn't disagree.

You did what you could. But you were a shallow young man, remember.

"I think I've been shallow all my life. Never doing enough. Never making a difference, like you did. You made a difference."

Harry. I got to do big things, but I started with little things. And that's how you have to judge yourself, how most everybody ought to judge themselves. Do I do enough little good things to add up to a good life? More good than bad, by a country mile. I sorta think you're in that category. Think about this one small thing, Harry. Tell me how many free rides you gave over the past thirty years, rides off the meter, rides for people who couldn't pay. Kids running away from a bad home. Kids running back to a good home. Out of work Joes going for a job interview. Poor moms needing a ride to the grocery. Little things. Poor folks needing a ride, Harry. You were there. And, trust me, I know all about you delivering bags of free groceries to a lot of people. Off the meter, Harry. That was you.

Chapin stood up.

Not sure when I'll be back again. When I am, I expect you to have cheered up. No more damn pity parties. We're all in this together, just like the dance band on the Titanic, *icebergs creeping up on the starboard bow. I come back, you and I are dancing on deck, nearer to our God for sure, or to our goddess Marilyn. Wait, wait. I do know when I'll be back. Marilyn is throwing me my annual birthday party on December 7. I'm pretty sure she has plans for you too.*

"Your birthday is December 7th? How come I never knew that?"

He did a riff on his guitar and laughed.

Getting old is a bitch, Harry. I wouldn't know, of course, since I never got past forty. You did know it at one time, that you and I have the same birthday. But it's not a fact that means much anyway. Just a coincidence. But I suspect that my party this year is going to be even better, now that we all know that Marilyn is sweet on you. Two galas for the price of one. Now, for real, I'm off. Tom and Steve are performing at some old places I did once, so I'll go watch them. Tom's fifty-two, Steve is fifty-one. I'd love to kid them about their gray hair.

A RAINY NIGHT IN OKLAHOMA

Are you really surprised? Did you really think that me and Sam and Will, the others, were the last great surprise of your life? And you say you know all of Chapin's songs? Did you forget about life being a circle, sunrise and sundown. Lost and found, Harry, lost and found. Of course, this means that you and I have to figure out a new plan for your future.

Harry Ducharme was drunker than usual.

"I need that damn ark of Noah's. I need B. J. Thomas. Annie Lennox. Hell, I need Credence Clearwater Revival. How many songs about rain are there? And, Lord kiss me, it's Monday and it's raining. Go find Karen Carpenter for me."

Ducharme was right. We were all expecting rain, but this much? Twelve straight hours? The last time it rained so much, the roof of my boardinghouse started to leak. I had to move my bed. The ceiling still has the water stains. Taxi business in the rain? A bust. People in no hurry to go anywhere. The exception? Closing time at the bars. Drunks always need a ride.

"I might spend the night here in this studio. Me and Bobby McGee. Me and my arrow. Me and my ghosts."

That got my attention.

"All the ghosts of my past. Hell, I might open up my phone lines again."

I wished he would. I had a question for him. About his ghosts.

"Lucky for us this is a warm rain. I once had a job in Minnesota. You want misery? Go out in the rain when it's forty degrees. No, this is wet and warm rain, almost romantic, except for the fact that it won't stop and we're all probably going to drown. Other than that, a walk in the park. Did I tell you that I was found next to a river bank in Iowa, damn close to getting some sort of old-school river baptism, but a couple of Quakers saved my soul? Quakers who disappeared in the ocean on a trip I bought for them. That story too? Yea, I remember, I told you all that. But here's a hot flash for you. Harry Ducharme never learned to swim. I hate rain. I hate the ocean. I am God's radio rock for sure. Me in water . . . straight to the bottom. Jesus Lord, I hate the rain."

Midnight in the rain, driving my taxi. A country song to be written. But I wondered . . . has there ever been a country song with a taxi in it? Semis and boxcars and buses, but a taxi?

It was raining that first night when I met Dwight. I feel like it's been raining ever since.

I was cruising on Northwest Grand, listening to the radio, when I saw her standing under the canopy of an all-night 7-Eleven.

She didn't wave at me, like she wanted a cab. She was just standing there in a bright yellow raincoat, holding a big red purse tight against her chest. I pulled over and rolled down my window.

"You need a ride, lady? Or is somebody coming to get you?"

She just shook her head, taking a step backwards.

So, here's the sum total of what thirty years as a cabbie has taught me . . . that woman was lost. She needed a ride. I pulled into a parking spot and got out. I went into the store, passing her, taking a quick side look. She was old and she was wet. I bought a couple of Hershey bars, and then I went back outside and stood by my taxi, like I was getting in, pausing to speak to her again.

"You sure you don't need a ride? I'm headed home now, so I'm off the meter. Be glad to give you a freebie."

Her purse began to cry.

I know, wrong words. Something in her purse began to cry. I shut my door and walked over to her. She still had not spoken. The look on my face was an obvious question to her. She opened her purse.

"I found it tonight. I went for a walk. I heard it crying."

She showed me the kitten, as wet as she was.

"Lady, we need to get it dry and fed. You too, probably, right? You come inside with me, okay?"

We went inside and it was suddenly obvious that the air-conditioning inside was Arctic cold and was going to make her and her wet kitten even more miserable. I bought a pint of cream and a roll of paper towels, then led her back outside where we sat on the bench together. I rubbed the kitten dry while she used the towels to wipe her own face and hands and hair. I was dealing with a child, a very old-looking child. I made her cup her hands together.

"Now, you keep your hands together, okay?"

It was like I was about to show her a trick. But all I did was pour some cream into her cupped hands and then hold the dry kitten as it lapped the cream out of her hands. I wanted Houdini to show up so I could ask him if he had ever done a better piece of magic than I was doing at that moment. Kitten full, I put it in my lap, where it went to sleep almost immediately. I handed the woman some more paper towels.

"Clean your hands. You'll still be a bit sticky, but you can give them a good washing when you get home. Now, how about accepting my offer."

She just stared at me, studying my face. A look of wonder and confusion at the same time?

"Harry?"

Harry, are you really surprised? Did you really think that me and Sam and Will, the others, were the last great surprise of your life?

"Sue?"

Shouldn't it have been obvious? Even after all those years? But, really, who was this woman in front of me? Who was the man in front of her?

"How are you, Harry?"

"I'm fine, Sue. How are you?"

If I had ever imagined meeting her again after all those years, this was not the scene, not the conversation I had imagined. She didn't look like Sue. Surely, I didn't look like Harry? But there we were. Under a 7-Eleven canopy, midnight in Oklahoma City, and the damn raindrops were waiting to fall on our heads.

"Sue, I'm not sure what . . ."

She closed her eyes and nodded. We just sat on the bench watching the rain, not talking. Rain falling, and a kitten purring. I wanted to hold Sue's hand, but I was paralyzed. All I could do was pet the kitten in my lap. I wasn't sure if it was the most profoundly sad or the most profoundly happy moment of my life.

Sue answered that question for me.

"Harry, I'm dying."

Of course, this means that you and I have to figure out a new plan for your future.

You could see it in her face, the struggle to find the right word. Me, I had no words at all.

"Harry, I'm sorry, tell me your last name."

"Sue, I need to take you home. We can talk there. You're having a bad night . . ."

"Oh, fuck, Harry, I'm having a bad life."

I wanted to look at her, to study her face, to see the old Sue. All I saw at that moment were shadows of her. A lined and pale version of her. A ghost of her.

"Stare much?"

"I'm sorry. You said you were dying. I'm still trying to get a grip on . . ."

"I said what?"

"You said you were dying."

The look came back to her face, the struggling look of someone trying to remember something.

"I'm sorry. I'm sorry . . . I meant to say something different."

I'm sure my expression gave me away, my relief.

"I meant to say that I wanted to die."

I was lost again.

"I am dying, Harry, but I want to die sooner."

My paralysis was gone. I reached for her hand.

"Come ride with me. Talk to me. Then I'll take you home."

She reached in her purse and pulled out a laminated three-by-five index card.

"That is where I live, up on Parkside Lane. You can take me for a ride, Harry whoever you are, but you can't take me home. My husband might be suspicious. If he's there. If not him, the woman who takes care of me."

"Harry Mason, my last name is Mason. You used to be in love with me."

"Oh, Harry, I said I didn't remember your last name. I didn't say I didn't know who you were. But you're wrong about one thing. I didn't used to be in love with you."

The moment balanced between wish and fear?

"Harry, I never stopped loving you."

The address she gave me was five blocks away, a five-minute drive. It took me two hours to get her there. We drove in the rain for those two hours, circling the entire Nichols Hills neighborhood again and again, long enough for her to tell me her story. Bits and pieces of it, sometimes more than once. Bits and pieces to put together to make a picture.

"There's a name for it, what I have, but I forget it. I'm losing all my memories, Harry, slowly and surely. When I can't remember my past any more, my body will still be alive. I'll be alive, but I won't even know it. It happened to my mother a long time ago. I know what's coming for me, Harry. I've seen it. A living breathing body in a wheelchair, dead. And I want to die before that happens, before I'm already dead and don't know it. I'm sorry, I'm not saying it right. When my time comes, I want those last few seconds to be full of the life I lived, every moment in my past to flash before my eyes, one last time. But if all my memories are gone, I will simply be a dying . . . vegetable . . . a vegetable that drools and pisses in her pants. The worst part now? I forget things that are not even old, things I said an hour ago . . . so, fair warning, if I repeat myself, you act like it's all new to you, okay? You act like everything is new to you too. My husband stopped doing that for me. He stopped acting for me. He hired a woman to act for him. He can afford that. He can afford to hire two women to act for him, an entire cast of actors, but he can't afford to act for me himself. That's fair. I guess he figured it out a long time ago. I was acting around him anyway, acting happy."

How many times did I drive past the gate to her property, her husband's property? I just kept driving. Another kind of circle, I suppose.

"I can fake it most of the time, Harry. Somebody meets me for the first time. We talk for a while. I'm a Sue that they can have fun with. Until they see me the next day, and we start over. I do remember some things, Harry, I work hard to remember things from my past. But I'm all by myself. Nobody helps me. I made the mistake of talking about you one time with my husband. I talked about you and your Dodge and how awful a singer you were and how we snuck into some old store and heard a man singing. Do you remember that too? But he asked about something from my past with him and I couldn't remember it. I kept all the letters from you, all the stuff we collected, but he found it and threw it away. No, no, that wasn't my husband. I mean it was my husband, but my second husband. My current husband doesn't know about you and me. He just knows that I'm not the person he married. My worst sin? I was never the woman he thought he married."

The kitten had crawled into my lap, but I kept driving.

"Harry Mason, Harry Mason, I'll never forget your name now. I promise. But they tell me over and over that it is all inevitable, me forgetting everything, even you, but my husband has enough money to make my life comfortable. I'm such a lucky woman. I hear that from the women who work for him. I am such a lucky woman. But I don't want that, Harry Mason, Harry Mason, first and only love of my life, Harry Mason, I don't want to die comfortably if it means forgetting you. I want to die now. I want you to help me. You're the only person I know who loves me enough to help me die."

We were parked outside the gate. I could see a well-lit palace at the end of the curving driveway.

"Thank you, Harry, for offering me a ride. You know the funny thing, funny ironic thing. I was going to kill myself tonight. Sneak out of the house, escape my keeper, and find a busy street and step in front of a car or a bus, anything big enough to make paste out of me, but then I found this kitten in a bush, drenched and howling, so I picked her up and walked to that store. There I was, planning to kill myself but not willing to do it because I was afraid the kitten would die if I wasn't there to protect it. And then you drove up, Harry Mason. You saved me and a kitten."

"Sue Alden, you are not going to die tonight. And I am going to take care of you. I'm not sure how, but I am going to take care of you."

"Alden?"

"I am taking you to your front door. I'll talk to whoever answers the door. Taxi driver found you a . . . yadda yadda yadda. You just act like we never met before."

"I can do that. I can act. But what I am going to do with my kitten? They won't let me have pets."

Of all the questions in the universe, I knew the answer to that one.

"I'll take care of the kitten. Trust me, I know exactly where it belongs."

Dwight must have been sleeping when I got to the Centre. The front doors were uncharacteristically locked and the lobby was dark. I banged and banged on the glass, the kitten tucked in my coat. It took almost half an hour, but I had time to spare. Eventually, I saw a flashlight beam bouncing around the lobby, finally shining directly at me through the door.

Dwight seemed actually happy to see me. He was in his pajamas.

"Harry, come in, come in, get out of that rain."

Then he saw the kitten and his expression went from happiness to suspicion.

"Seriously? Another cat?"

"Forget the kitten. I want to talk to you about your offer."

That got his attention.

"I want to see that apartment again."

"I can certainly arrange that."

"Dwight, I want to see it right now."

He was not expecting that.

"Harry..."

I ignored him and went for the stairway leading to the mezzanine. He followed me. I spiraled up the stairs and went straight to the translucent door. When I turned back to look for Dwight, I was surprised to see him puffing as if out of breath. I should have been more concerned about him, an old man having just raced up some stairs, but I simply waved at him to hurry up.

Inside the apartment, I went straight to the armoire, opened it, and looked down. My box of records and letters, my life, was still there.

"I accept your offer."

His eyes widened at the same time his breath and posture returned. Dwight was a happy man.

"But on some conditions."

"I will do my best."

"I need more space. The second room here, is there any space behind the wall? Empty space to be used for more space for me?"

"I will need to check some of the building plans, but I would expect so."

I was leaning against the closed armoire.

"I need space for two more rooms. I want a bathroom with a shower, some sort of shower that I can just walk into, not step over a tub ledge."

I could tell that he was becoming leery.

"And I want different furniture. All this stuff is very fine, and I thank you for that, but it is not me. I'll give you a list. I need it within a week."

He just stared at me.

"I keep the kitten with me."

He shrugged.

"After I move in, I'm having the locks changed on the door. You do not get a key."

The suspicion returned.

"And if I invite somebody to stay with me, you do not object."

"No, Harry, no!"

He was surprisingly adamant, waving his hands as if trying to warn me away from taking a step toward him.

"The offer is for you only. Only you. I will do everything else for you, but I cannot have any other living person in the Centre. It is forbidden!"

I looked around the apartment again. The kitten was asleep in my coat. Purring.

"Dwight, I'm not negotiating with you. If you really want me to live here, it's all or nothing. And if you agree and then double-cross me, go back on your word, I will bring a barrel of gasoline here some night and I will burn this building to the ground. It's already a firetrap. It wouldn't take much. But I will burn it to the ground, with or without you inside."

Yes, I shocked myself. Where did that come from?

Dwight shrank in front of me.

"Harry, if those are what you want, I'll make them happen."

Somebody else was in the room. I couldn't see them, but I could hear them breathing. Dwight was oblivious.

"One more thing, Dwight. I want you to shake hands with me. A deal is a deal."

Harry, you finally took the bait.

Houdini was in the backseat as I drove to my boardinghouse. The rain was barely a drizzle. I was doing my best to ignore him.

If you move in, you will never be able to move out. You're crossing your Rubicon, my young friend. You can never go back to your old life.

How could I ignore that line?

"Harry, not go back to my old life? You tell me, where's the downside to that?"

As you wish, but you really are a bad negotiator. Dwight has been desperate to get you to move in there, you could have asked for a lot more. Didn't you ask about a swimming pool at one time? Dwight could have made that happen. That big underground garage could have been converted. He could have made that happen.

"I got what I wanted." And then it hit me . . . Houdini did not know about me finding Sue.

Alas, my young friend. So did Dwight. He finally got his replacement.

A PARTY FOR SUE

I assume that you are going to name it Marilyn, right?

I was asleep when I heard Monroe. I was asleep, so I must have been dreaming. But then she nudged my leg and I was awake. She was sitting on the edge of my bed. The kitten was asleep on my pillow.

Harry, you are really cute when you're asleep, but you need to work on that snoring thing. Ladies do not like sleeping with a man who snores.

"Is it still raining?"

She bounced off the bed and went to the shaded window, pulled the blind strings, and flooded the room with light.

A new day, Harry, the first day of the rest of your life. God, how I hated that line.

I got out of bed carefully, trying to not disturb the kitten. Monroe kept standing by the window, looking out, talking without looking at me.

What's your plan, Harry? Move into the Centre and take Sue with you? Act as if you're both twenty again? I do have to give you credit for how you handled Dwight. And I do have to give you credit for a heart of good intentions. But you will still be living by the rules of the living. Sue will not get better. You will get older. She is right. It will be an ugly way to die. Are you really ready for that, Harry? Do you want your last memory of her to be her in a wheelchair, sitting in her own waste, her eyes glazed over, not knowing who the hell Harry Mason is?

"Marilyn, you're asking the wrong questions. The right question is . . . do I want all that to happen to her and for her to be alone, surrounded by people who don't love her? No, if she is going to die like that, her mind gone before her body, I want the last thing she 'sees' to be me."

She turned to face me.

Harry Mason, you are an absolutely seriously sentimental sap. Anybody ever tell you that?

"Marilyn, I've always been in love with her."

You say that as if love explains everything.

"I don't care about everything, Marilyn. I just care about her."

Well, Harry, you're talking to a woman whose experience with love has not been all that great, but you and I are about to become co-conspirators. We might even have to ask Will and Sam for help, your singer friend too. I suppose that since you're going to be our new landlord, we should get on your good side.

"Are you and Houdini both saying that all this was part of some plan by Dwight from the very beginning?"

Dwight has been trying for years. He's tired of dealing with all us charming ghosts. He's tired of waiting for Cori. He's an old man, Harry, older than you think. He's also a crafty old bastard.

"And you knew this all along, and you never talked to me? You let him con me?"

Truth? You want the truth?

I was getting angry.

The truth is, Harry, you're the right person for us. Dwight thought you were the right person for him, but me and Sam and the others ... we knew you were the right person for us as soon as we got to know you. As long as Dwight was around, we were never going to be truly free. Dwight thinks he can teach you to be him, Harry. The Centre actually is a hard job. But we don't want you to be him. We want you to be the person who sets us free.

"Marilyn, all of you are crazy. Being dead has made you all crazy. None of this makes sense."

Another truth. Until you found Sue again, Dwight had no chance of you coming to live in the Centre, but he had nothing to do with that happening, you finding Sue.

"And who did?" I was angry and accusatory.

Harry, I have no fucking idea. The worst lie of our childhoods ... that God moves in mysterious ways . . . except for the God thing, it's still absolutely true. It's still a goddam mystery to all of us, the who's in charge question, and all we do is try to play with the hand we're dealt. Right now, you just pulled a Sue card out of the deck and you need to figure out how to play it, and that means more than kidnapping her to come live with you in a theatre of ghosts.

"Marilyn, I'm a lousy poker player."

It was all too much, too many people pulling at me, too many ghosts.

"After all these years, she is back, and she wants to die. I just want to take care of her. All I want. I need to figure out how to do that."

Well, Harry, welcome to my world. And since you're here, you're not the only person who has to figure it out. I need you here, Harry, me and the others. We're all going to figure this out. And the first thing we need to do is throw a party for her, a small party, so we can meet her. Let me talk to Sam and Will. We'll leave it up to you to figure out how to get her here. Trust me, she's going to think you're crazy, Harry, crazy like us, remember?

"Thank you."

I still want that kitten named after me.

I had to become a stalker. I couldn't call Sue, couldn't simply drive through that gate and knock on that door and demand that her bags be packed and that she be free to go with me. That would be crazy.

Dwight started renovating my new space at the Centre. He told me that he could have it done in a month. Evidently, tearing out walls inside an old building was not as easy as I supposed. And plumbing needed to be installed. Work still had to be done on the private garage he had shown me earlier.

I had time to figure it out, how to spirit Sue away, assuming that she wanted to be spirited. I just needed to see her again. I spent my days driving past that gate, slowing down to see if she was outside. I had a cover story all prepared that would have justified me going through the gate and honking to get her attention, even if somebody was with her. A story about her leaving something at the 7-Eleven that night I found her, and the manager wanted me to return it to her. All I needed was a minute alone with her to make a plan to see her alone again.

Three weeks, and she never appeared. I was almost desperate, and then she found me in the most obvious place . . . the 7-Eleven, at midnight. She was sitting on the bench outside.

"Harry, where have you been? I come here every night. When everyone is asleep is the only time I can get out. I made myself a map so I know how to get here and back, but I come every night. I was scared that you would forget me."

"As if that's going to happen."

"Promise?"

"Sue, of course. The important thing now is that I know how to find you. And we need to talk. I want you to meet some friends of mine. They want to have a party for you."

We sat on that bench for an hour, facing each other as I talked. I told her about the Centre, from that first night meeting Dwight to talking to Marilyn Monroe a few weeks ago. I told her about the other ghosts. I told her about Houdini and Harry Chapin and grumpy Mac Duncan and one-legged tap dancers and trained seals and a screen that could not be touched by the ghosts. She never said a word until I mentioned the cats.

"Where is our kitten, Harry? Is she okay?"

"She's living with me. I named her Marilyn."

"You named her Marilyn? Seriously?"

For a split second, I thought she might have been disappointed, but all she did was stifle a smile, putting her hand over her mouth as if to hide it.

I told her more. I told her about how everyone hated Houdini, about a singing nun who married a priest. I told her about everything except the apartment that Dwight was preparing for me. And Peyton's Library, I didn't tell her about that.

She seemed spellbound.

"Harry, were you always like this? I don't remember."

"Excuse me?"

"Did you always tell me stories like this? Were you always so . . . wonderfully crazy? And you are wonderful, truly wonderful, but, Harry, you are also truly crazy."

"Sue, you have to believe me."

"I have to believe that you see and talk to ghosts. That is what I have to believe? Wouldn't that make me crazy too? My brain is turning to mush, Harry, but I'm not sure I'm crazy yet."

"You have to believe me, Sue. You have to."

She looked around the 7-Eleven parking lot. For help? And then I saw the worst look on her face that I could have seen. She was thinking. And her face said that she was thinking that the only person who mattered to her, that could save her, was utterly delusional and that she was all by herself again. That she was alone again.

"Where's the kitten, Harry? I want her back."

In for a penny, in for a pound? I told her the truth.

"She's back at the Centre. Marilyn and Sam are taking care of her."

"And Sam is Mark Twain?"

I nodded.

"And Marilyn Monroe kissed you?"

"Her ghost, but she said it was actually me kissing you."

"And you are Harry Mason, the boy I love with all my heart?"

I closed my eyes and nodded. I kept them closed and did not speak until I heard her take a deep breath and exhale softly.

"Sue, they want to meet you. They have a party planned for you."

That was too much for her. She exploded in laughter.

"Of course, they do. My very own debutante ball coming-out party."

She started crying as she laughed, but not happy tears.

"I can't do this again, Harry. I just can't. I'm here talking to a ghost from my past who tells me how he talks to ghosts now. And all I really need is for somebody to help me die."

She stood up and tried to kick my legs. But she was too hysterical to hit anything. I stood up and wrapped my arms around her, holding her against her will as she cried. If the store manager had been paying attention, he might have called the police and reported an assault or kidnapping. But I held on. It was the first time I had held her in almost forty years. I wasn't going to let go. We stood there . . . forever? We stood there until I felt her going limp in my arms, and then we sat down again, but closer.

"Sue, please trust me this one time. Come with me to the Centre. Meet my friends. And then, I promise. I will do anything you want me to do."

She leaned forward and put her head on my shoulder.

"Anything?"

"Yes."

"Anything?"

"Yes."

I wasn't going to help her die. I lied to her.

She leaned back and looked at me. It was my turn to laugh and cry.

"Sue, you look like hell. Makeup smeared and snot coming out of your nose. I'm going to dump you for a pretty girl."

She sniffled, and then she punched me softly in the chest.

"Harry, I'm the prettiest girl you're ever going to get. And, yes, I'll go to your so-called party. Why not? It's not like I have anything to lose. But I tell you now, Harry Mason, if this is some sort of costume party with your friends playing roles, I will kill you. And then you'll be a real ghost for sure."

Was there ever going to be a better time to do it? I leaned over and kissed her. Softly, afraid she would push me away. She kissed me back. She touched my hair.

"But you have to make me a promise," she said.

"I already said I would do anything you wanted."

"No, this is different. I want you to tell me this story again if I ask you. I will forget a lot of the details. If I ask, you have to tell it to me all over again, until I remember it. Tell me again like it's the first time. It's a wonderful story, Harry, even if I do think you're full of shit. And I want you to tell me more stories from the past, okay? If you tell them to me enough times, I promise I will remember them. And then I'll probably forget them. But until you help me die, you have to tell me stories about me and you, over and over."

Harry, we are going to have so much fun.

"Marilyn, I just worry about her being overwhelmed. I remember the Big Party when I first met you. I don't think Sue will enjoy that."

Harry, who I am?

I knew the routine coming.

"You are Marilyn Monroe."

The very person. And I have never thrown a bad party. For you and Sue I have booked the honeymoon suite. Let's just say we're going to have a Little Party.

"The what?"

Peyton's Library. So, you can forget about Dwight or Houdini and almost everybody else being a guest. Only the A-List of showbiz ghosts. Me and Sam and Will for sure, your singer friend Chapin, and Patsy Cline ... you told me that Sue liked her ... and maybe one or two surprise guests too. All on the down low. You bring her to your private garage and lead her to the stage. We'll be waiting for you.

"Marilyn, I want her to come live with me."

Leave that to me too.

"She wants to die."

Harry, if I was her, I'd want to die too, the sooner the better. But you and me will figure out Plan B later. You just make sure you get her out of that mansion without anybody seeing you. I will also light a fire under Dwight to get that work done you wanted on that apartment.

"Will you tell him about the Little Party?"

Sure, but not where it is to be. Just a party. And I will make sure he is gone for the night. Trust me, Harry, he is so scared you will change your mind about moving in here that he will do anything to keep you happy. And, for the record, he has to keep me happy too.

"Nice touch, Harry, nice touch."

Sue and I had just pulled into my private garage, the former dry-cleaning shop, to discover that the walls were covered with movie posters, almost all of them posters of Marilyn Monroe movies.

"You named our kitten Marilyn, and the last movie we saw together, according to your memory, was a Marilyn Monroe movie. We're surrounded by Monroe posters now, and you tell me that I'm about to meet her ghost. Do you realize how incredibly disappointed I am going to be if all this is *not* true?"

"Sue, trust me."

She just rolled her eyes.

Getting to the stage took longer than I expected. I had forgotten to bring a flashlight, so I had to feel my way along the halls in almost total darkness, with Sue holding my hand as she followed behind me. We were almost to the stairs leading directly to stage when she shrieked.

"Harry, something just grabbed my foot!"

I should have warned her earlier.

"It was one of the cats. Don't worry. They won't hurt you."

We stopped so she could catch her breath, fright compounded by laughter.

"Right, right, the ghost cats. I forgot about them."

"Okay, Sue, we are almost there, so I have to ask you do something for me, something that Marilyn asked."

"Riiiiiiiiight."

"When we get to the stage, you have to keep your eyes closed until they all arrive. You can't peek, okay? You can look around at first, but you have to close your eyes when I tell you."

"Harry, remember what I told you last time . . . be prepared to tell me this story again and again. Hell, this is so much fun now that I might even remember it myself."

As we walked out on the stage, Sue held my hand, but once we got to the center of the stage, she dropped my hand and just stared. The overhead spots bathed us in blue lights.

"Where did we always sit, Harry?"

I stood beside her and pointed to the top row of seats in the balcony. She looked up but did not speak. Me, I kept looking at the ground floor seats, afraid that some ghosts might be crashing the party. But it was empty. I looked up to the projection booth windows. Dark.

"Did we ever go all the way in this theatre?"

"Sue, lord no!"

"Second base?"

"A few times."

"A few million times, I seem to be recalling now."

I heard John Lewis's staff pounding the stage. That was Marilyn's signal that she was about to arrive with the others.

"Sue, you have to close your eyes now."

I walked her to the side of the stage and then gently turned her to face the other side, her eyes still closed.

"No peeking."

Marilyn and the others did not walk out onstage. They simply appeared about twenty feet away from me and Sue. I knew them all except for one woman I had never seen before.

"You can open your eyes now."

I had my arm around her shoulder, so I could feel the sudden, almost spastic, intake of breath. Her entire body tensed up.

"Harry . . ."

It was not a question, nor any sound I had ever heard before. It was Sue as a child, Sue afraid and brave at the same time, Sue in some sort of Wonderland. Had I been the same the first time I was here, meeting Houdini and the others?

"Harry, I know her. Not sure how, but I know her."

Her body relaxed and she stopped talking. I looked to Marilyn for some signal about how to proceed.

She was in the center of the line facing me and Sue, holding the kitten named Marilyn, flanked by Sam and Will and John and Patsy and Harry Chapin and a woman I did not know. I kept trying to imagine what Sue was seeing. Was she seeing ghosts? Was she still suspicious of me? For s split second I was afraid that Marilyn would do some magical ghostly thing, turn herself into Tinker Bell, whatever, and it would all be too much for Sue to absorb at once, but all she did was wave at Sue. Then she turned to Sam and gave him the kitten, whispering in his ear as she did it. I learned something new at that instant. It was possible for a ghost to blush. Sam seemed both shocked and embarrassed, but then he laughed. He turned and whispered to Will next to him, evidently repeating what Marilyn had just said. Will had that deer-in-the-headlight look too. Marilyn looked over at me and winked. But then I realized … she was not looking at me. She was winking at Sue. And then she spoke as she walked over to us.

Sue, we meet at last. Harry has been telling us all about you.

Sue was evidently a bit overwhelmed, and she reflexively extended her hand, which Marilyn ignored as she walked straight over and wrapped her arms around Sue in a hug.

We are going to have so much fun tonight. Sam has some stories to tell, Will has a new trick to show, your Harry's hero Harry will sing with Patsy. Fun, or else my name is not Marilyn Monroe.

Sue's first words?

"Is my kitten okay?"

Sue, your kitten is now in kitten central with me and Sam and a few hundred other cats. Safe and sound here at the Centre. You should come visit more often.

With that comment, she turned to me.

And Harry here is coming to live with us and he'll be in charge of all the cats. You come visit, you get a double: Harry and your kitten. And, of course, the rest of us. That's a win-win for sure.

With that, she motioned for Sam to bring the kitten to Sue. As he handed the kitten over to Sue, with a bow and a tip of his white hat, Monroe made him blush again.

Sam, you wanna tell Sue here what I told you a minute ago?

Sam was evasive.

Oh, Marilyn, that is to be our little secret, I assume.

Monroe waved him back to the line, but she then leaned over and whispered something to Sue, whose eyes widened at the same time she almost did a spit-take, laughing as if she had heard the funniest, least expected, joke in her life. I remembered how she used to laugh like that when we were younger.

Introductions began, each ghost coming over to be formally introduced by Monroe. I was still wondering if Sue actually believed she was surrounded by real ghosts. Last to be introduced was the woman I did not know.

Harry, this is Whitney Randall.

That was it. Just a name. A young woman dressed like she was the wife in a 1950s television show, complete with apron. I waited for more. And why introduce her to me but not to Sue? Whitney was obviously a ghost. I knew all the signs. I looked at Monroe, but she was staring at Sue, who was staring at Whitney.

"Whitney?"

Thank you very much, bitch, for forgetting me.

"Whitney!"

The two women lunged at each other and hugged like teenagers reunited after being banned from each other by their judgmental parents. They both kept hugging, breaking apart, and hugging again. I looked at Monroe, who was obviously very pleased with herself.

"Harry, Harry, this is Whitney, my very best . . . hell, my only . . . friend in Hollywood. We shared an apartment. We went to parties together. We were both going to be stars. The best times I ever had in that town . . . Whitney was with me. Whitney, this is Harry . . ."

Oh, I know all about you, Harry Mason.

I assumed that I was about to be flattered.

You're an asshole, Harry. Anybody ever tell you that?

"Whitney!" Sue shrieked.

Monroe was trying not to laugh.

Do you know how many times you made her cry, even when you were a thousand miles away back here in Joke-la-homa? How many times I got tired of hearing her talk about how wonderful you were and how she missed you.

Sue saved me.

"Whitney, you were just jealous that you didn't have your own Harry. Or, should I say, your own Harriet? Or am I getting you confused with somebody else?"

Whitney calmed down. What could I say to her?

"Whitney, you're right."

Monroe nodded at me. It was the right thing to say. Whitney was now on my side.

Okay, as long as we all agree that Harry is an asshole, isn't it time we got this party started. Sue and I have a lot of catching up to do. And I sure as hell want to finally see this so-called library that Marilyn talks about.

With that cue, Monroe snapped her fingers.

As Fred MacMurray used to say, "Follow Me, Boys." Sue, you and Harry stay behind me, the rest of you follow them.

With that we were led to Peyton's apartment and then to the magic door to Peyton's Library. With us assembled there, the room temperature began dropping. Sue began shivering. I knew what was coming.

"Close your eyes, Sue."

I led her through the door into the warm library. The open fireplace was blazing. The others followed me and Sue, but stayed behind us once we were all inside and Marilyn closed the door. I stood behind Sue, my hands on her waist for support, and then I told her to open her eyes. Not tension this time, like when she saw Marilyn for the first time. No, she went limp and fell back against me, letting me hold her up. I wrapped my arms around her, feeling her heart race. Except for the crackling of the fireplace, the room with no walls or ceiling was tomb silent. Finally.

"Harry, you . . . win."

You ever go to a party with ghosts of famous people? If you get invited, be sure to go.

For the first hour, it was like a private cocktail party. Guests mingled, drinks seemed to have been downed. Sam smoked cigars, most of the others were puffing on cigarettes. Everyone took time to take Sue away from me and talk to her. Whitney and Sue drifted in and out of a long-delayed conversation. Eventually it was showtime. Sam stood as we sat in a circle around him, telling us a story about a jumping bullfrog with a belly full of buckshot. We had all read the story when we were kids, I was sure, but hearing him tell it . . . it was new, and funnier. Me, I was simply watching Sue be happy. Tableaus were staged, to melt away and be replaced by new variations of still life. My favorite? Sue and Marilyn on the couch together as Sam was performing. The kitten was in Sue's lap. Sue was pushing sixty, like me. Marilyn was forever thirty-six. But all I saw was mother Marilyn letting her daughter Sue sit close against her and press her head into her shoulder. Marilyn had her arm around Sue's shoulders as she nestled there. I saw their eyes focused on the same thing, Sam, but Marilyn would sometimes tilt her head down and kiss Sue on the top of her head, whispering to her, as if assuring her child that nothing bad would ever happen to her. Once, I thought Sue had fallen asleep, there under Marilyn's arm. Her eyes were closed, but then I saw her hand stroking the sleeping kitten.

Sam closed his performance by blowing cigar smoke rings, bowing and yielding the floor to Will, who surprised us all by not doing rope tricks. Instead, he told a story about meeting his future wife, Betty Blake.

She was a friend of my sister, and I knew she was the one, but I wasn't ready to settle down. Her father and mine weren't too happy with my wandering ways. But we met up again in 1904 at the St. Louis World's Fair. We get hitched and I keep traveling with a Wild West show. Of course, not sure how it happened, Betty tells me we're gonna have a baby. I think I can take my rope tricks to vaudeville, make a good living, but somehow rope tricks were not the hit they shoulda been . . . One night I drop the rope and start talking. Evidently, I was a better talker than I was a roper. I was a star in the Ziegfield Follies after that, but Betty was still the star of my life . . . I'll never forget the last time I saw her. Me and Wiley were flying up to Alaska . . . not my best decision, obviously . . . but after we took off, I made Wiley circle low back over the airport so I could wave at Betty one more time.

Among the living and the dead in that room, not an eye was dry.

Harry Chapin was next.

After listening to Will, I think I might have to change my song selection. I was going to sing about a big rock falling on a town.

One of my favorites.

But I think I'll tell you about Sandy.

He sang "I Wanna Learn a Love Song." Young man, older married woman, guitar lessons.

I was beginning to sense a theme party in progress.

Marilyn got up from sitting next to Sue, offering her place to Whitney. Then she motioned for me to make room for her on the couch I was on. As Chapin began to sing, she nestled her head in my shoulder, just as Sue had done with her. I felt awkward for a second, sitting across from Sue like that, but she was smiling at me, making it clear that she was perfectly fine with the couple across from her. More than fine . . . happy to see it. We locked eyes, and all I could do was mouth *I love you.* I could read her lips too. *I know.*

When Chapin finished, the Library was silent, again. He sat down next to John Lewis, who patted his knee. I wondered if anybody else was getting sleepy, like I was. Just then, Patsy Cline stood up . . . and woke me up.

You folks are getting too much sappy sad love stuff. I've got a song to keep you on your toes. A sad song about bad love. Thing is, in a big way the title is about all you folks here tonight, even you, my friend Harry Mason. Just the title. If I find Willie again, I'll have him write some new lyrics just for y'all.

As Cline strummed some warm-up chords, I leaned over and asked Marilyn a question that had been bugging me all night.

"What did you say to Sam back there on stage?"

She turned her head and whispered in my ear, her breath like a kiss.

So, I handed the kitten over to him and, in my sweetest little girl voice, I told him to be nice to it because it was the only time he was ever going to touch my pussy. You know, I figured out that Sue was my kind of girl when she laughed like she did when I told her. You be nice to her, Harry Mason.

Just then, Patsy Cline started singing "Crazy."

You can thank me later.

The party was over. Good-bye handshakes and hugs were exchanged. Everyone's favorite moment was when Sue hugged John Lewis. The old man evidently was not a natural hugger. As each one said good-bye, Sue was distracted by the next person. She never saw how each guest simply faded away. Up last was Marilyn, our hostess.

Last call, folks. This joint closes in a few minutes, but I still have something to show you.

With that, she rubbed her hands together and then opened them to reveal a key.

Sue, I have a surprise for Harry here. His new apartment is ready. Time for him to take possession.

She led us off stage, down to the first floor, up the aisle, and into the lobby, where Sue made us stop.

"I remember this. I loved this. The mirrors. The chandeliers. And, oh, those curtains."

Marilyn and I stepped aside and waited as Sue slowly walked around the lobby, touching the glass and wood and cloth.

"Harry, are you really going to live here?"

I nodded.

"Can I live here with you?"

Marilyn muttered, but I could hear her.

Well, that was easier than I expected.

"But you still have to keep your promise."

More muttering.

Harry, the questions don't get any easier. We need to talk in private.

"Sue, we'll make everything work for you."

I was stalling for time. At that moment, I was too happy that she wanted to live with me. Helping her die? Time for that later. She let it slide, for then. Marilyn changed the subject.

You lovebirds can go all Romeo and Juliet later. For now, Harry needs to sign the lease before Dwight gets back.

"Lease?"

Figure of speech, Harry. Please keep up.

Two minutes later she unlocked the door to my apartment, stepping aside to let me and Sue go in ahead of her.

I was surprised by how precisely Dwight had followed my instructions. The extra rooms were exactly what I wanted. I couldn't put my finger on it, but something was still different than I expected. Sue, however, was pleased.

"This is where we could live?"

Sue, you can thank me later. I saw the list that Harry gave Dwight, about what he wanted. As you know, being a Hollywood veteran yourself, only gay men have any interior design sense. Dwight and Harry are hopelessly straight. Harry wanted something out of the Fifties, but if we left it to Dwight, we would be looking at secondhand furniture he picked from up from the curb of the Salvation Army. I contacted an old friend of mine, Ed Willis. He took it from there.

I had one final thing to check. I opened the armoire, but the box of letters and albums was not there.

Relax, Harry. Look under the bed, where you had them in your old dump. Sue, you might be interested.

Losing track of time was happening more and more to me. How long did Marilyn and I sit and watch Sue go through that box? How many times did she say, *You saved everything?* And then say it again ten minutes later? Hundreds of letters from her to me. Each one touched by her, postmarks noted, but not read. I knew we could do that later. The other relics from ancient history? The receipts and movie ticket stubs, the school paper clippings about her high school stardom. The few photos of her and me together. Her graduation picture. More. All that was missing was everything from 1960 to 1997. Letters and other stuff spread out all over the bed. She would sometimes stop, a letter in each hand, and look back at me.

"Sue, sometime, would you read those letters to me. Read to me, and maybe you can tell me about other things that were happening to you then that weren't in the letters?"

Good for you, Harry, good for you.

HARRY SWIMS

I was beginning to think that Houdini had been right. I should have asked Dwight for a pool.

The morning after the party, I was swimming at the Y. Marilyn, Sam, and Will were all sitting on the edge of the pool, their feet in the water. They were all wearing white robes.

"I'm telling you now. If you're naked under those robes and decide to go swimming, I'm not moving into the Centre. All bets are off."

Sam and Will looked confused, but Marilyn explained.

Harry and I go skinny dipping here a lot.

"We do not!"

Will and Sam looked at each other and then stood up and reached for the belts on their robes.

"I'm serious." And I was. "I can spend the rest of my life happily without seeing you guys naked. Stop it!"

Both men sat back down, exchanging grins. Marilyn was innocently looking up at the ceiling. Then she looked back at me, not anywhere near a smile.

Harry, you called this meeting. Whether you did it consciously or not, doesn't matter. You've got the gavel. We all know what you need, but none of us has an answer for you.

"Sue wants me to help her die. I told her I would, but how the hell am I supposed to do that?"

I was surprised when Sam spoke. I was so used to Marilyn being in charge.

Young man, Sue is a lovely child. But I agree with Marilyn. If I was her, I would want to die too. And, as we all know now, you did promise to help her.

Will nodded in agreement and spoke as Marilyn remained silent, looking down at the pool water.

Harry, we want to help you. More, we want to help Sue. Sam is right. She's a lovely person. But she doesn't love us. She didn't ask us to help her. She's asking you, she's asking you to do the right thing for her. For her, not you. And, get down to it, she doesn't fear death. She fears life. Look at us, Harry, the three of us. We're all dead, but it's not a bad life.

"But you don't understand. I lost her for almost forty years. I can't lose her again."

Marilyn snapped.

Harry, don't be so damn selfish. You're going to lose her anyway, after . . . after . . . she loses herself. You think you can save her? You'll end up saving some shell of her, and you'll end up with nothing except that shell. And that is all you'll remember when you die, and trust me you are going to die, your last memory of her will be that shell.

"But you don't understand . . ."

No! You . . . you, Harry Mason . . . you . . . do not understand. You made her a promise. You gave her hope. When you figure out how to keep that promise, you talk to us. You tell us what to do, and we'll do it. But do not ever . . . ever . . . tell the dead that we do not understand.

I kept swimming for another hour. Doing slow laps, floating, letting myself sink to the bottom and then rising. Back and forth, up and down. I would be sixty in a month.

I shouldn't have been surprised. Houdini was in the water with me. I was floating on my back, my eyes closed. He was floating beside me.

Harry, I wish I could help you.

I opened my eyes and started doing a slow breaststroke away from him. Of all the ghosts in the world, I expected the least from him. He had nothing to offer me, right? Doom and gloom Houdini. But he was waiting for me at the other end of the pool.

Harry, I am not your enemy.

I started swimming back to the opposite end. He beat me there.

Harry, please.

The tone of his voice? As every parent understood, the difference between an inside versus an outside voice? Houdini usually spoke with his outside voice, but not now. He and I were on the inside, surrounded by a dozen oblivious swimmers, the two of us absolutely alone.

"I don't think anybody can help me. I wished for something for almost forty years. My wish came true. It was not . . ."

It was not your real wish. You wished for the past to come back. Harry, you cannot freeze the past and save it. All you have now is the present, and the future.

"And then the forever?"

It does not exist. And this is how I help you, Harry. I am either right or I am wrong. Marilyn and the others are right, or they are wrong. As soon as you figure out who is really right, you will know what to do. Believe in me, you hold on to Sue for as long as you can. Believe the others, you let her go.

I'll be sixty in a month. I should be smarter than I am.

More than book smart. Life smart. I went to college, but I dropped out. I read a lot of books in those few short years, very few since then. I haven't owned a tv in twenty years. Don't have a phone. I used to go to the movies a lot, not so many in the past few years. I subscribed to *The Oklahoman*, but as soon as I moved into the boardinghouse it kept getting stolen before I could get it at the front door. I unsubscribed. I read copies that are left in my taxi, copies left at a Denny's or an IHOP or the Y lobby, and the library has a newspaper section. For a long time, I had magazines delivered to a post office mailbox. Serious magazines. Popular music? Forget it. A computer? Nope. I still listen to the radio a lot, oldies, and Harry Ducharme. If I have any source of current news, I suppose it's him. But I *am* smart enough to know that he might not be a reliable source of reality.

I need to be smarter than I am. I need to be smart so I can take care of Sue. I need to know more about what is wrong with her.

A few blocks away from the Centre is the downtown public library on Dean McGee Avenue. I suppose that if I had to divide up the time of my life, the taxi would come in first, then my room, most of that time asleep, then the Y swimming pool, and then a couple of hours a week at the library. I don't have a library card. I simply browse. I catch up on the newspaper and, like some sort of muscle memory of an amputated limb, I look at a few magazines.

The people at the library are good people. They know my name. I've had them as passengers. I've even delivered books for them to a few shut-ins. I needed to be smarter about Sue, so I went to the library and asked for help. They're good people.

The young woman at the Information Desk was new or, was it simply that I seldom went to the library on a Sunday? Her nametag said "Sharon Billinger: Book Lover," and she had that look I always envied when I saw it in anybody . . . the *I finally have my dream job and I am looking forward to the rest of my life* look. I told her about Sue, and she nodded without breaking eye contact with me.

"My grandmother has that too. Sue is your wife, right?"

Why not?

"Yes, for almost forty years."

"Okay, Mr. Mason, let me do some research and get you a list of material that we have here now, and I can order other things through the interlibrary loan system. Can you give me a half hour?"

True to her word, Sharon soon had a printout of magazine articles and catalog references on where to find them. She even had a list of videotapes I could watch on the library VCRs. As she went through the list with me, I wished that she could have seen Peyton's Library. I would have liked to watch her face as she stood there looking around.

Five hours later, as I sat reading another article, awash in facts, Sharon tapped me on the shoulder.

"Mr. Mason, we're closing soon. I can hold all this for you if you want to come back tomorrow. I'm sorry we can't let the magazines leave the building. People tend to tear out pages when they're out of our sight. But if you have some articles in particular that you want to read, I can stay late and make copies for you."

The middle of November. It was dark outside. Chilly. How old was she? Early twenties? A lovely young woman.

"No, no, thank you," I said. "I think I've read enough. You've been very helpful."

"My pleasure. I wish I could steer you to some more optimistic sources. I went through a lot of this with my grandfather. It was rough on him."

"How is he doing now?"

She looked away for a second, cleared her throat, and turned back to smile at me.

"He died when I was eighteen. I guess he was just worn out."

"And your grandmother?"

"She's in a nursing home now." She almost shuddered. "Not a good one."

"Do you get to see her often?"

That was too much. Her eyes teared up.

"Oh, Mr. Mason, I tried to help her, me and my parents. They still go see her, but I can't handle it. She doesn't know me, or them, or even herself. She's . . . she's not herself anymore."

I wanted to put my arms around her, as I saw her struggle to compose herself.

"Mr. Mason, you need to take care of yourself. Your wife is going to need you. But you need to take care of yourself first."

"Sue, would you like to go swimming with me?"

Midnight at the 7-Eleven. She was a bit skeptical.

"Harry, it's late. I don't have a swimsuit. You got any other ideas?"

"I can remember a few times in the past when not having a suit didn't stop you."

Was it in one of the articles I read? Be careful about comments about memory and the past. People like Sue might not remember the past, but in the present, they are painfully aware that they do not remember. This was the night that I realized that I needed to juggle two versions of Sue . . . the woman suffering the slow erosion of her past . . . Sue as patient . . . and the Sue in my own past . . . the Sue I loved, who had gone away but who still had a life after me, if only I could help her share it with me. Medical schools were right. Doctors should not become emotionally attached to their patients.

"I'm sorry, Harry. I don't."

"Let's go for a drive."

We had been meeting almost every night after midnight. I had put off actually moving into the Centre until she was ready to go with me. The big problem? The transition was irreversible. Sue Alden would have to disappear from the world of the living, never to return. That disappearance would be frontpage news: *Wife of Prominent Banker Missing.* Sooner or later, the women taking care of her would remember a taxi driver who brought her home one night. Two and two would be put together. The field would narrow. Harry Mason would be questioned. Past relationships would be uncovered. All in all, for Sue to live with me, we would both have to disappear.

The small problem? She wanted to hold on to a lot of material things in her life. Clothes, framed pictures, a few pieces of her favorite furniture, one chair in particular, a chair she had kept from her teen years at home. I thought she was being unreasonable, that I didn't see us being able to drive a U-Haul truck up to her front door and load up her stuff, but Marilyn corrected me when I told her later.

Harry, we all have things from our past that we want to hold on to. I know you think that old Harry Mason is the only important thing for her to keep, but everything she wants is part of the past she does remember. She wants to keep that past. Let me and Will work on this.

"So, no swimming?"

"Harry, no suit, no swimming, and besides, where would we go? And trust me, skinny-dipping when we were kids was when we both had much better bods. Hell, right now I don't like seeing myself naked, much less letting you see me naked."

She had a point. All the public pools were closed. The Y was closed. That would have been the best place, indoors and warm. The outside temps made swimming in the lake, which we had done a lot when we were young, made that unappealing. As for how we looked naked, she was right. I wasn't really ready either.

"No problem, we'll do it eventually." I was going to ask Dwight about the pool he promised. And then Sue surprised me.

"On second thought, I do have an idea, but you might not be comfortable."

An idea? About swimming?

"We can go to my place. We have a pool there."

She was right. I didn't see that happening. She was back to the old Sue, the rulebreaker.

"Harry, we actually have two pools. Remember, my husband is richer than God. A big pool next to the big house, and a small pool next to the guesthouse. Big house, big pool, small guest house, small pool. And the guest house blocks the view of its pool from the big house. We can sneak in and, unless we turn on the lights and start blasting music, nobody would know we were there. I'll do it if you will."

"Sue, it's about forty degrees outside."

"Richer than God, Harry. Both the pools are heated."

"You'd go skinny-dipping . . . what, fifty yards away from your sleeping husband?"

"Oh, he's sleeping, but not at home. As for skinny-dipping . . . no, that's still off the table, but as long as we stayed in the dark, we could get down to our undies."

"Sue, you might be the woman of my dreams."

She slugged my shoulder.

"Might? Fuck you, Harry."

Sue and I talked about the past, ours and hers, as we had done for the past month almost every night. I would ask a lot of questions to pull those memories out. It soon became obvious that my past was a lot less interesting than hers.

"You actually met Errol Flynn and Humphrey Bogart?"

"Harry, it was a small town. And we were all like kissing cousins. Studio work, dinner parties, cocktail parties, screenings. But you have to remember, me saying I met somebody is not the same as saying that they would remember meeting me."

The subject I did not want to discuss with her? What went wrong.

"So, tell me about the parties."

We were sitting in the shallow end of the pool, our butts on the bottom, warm water up to our chests. I waited for Sue to respond, but she just sat there, her head resting against the edge of the pool, eyes closed.

"Sue?"

She kept her eyes closed.

"I also met Harry Cohn."

Did she assume that I knew about him?

"Marilyn and I talked about those times. She told me how she had him banned from the theatre. You wanna know a secret, Harry?"

I wasn't sure I did.

"I met Marilyn at a party. I was one of the wannabes. She was a star.

She was nice to me then, but she didn't remember meeting me when we talked a few weeks ago. She remembered the specific party, but not me. That's okay. Thing is, I remember her, what she wore, her voice, but I don't remember the party."

"Sue, you know you don't have to tell me anything you don't want to."

"Hell, Harry, there's a lot of things I want to tell you, but I can't remember shit."

"So, how about this. Tell me about your friend Whitney."

"Ah, Whitney. I was shocked to see her at your party. I should ask Marilyn how she arranged that, how she knew about me and Whitney. But it makes sense, I suppose. She seems to have adopted me. You and Marilyn Monroe . . . my parents. I saw Whitney and wasn't sure who she was at first. I just knew then that I had known her in the past. A long time ago. My best friend, and I wasn't sure who she was. But it came back. We talked and talked. My best friend from the past. Hell, I knew her longer than you and I were together. More of my life shared with her than with you. She was in love with me, I'm pretty sure. But it was one-way. How naïve was I? Until she actually told me that she loved me, actually tried to kiss me, I had no clue she was a lesbian. I was a clueless Okie in Hollywood. She could have been a great actress, for sure. But we stayed friends. How many times did we keep each other from quitting the entire business? We were going to make it big, together. But they killed her."

"She was murdered?"

"Harry, she committed suicide, but they killed her. Me, I told her at your party that she killed herself for the wrong reason. A failed career? Surrounded by asshole incompetents? She was a lesbian? Not good enough, I told her. And the wonderful part? She agreed with me."

"You know that she can still be your friend at the Centre, right? And the others."

She ignored me.

"Harry, I'll miss them all, you too. But I want to die. You want to know another secret? It's not easy killing yourself. I tried. In this very pool. I thought I could drown myself. How stupid is that? My damn body is turning to crap but it refused to let me drown. I was doing both of us a favor, but it wouldn't cooperate. I couldn't drown myself. I couldn't throw myself in front of a bus right before we met again."

A warm pool, morning a few hours away, we scooted into the deep end and began floating.

"I'll do it soon, Harry, move in with you. And then you can help me die, like you promised."

"I'll take care of you, I promise."

HARRYS HAVE A BIRTHDAY

What kind of dessert do you like, Harry? Me, I'm partial to chocolate caramel sundaes, but it's not my birthday. Your friend over there has already put in a request for coconut custard pie.

Marilyn was sitting on the couch in Peyton's Library. She had a steno pad flipped open and was jotting notes. She also had on some reading glasses, a look I had never seen before. Harry Chapin was on another couch, guitar in lap. It was early morning and I needed to head back to my boardinghouse room.

Just as I said, "I like chocolate cake," Chapin strummed his guitar. *That's good for me, as long as I get the pie too.*

Marilyn muttered. *Great minds think alike.*

"Dessert is not my problem, Marilyn. What to do with Sue is my problem."

She kept jotting on her pad. Chapin kept lightly plucking strings.

"Hello? Planet Harry calling Marilyn."

She turned and looked over the top of her glasses at me, then over to Chapin.

First things first, Harry Mason. I'm throwing a party for you guys. Dwight might think he runs the Centre. You might think you're replacing him. But I am the Social Secretary. And, just for the record, I can walk and chew gum at the same time. This party and your so-called problem with Sue are connected. Both you guys . . . capiche?

Chapin looked at me, then at Marilyn.

Yes ma'am.

"Marilyn, as usual, I have no idea what you mean."

I mean that if this party goes as I plan it, half your problems will be solved. Now, with dessert out of the way, the next question for you guys is about the guest list. The usual suspects?

"Who are they?"

The usuals are . . . everybody. Unless you specifically exclude somebody, everybody gets invited. Not everybody shows up, but the proverbial door is open. Of course, my birthday is always packed.

Chapin piped in. *Do we have to invite Houdini?*

She turned to me.

Since this is your first, it's up to you. In or out.

I looked at Chapin. He just shrugged.

"In."

Chapin sighed, *God help us.*

Marilyn laughed.

Harry here still hasn't forgiven me for asking everybody to sing their favorite song of his at his last birthday party. A lot of bad singing, but we were having fun until Houdini started lecturing us about an apparent lack of preparation, which, to me, was the whole point. A lot of drunk ghosts singing from lyrics on a piece of paper.

I could see Houdini doing that, spoiling a party, but I wanted him to come anyway. He had still not met Sue.

"Okay, I'll leave it all up to you, but Houdini is invited, okay?"

Yessir.

"One last thing. Is your couch offer still good? I'm bushed."

Monroe and Chapin stood at the same time. She pointed to the couch as he waved at me.

Sweet dreams, Harry.

I'm one of those guys who can usually go to sleep in thirty seconds. No tossing and turning. Counting sheep, I never get very far. I lay down on the couch and looked up. The room was darkening, and the stars in the sky were beginning to appear. I could still feel the warmth from the open fireplace. Only the glowing embers remained. I was alone in Peyton's Library, wishing that Sue could be with me at that very moment, lying next to me on that couch, both of us looking at the stars as we closed our eyes and went to sleep. It would be the best moment of our lives, to die together at that moment.

Good night, Harry.

I must have been asleep, but I heard the voice. A man's voice, someone I had never heard before. I must have been dreaming. I tried to wake up.

I'm glad you're here.

"Happy Birthday, Harry."

I was driving Sue to the Centre for my party when, exactly at the stroke of midnight, I heard Harry Ducharme wish me a happy birthday. Even Sue was impressed, for about two seconds, until we heard the rest of what he had to say.

"I suppose that all my Lefty listeners are disappointed that I'm not congratulating Noam Chomsky, who was born on this date too. Or maybe I should be reminding everybody about it being Pearl Harbor Day, as if we could forget that. Thanks to FDR and that Day of Infamy speech. No, folks, I am talking about Harry Chapin, who would have been fifty-five today. Thing is, I'm betting that most people have forgotten about him. Man gets a Congressional Gold Medal for his humanitarian work to end hunger in America. He has food banks named after him. He wrote some great songs. But does that snot-rag Songwriters Hall of Fame include him? Hell, no. But I think I told you all this awhile back. Tonight, to show you how much I respect the guy, I'm going to play the only Chapin song I do *not* like. No, knowing what you're thinking right now, no, I do not have to make any sense."

I had told Sue about me calling Ducharme one night and asking about a certain Chapin song, but hearing him tonight I knew I would have to tell her again. Just as I finished my story, we heard the opening lines.

Hello honey, it's me . . .

Sue scooted across the front seat to sit closer to me and said what I had always thought.

"Wouldn't it be great if they met."

I remembered Ducharme's name on Dwight's list.

"It could happen."

I was sort of disappointed. For some reason, I had expected the Centre to be lit up for my party like it was for Marilyn's. Then again, as she reminded me later: *Harry, you and your singer friend are not me.*

Still, Sue was impressed. At least the marquee was lit: "Closed Tonight for Private Party." I pulled up to the front, knowing that Marilyn had arranged valet parking for my taxi. Chapin was waiting for me at the door.

Happy Birthday, Harry.

"Same to you, Harry."

The lobby was full, and as Chapin and I walked in they all broke into applause. You want a definition of surreal? Walk into a room to see Will Rogers, Samuel Clemens, a priest and a nun, a one-legged tap dancer, Patsy Cline, dozens of other people more famous than you, all of them happy to see you. Dwight was there too, beaming like he had won the lottery.

Chapin and I locked arms and took a bow. Where did that come from? It just happened. Sue was behind us, giggling. Up on the mezzanine level, a brass band was playing "Downtown." The party was off to a great start.

As Chapin and Sue and I walked down the aisle to the stage, past an auditorium almost full of ghosts, he leaned over and told me what was about to happen.

I've had a couple of these. All nice. Everybody sings my songs and I get to have a lot of coconut cream pie. But this is your first, so I can't predict anything for you. All I know is that Marilyn will have something special planned.

And there she was, up onstage in the spotlight. Even for her, it was spectacular. She was dressed like a beauty queen winner. A white evening gown, a dazzling diamond tiara, and a wand in her hand more like she was some Good Witch from the *Wizard of Oz*. The icing on the cake? Across her chest was a ruby-red sash with sequined white lettering: *Miss Golden Globes*.

As Chapin and I walked, the brass band followed, playing "Seventy-Six Trombones."

At the foot of the steps up to the stage, Will Rogers took Sue's hand and led her down to the front row to sit between him and Whitney Randall as Sam led Chapin and me to our seats onstage. Seated, I whispered to Chapin, "I'm surprised there aren't any cats." He snorted a laugh.

Marilyn took charge.

Ladies and Gentlemen, you too Harry . . . waving her wand at Houdini in the front row, scattering a swirl of pixie dust . . . *we are gathered here tonight to honor our old friend Harry Chapin and our new friend Harry Mason. For tonight I've changed the format somewhat. As you know, I can do as I please* . . . cheers from the audience . . . *but we will have our traditional ending. All you will be serenading our Harrys with a birthday song* . . . more cheers.

I made sure I knew where Sue was sitting, so I could watch her.

Marilyn looked directly at me and Chapin and spoke softly, but everyone in the now-silent audience heard her too.

Fair warning. I am about to break your hearts. Both of you. I'm going to make you cry and be happy at the same time. I'm going to break your hearts because I love you. I'm going to break your hearts and then put them back together again. You first, Harry Chapin.

She walked back to the center of the stage and pointed her wand toward the projection booth, a gesture commanding the show to begin. The curtains began opening, rippling up and then apart, as Chapin's recorded voice filled the auditorium.

It's got to be the going, not the getting there, that's good.

Marilyn had disappeared, but we all heard her.

Harry Chapin, this is your life.

The last sheer curtain parted and the screen was filled with an image of Chapin . . . as a young boy, sitting on a stone wall, striped shirt, high-laced sneakers, hands knotted together, with a look on his face like he was thinking about the future.

Beside me, Chapin was frozen, looking up at himself on the untouchable screen. Marilyn had surprised him for sure.

For an hour, we watched the story of a life. Photos of him as a child, his parents, drummer father and strong-willed mother, his brothers Tom and Steve and him in their early club days, him at Congressional hearings in a suit and tie, him sitting on the stage with Robert Redford and other stars, him performing, him in a radio studio with Bill Ayres, him with his children, him with his wife Sandy. Each scene had its own song. Between the scenes from his life, interviews with people who knew him . . . Bruce Springsteen, Billy Joel, Kenny Rogers . . . famous and unknown singers and politicians. Their words, his words, a short life in an hour.

Marilyn had been right. His heart was broken. He had held himself together until it got to the pictures of Sandy and his children Josh and Jen and Jason and Jono and Jaime. I heard him sniffling first and then weeping. I put my arm around his shoulder. I looked for Sue in the front row. She was crying too.

The film ended with a scene of his family and friends singing "All My Life's a Circle."

Fade to black.

The stage was dark. The auditorium too. Except for Chapin weeping, we all sat quietly until Marilyn walked back on stage.

Harry Chapin, come up here and get your birthday kiss.

As he stood, wiping his nose on his sleeve, the auditorium erupted in applause, loud and raucous cheering as the ghosts rose to give him a standing ovation. I rose too, wishing that Harry Ducharme could have been there with us.

Chapin and Monroe embraced and it was obvious that she was whispering something to him that made him laugh and feel better. As they huddled, Sam's friend John Lewis brought out a guitar. It was Chapin's usual role, to sing on his birthday. He sat on a stool and tightened some guitar strings before he spoke.

Thank you, Marilyn, as always. And, yes, you surprised me, in a good way. And thanks to all of you . . . sweeping his hand toward the crowd . . . *but this is a party for two, remember. Marilyn and I have prepared our own surprise for the other birthday boy, my friend Harry Mason over there* . . . gesturing toward me . . . *so this song is dedicated to him and* . . . pointing to Sue in the front row . . . *his friend Sue. We even got Mr. Lewis here to help us. He's going to sing too* . . . a buzz in the audience, nobody had ever heard Lewis speak, much less sing . . . *It's a song about a man who sings opera late at night in his dry-cleaning shop. Mr. Lewis is going to sing the part. I think you're going to like it.*

Harry Chapin sang "Mr. Tanner" for Sue and me. That's how I felt. Like Sue and I were the only people in the theatre. I looked for her down front, but the seat between Will and Whitney was empty. As John Lewis began singing Mr. Tanner's solo, Marilyn appeared in the seat beside me and patted me on the knee.

Relax, Harry. She is still here. Other side of the stage. She can hear it all.

Minutes later, Chapin was sitting beside me again as Marilyn took center stage.

Hell, Harry, if she surprised me like that, no telling what she has in store for you.

"I sorta think my life has a lot less interesting material to work with."

From center stage, Marilyn shushed us.

You boys, quiet! Or else I send you to the principal's office.

She pointed her wand at the projection booth again.

I whispered, "Harry, you were a movie. I'm a short subject, probably just a short cartoon."

Harry Mason, this is your life.

I was wrong. I was almost an hour too. Not an hour of famous people talking about me, not an hour of me in front of Congress or on a stage. But an hour of pictures and 1950s and '60s music. How did she find baby pictures of me? Damn pictures of me at six weeks old. Pictures I had never seen. Some of the pictures I recognized. They were from my private box. But, seriously, pictures of my parents before I was born? Even pictures of my crazy brother Frank? Me in the Air Force? I quickly recognized the pictures from my high school annual, me in the pool, me in front of the swim team. I was wrong about no pictures of me onstage. There I was giving a speech when I was running for student body president. Hair puffed out and slicked back, my James Dean phase. Me as a hotel clerk. Even a picture of that goddam Chet McKinney. Me as taxi driver. Me stoned out of my mind.

Chapin had disappeared. Sue was sitting beside me, enthralled at the giant images over us. Midway through my hour, Sue finally appeared onscreen in actual film of her on our school stage. More, there were outtakes of the few movies in which Sue had appeared, even if only in a crowd shot, there she was. I did what Chapin did. I started to cry, but so did Sue.

As the story of my life ended, Chapin appeared on stage with Marilyn. Both of them turned and motioned for me to come to them. I was wrong. As I stood up, Chapin waved me off.

No, no, Harry, we want Sue to come up here.

I expected her to be surprised, hesitant, but she popped up and was center stage in a few seconds. The three of them huddled, with Sue glancing back at me. Marilyn put both her hands on Sue's shoulders and seemed to be asking her a question. She nodded, looked back at me, and then she exited to the other side of the stage. Chapin became the master of ceremonies as Marilyn came to sit next to me. As a small band of ghost musicians formed onstage behind him, Chapin introduced Karen Carpenter.

Folks, we have a treat tonight for sure. You endured my singing. Your reward is here, with a song just for Harry. Look, we're all ghosts here, but only one of us has the voice of an angel. Ladies and gentleman, Karen Carpenter.*

A hush fell over the audience as Marilyn reached for my hand.

Put this on that long list of things you will thank me for later.

I knew what was coming, the song. I knew I would cry. I might have been the only man in history who would have wanted somebody else to be sitting next to him at that moment. I wanted to trade Marilyn Monroe for Sue.

Carpenter stepped into the spotlight as a clarinet began to softly play, then drums, then horns, and then a guitar. Then her voice.

Long ago . . .

I thought I was prepared. I was not. It was all too much, and then it became more.

Sue stepped into the spotlight to stand beside Carpenter.

"And, oh, so far away . . ."

Sue's voice came back to me, from all the times I had heard her sing when we were young. All the times. On that small high school stage and all those high school musicals, and when we walked late at night, that time we were watching planes take off at the airport . . . when she sang "Fly Me to the Moon" and she laughed when I told her that she should be a singer and forget about acting. Her voice.

Five minutes. I think I held my breath for five minutes. Sue had become a star.

As they ended, Sue and Carpenter took their bows as a thousand ghosts stood to clap and call for an encore. Me, I was frozen to my chair.

Harry, just so you understand, Sue has now officially performed on the stage of the Centre Theatre. It might not be a rule, but I'm not taking any chances.

Just as Marilyn stood up, Sue waved at the crowd and then rushed over to us and pulled me up out of my chair and hugged me. She was sixteen again. The crowd kept cheering.

"Harry, Harry, were you surprised? Did you like it? It was Marilyn's idea.

Our secret. She would bring me here when you weren't around. Well, her and Will and Sam, they took turns. Karen and I would practice. I mean, I practiced. Karen is always prepared. Did you like it? Please tell me you liked it."

"Sue, it was . . ." I was at a loss for words.

Marilyn answered for me.

Sue, what Harry is trying to say is that you were perfect, goddam perfect.

Sue hugged me again, then she hugged Marilyn. Chapin had come over and joined us. Sue hugged him too. Sam joined us. Karen and Will too. More hugs. Hell, I was hugging Sam and Will and the others. A hug party, and the band played on.

The next thing I knew, I had been dragged to the center of the stage and left alone in the spotlight. Standing around me, just out of the light, were Sue and the others. From the darkness surrounding me, I heard Marilyn whisper.

Tell a joke, Harry. Tell your best joke. Make us laugh.

Tell a joke? Then? At that moment? A joke? I heard Sue whisper.

"Tell the joke that I hate, the one that is never funny. As bad as my memory is, Harry, I can't forget how bad that joke is."

I took a deep breath.

"You know the best tip you can leave a waiter?"

Sue started to snicker.

"Never bet on a lame horse."

Complete silence. Complete and utter silence. I had been invited to a perfectly scripted party and just as I was about to thank everyone for a perfect evening, I was told to ad-lib a joke? I had another question. Why?

Marilyn stepped into the circle of light with me. She was slowly, very slowly, clapping her hands.

Harry, that was terrific . . . terrifically awful. Sue warned me that you were a worse joke-teller than you were a singer . . . turning to the crowd . . . but we don't care, do we. We're all wild about Harry, right? The crowd finally cheered.

And we all appreciate you performing for us, lame or not, right? More cheers. *Now, I am changing the rules again. No more group sing-a-long for a finale . . . She pointed to Harry Chapin in the darkness outside the circle . . . You get up here with your fan club president Harry Mason and the two of you get ready to be serenaded.*

With that, she stepped out of the light and Chapin stepped in to stand next to me. The crowd began stomping their ghost feet in unison. The band began the opening chords of "Happy Birthday" and then another spotlight beam shot down from the projection booth, forming a circle of light about ten feet away from us.

Marilyn stepped into that circle . . . wearing the same luminous dress she had worn in Madison Square Garden the night she serenaded JFK.

The ghost crowd went from loud to deafening.

Chapin whispered for both of us.

Holy Jesus!

"Harry, I want to move in tonight."

The party was over, but the unofficial after-party was in full swing. The big audience was gone. Onstage, a few of us were treating ourselves to the buffet table and open bar. I wasn't drinking, but I was going through chocolate cake like a starving man. Chapin, wearing a tuxedo, had a plate of pie in one hand and a plate of cake in the other. Patsy Cline, dressed as a nurse, was stealing bites of his cake when he wasn't looking. Marilyn was wearing a nun's habit, but she was still the hostess, walking around holding the kitten named Marilyn. Sam was dressed like a cowboy. Will was dressed like Mark Twain. Karen Carpenter, wearing what looked like a communion dress, was not eating. Houdini was there too, but not mingling. Sister Jeannine and her husband Father Bill, still in their clerical gear, were serving at the punch bowl. Bob and Harv, from Iowa, were still wearing their barbershop quartet outfits, including the boaters. Whitney Randall was dressed as Gloria Swanson playing Norma Desmond. Dwight was wearing a blue seersucker suit, but obviously the happiest man at the party, even more than me. Sue and me? And John Lewis? We were dressed as ourselves.

It was the best party of my life, and then Sue told me that she wanted to move in with me that very night.

"Sue, I thought we had to make some plans. Your stuff you wanted, how to not get caught. You know, plans."

Marilyn walked past me and leaned over to whisper.

Don't fuck this up, Harry.

I immediately knew what she meant. She was right. I had hesitated once before.

"You're right, Sue. Let's do it tonight. All that other stuff can be sorted out later."

"Really? We can?"

Things were falling into place, finally.

"Of course. But you realize, of course, that there is only one bed in my apartment here. We'll have to share it."

Everybody else on stage had stopped and turned to watch me and Sue.

"Oh, in that case, forget it."

Marilyn and the others laughed before I recovered.

"A deal is a deal, Sue."

She did a mock sigh.

"Oh well, I'll do it."

Everyone applauded, and then Marilyn started twirling her rosary beads.

Then this party is over. We'll get together again soon, but for now I'm going to escort this blushing couple to the honeymoon suite. Everybody come say their good-nights.

A line formed and each ghost came over to say good-night and wish us well. Everybody except Houdini, who had disappeared. The last person in line was Dwight. He took my hand to shake, and he did not let go. Almost trembling, almost weeping, he spoke.

"Thank you, Harry. Thank you for everything. I knew it had to be you. Thank you."

Marilyn stepped in and pulled Dwight aside and led him over to stand with the others.

You two follow Sister Marilyn.

Down the stage steps to the auditorium floor, up the carpeted aisle, into the lobby lit only by dim lights in the concession cases, up the wide stairs to the mezzanine, Marilyn led us to the door of our new home.

You want a wake-up call in the morning?

Sue stepped over and put her arms around Marilyn, holding on tight, resting her head on Marilyn's chest, looking back at me as she spoke.

"It was all perfect, Marilyn. Thank you for helping me be a part of it. Thank you for bringing Whitney back. Thank you for helping Harry. I never thought I would ever be this happy again in my life."

Sue, before you go all Oscar acceptance speech on us, there is one more thing.

As if on cue, we all looked down. The kitten was circling us.

You are now officially in charge of taking care of Marilyn. Litter box is in the bathroom. My work here is done.

With that, she opened the apartment door, handed me the keys, and walked away.

Sue and I had a new home, a cat of our own, and issues to be resolved . . . eventually. Tonight, we simply had each other. In a few minutes, we would be sleeping together for the first time in almost forty years. Yes, sleeping. We were both exhausted. Sleep was what we needed.

Inside, the only difference from the last time we had seen it was that the walls now had decorations. Dozens of photos that had been used in the movie of my life were now framed and on the walls. Fresh living flowers were on a table. The only clothes we had were on our backs, but we could get more later. We had everything we needed for that night.

Like virgin newlyweds, we undressed in separate rooms and changed into our bedclothes. Marilyn had left a new pair of matching pajamas on the bed, old people's pajamas. Blue, with a pink flamingo stitched over the breast pocket of each top. When we saw each other, we knew that those pajamas might be a one-time-only experience.

As we were about to get into bed, the kitten Marilyn started meowing below us. Sue got down on her hands and knees and tried to coax it out from under the bed.

"Harry, there's a box under the bed. Did you know that?"

"Sure, that's the box of letters and pictures we looked at before, all the stuff I kept from you, other stuff from our past."

"You kept all the letters and pictures from our past?"

I looked at her face. She was serious. She didn't remember. I looked away for a moment, remembering the future.

"Yes, yes, I did. Come to bed and get some rest. We'll go through all of it tomorrow. Okay?"

"Promise?"

"I promise, Sue, tomorrow."

She crawled back in bed with me, the kitten on the covers at our feet. Both were asleep in a minute. Me, it took a lot longer than usual.

HARRY HAS TEN SECONDS

Harry, we have a problem.

I was blinking in the dark. Something was shaking my leg. Somebody.

Harry, Marilyn told me to get you. We need you down onstage.

It was Will Rogers. I tried to focus, my eyes and my brain. I could hear him, but I couldn't see him. I wasn't quite awake yet.

"Will, can this wait? I am really . . ."

No, Harry, it can't wait. We need you right away.

"Okay, okay, give me a second. I need to tell Sue . . ."

No, Harry. Marilyn specifically said to not disturb Sue. So, please, please, hurry. Get down there right away.

"Will, can you tell me . . ."

Harry . . . Houdini has lost his mind and is about to do something crazy. He's screaming about wanting to prove something to you.

I heard the shouting as soon as I got down to the lobby. Through the lobby doors into the auditorium, I finally understand the words. Marilyn and Will and Chapin were taking turns shouting their version of one thought.

Harry, don't do it. Please don't do it.

Houdini was pacing back and forth in the center of the stage. The others were off to the left. The curtains were wide open, the screen exposed. Marilyn saw me and ran to meet me as I ascended the steps to the stage.

He kept insisting that he wanted to talk to you. I tried to put him off, but he's melting down. Said that only you would understand. You got any idea what he's talking about?

I looked at her face. She was uncharacteristically nervous. The others had stopped shouting, but Houdini kept pacing, waving his arms, muttering to himself. Four ghosts and me onstage at the Centre.

I am either right or I am wrong. Marilyn and the others are right, or they are wrong. As soon as you figure out who is really right, you will know what to do. Believe in me, you hold on to Sue for as long as you can. Believe the others, you let her go.

"I'm not sure."

Well, you might start figuring it out. He refuses to listen to us.

"Where is Dwight? Shouldn't he be here too? He's dealt with Houdini longer than anybody else."

Marilyn took a deep breath and exhaled in exasperation.

Harry, Dwight is gone. Forever. As soon as I gave you the keys to your apartment, he left the building, just like Elvis. You're the new sheriff in town. We're counting on you.

"I have no idea what to do."

Houdini saw me and stopped pacing. He had the look of a man standing on the ledge of a building. But that look softened as he focused on me.

Thank you for coming. The rest of them . . . gesturing to Marilyn and the others *. . . they hate me. They've always hated me because I told them the truth. They're trapped in their own illusions. And I fear that they have seduced you into that illusion. And you know what else, Harry, they have never given me a birthday party. They have never respected me. A party would have been easy for them. Just some small gesture of friendship. A party for the world's greatest escape artist. Was that too much to ask?*

Marilyn tried to interrupt him.

Harry, we're sorry. You're right. We've been unfair to you. Your birthday is in March, right? Plenty of time for us to plan a blowout party for you.

Was it as obvious to Houdini as it was to me? She was negotiating with him, stalling for time. Anything to keep him calm. It did not work. He ignored her and kept looking at me as he spoke softly.

Harry, all I wanted to do was help you. You were my only friend here. But I am tired now. This charade has to end. If I were a poet, I would say that we are such stuff as dreams are made of and our little life is rounded with a sleep. A poet could say that. To die to sleep, to sleep, perchance to dream. A poet's words. That is the best I can say to all of you, that your illusion is a dream. And it is time for all of you to go to sleep.

With that, he turned and walked toward the screen.

I could see it in all their frozen faces, the paralysis of their ghost bodies. All of them, even Marilyn, were terrified. They did not move.

The screen began to blaze white, light almost pulsating off of it. One last chorus from three ghosts.

Harry, please do not do it.

Houdini stood inches from the screen, his back to us, and then, as he raised his hand, he turned back to look at me, as if asking my permission.

He touched the screen, resting his palm on it. It blazed brighter, and then he stepped through the screen, disappearing. The screen started to dim. Seconds passed, the four of us left onstage did not move, and then he walked back through from the other side of the darkening screen.

There, do you not believe me now? The screen is a myth. The Rule is a myth. You are all free now.

The only sound in the universe of the Centre was my breathing.

I looked at Marilyn. She was crying.

Houdini spread his hands wide, as if welcoming an old friend.

You are free.

Will and Chapin came to stand with me and Marilyn, all of us mute.

Those moments when you have nothing to say, but you know that something needs to be said? We were there, all of us without any words.

I heard a door open and close on the other side of the stage. So did the others. I looked toward the auditorium. It was full of ghosts, main floor and two balconies. SRO. Another door opened and closed, just as the screen began to softly glow again.

On the other side of the stage, a young man stepped out of the darkness and walked toward Houdini. Marilyn and the others around me took a deferential step backward, their heads down just a little, as if to avoid eye contact. The young man looked familiar, but I couldn't place him. He walked straight toward me, walking past Houdini without acknowledging him. Standing in front of me, he finally spoke, a voice I had heard only once before.

I'm glad you're here.

He then turned to Marilyn, put his hand softly under her chin and raised her face to look at him. She took his hand in her own and kissed it, and then introduced him to me.

Harry, this is Peyton Davis. We're all his guests.

I could still not speak. It made no difference. He merely nodded at me and then turned to whisper something to Marilyn. She shook her head up and down in some sort of acknowledgment that she understood what he was commanding her to do.

He walked back to the other side of the stage, again ignoring Houdini, who was obviously confused, and then he disappeared into the darkness. Two doors opened and closed.

Marilyn walked to the center of the stage and faced Houdini.

I'm sorry, Harry, but I have to do this.

He squinted and was about to speak, but she cut him off.

Ten.

Next to me, Will Rogers flinched.

Nine.

Houdini turned his head from side to side, as if looking for help. He made eye contact with me, but I was helpless. Rogers left my side and walked over to stand with Marilyn. He continued the countdown.

Eight.

A thousand ghosts sang.

Seven.

Chapin joined Will and Marilyn, speaking.

Six.

Houdini seemed frantic, his body beginning to blur as he raised his voice.

Don't you realize that you're all going to disappear too! You're all going to die!

Two thousand ghosts sang.

Five.

Marilyn spoke again.

Harry, you never understood the Rule. Neither did Dwight. Touching the screen does not destroy the Centre. It destroys the one who touches it. Do you understand what is about to happen to you in four seconds? Houdini looked at me, almost pleading. He understood. I wasn't sure I did. *You are already dead, Harry. We all are. But we exist. We will exist forever. But you touched the screen, Harry.*

Houdini was almost transparent.

Marilyn held up three fingers.

I'm sorry, Harry.

Houdini had touched the screen. He was becoming nothing.

Two.

He took one final look at me, his lips trying to form words which I did not understand. His eyes were wide open. Astonishment? Fear? Anger? Something, but not peace.

One.

Then he was gone.

And I was alone in an empty auditorium.

"Marilyn? Will? Harry?"

Silence. The Centre was empty.

The silence was broken by the creaking and cranking of old pulleys. The sheer curtain slowly closed over the screen, followed by the other two, the last one rippling down in waves. I was alone, still in a spotlight.

"Marilyn?"

Still no answer.

I walked over and touched the outer curtain. It was real. I got down on my hands and knees and slammed my palm into the wooden stage. It was real. I looked back up at the projection booth. A light was still on inside of it.

And then I heard Peyton's voice.

Relax, Harry. Everything is as it should be. Go take care of Sue.

I walked back to my apartment. Sue was still sleeping. The kitten Marilyn was still asleep at the foot of the bed.

Houdini had been right. I finally knew what to do. I had a promise to keep.

HARRY MAKES PLANS

"Christmas is coming, and evidently I'm on somebody's naughty list."

Harry Ducharme was leaving town. I was not surprised.

"All those oil derricks at the Capitol? That should've been my first clue. Me, I'm water, Perrier water, in an oil world. My bosses knew that when they hired me, and I suppose I owe them thanks for ignoring me for so long. Over two years? That's not a record for me, but damn close. I always figured I would get a new gig near the ocean, but I'm headed to . . . you hear that drumroll? . . . I'm headed north. Of all the places I said I would never go again, it was any place with cold weather. I'd like to tell you that I had all sorts of offers, but I took the only one I got. An old fan of mine from my days as a morning dj found me. He owns his own radio station now. Did I say old fan? I meant old from a long time ago. He was probably seven back then, but he remembered me. Hell, I barely remember me from back then. But he made me an offer I couldn't refuse. Same late-night schedule, but in a college town. Smaller demographics, and I take a pay cut, but I'll be water in a water town. Nobody upset at me joking about porn or Newt Gingrich, same thing in my world. Of course, college town means they will have to be introduced to real music, not the crap they hear now. So, here's my warning to Iowa City, Iowa: Harry Ducharme is coming to town. Your football team might not be in the same league as the Sooners. But you've got that damn field of dreams. You built it, so Harry Ducharme is coming. Despite it being thirteen degrees at this exact minute, I'm still coming. The Quakers found me in Iowa, Springville, little town thirty miles east of Iowa City. So, I guess I'm going back to where I started."

It had been a week since my birthday, and for that week Sue and I had been alone in the Centre, except for one notable spook. Mac Duncan was still in the projection booth.

The first night after my birthday I heard movie music. Sue and I went down to the auditorium to discover that *Some Like It Hot* was showing on the screen. Every night that week, at seven o'clock on the dot, another Monroe movie played. Duncan was not a ghost, so I had to invent a new category for him. Mac the Spook.

After that first showing, Sue asked me if I had arranged it for her. She loved it, but she did not remember seeing it with me a long time ago. The next night, we saw *The Seven Year Itch*, the one we had missed. She loved them both, and I knew that we could watch a hundred movies that she had seen before and they would all be new to her. But she loved them in the moment, the joy new to her. I didn't mind seeing them again, and I acted like they were new to me too. Sue was happy, so I was happy. She thanked me, but I knew that I had to thank Mac Duncan . . . and ask him a few questions.

"Mac, why are you still here?"

"Mr. Mason, where else I got to go?"

I kept staring at him in the dingy booth, looking for some physical characteristic that would explain him. How old was he? Why were there no wrinkles on his face? As long as Dwight had been around, except for that one night in the lobby, Mac and I never crossed paths.

"But this place has been closed for a couple of years."

"I got a contract. Small print guarantees me a job for life."

He wasn't answering my question, just like everybody else. Then, out of the blue, I had one of those weird revelations. I mean, not a literal insight, more of an observation. Mac was a small man, a small grumpy man, and I thought of a dwarf in *Snow White*. Grumpy. He saw me smiling.

"This here is my life, what I do, show movies. Ferby never respected that.

Hell, he kept trying to act like I didn't exist for real. I think you're different. Miss Monroe told me that you were different. I trust her. She gave me a list of movies that you and your missus would like. Asked if I had prints. I told her that I could get any movie ever made. Not just her movies. Pick your favorites. I have connections. Good union connections. I can even get those old Disney movies, and those bastard fuckers are tough to deal with."

"Mac, how long have you been here?"

"I was here before Mr. Davis. Took me a long time to warm up to him. He was no-nonsense for sure."

There was an obvious question that had to be asked.

"You know this place is full of ghosts, right?"

He gave me one of those *Ask a stupid question, get a stupid answer* looks.

"I was here before you were born. I met Marilyn the first time she showed up here. Ghosts? I've seen more than ghosts in this old building."

Miss me, Harry?

I always assumed that Marilyn and the others would come back, but it took longer than I expected. Even Sue had been worried.

"You did make a rather abrupt exit. But, yes, to answer your question. We did miss you, and the others. You have to admit, everything that happened at my party might have left me confused."

Harry, we all needed a break from the Centre. It was a bad scene for us, ghosts or not. Houdini was a soul-sucker, but he never really understood that he was part of us too. Our world. He could have been happy with us, had fun with us, but he kept thinking that his old-world rules applied to ours. It was sad to see him do what he did to himself. He hated Dwight, so we all thought that he would ease up when you arrived. You were kinder to him than Dwight was. That should have been enough. It wasn't. And, hey, I also told everybody to leave you and Sue alone. You're on your honeymoon. So, tell me, how are things?

How were things? Everything I predicted about Sue disappearing had come true. She was front-page news for a day, page-six news the next, interviews with a concerned husband and defensive caregivers. People like Sue were known to wander off. She herself, duly reported, had done it many times. She could not have gone far. Perhaps someone had taken her in and not yet called the police? Foul play? A week passed. No leads, no clues, Sue was put in the category of "Awaiting further developments" and forgotten.

Late at night, she and I would drive by her old home, and she would say, "I used to live there?"

How were things? Seven days of being with her, every conscious moment, only confirmed the decision I had made when Houdini took one final look at me and then disappeared. We were in a . . . mobius strip? . . . every day a circular trip. In a moment, in a short moment, she was herself, smart and happy and witty and optimistic. As we watched a movie, she would laugh and lean into me. We would sit in the balcony, in our old spot, but the next day she would have forgotten the day before. We could have watched the same movie again, and she would have been happy. Sometimes, at the end of a movie, she would ask me what the title was. Her short-term memory was gone, the ability to hold on to the present. But when we looked at the old pictures, or I drove her around in the dark, and I would say *I remember when* . . . something would happen and she would start to remember it too. It was only when I said *Do you remember when. . .* that she did not remember anything, that she became defensive, and then sad, and then angry, and reminded me about my promise.

How were things? I was glad that I didn't believe in God. I would demand that he justify his existence. Ask Him about His so-called cosmic design. How did he justify what was happening to Sue? Where was the goddam design in that?

"That's how things are."

Marilyn and I were standing in the small garage where my taxi was parked, surrounded by posters of her. Sue was asleep up in our apartment. She was tired all the time.

So, are you okay, Harry?

I thought that was an odd question, but then I remembered a young librarian.

"It's not fair, Marilyn. What I have to do. But I know it's what I *have* to do. You and the others, and Sue . . . you're right. Especially after what happened last week, seeing Houdini disappear, I know that I can only hold to her if I help her die."

The fairness thing? Jack said that life is unfair, but he was talking about the consequences of being in the army, stationed in Antarctica or in San Francisco, killed or not. The randomness of it all. He said it in March of '62, I died in August. A month before I died, he and I talked. He was pulling away from me, and I told him how unfair he was being. I reminded him about what he said a few months earlier, it was in all the news, and he explained what he meant. So, I'll tell you what I told him. "Fair" is the wrong standard. In love or war. Right or wrong. Those are our choices. Harry, you're doing the right thing.

"I need your help."

Harry, you're the boss now, boss of the Centre, tell me what you want.

"I just need you to be around, spend time with Sue, and . . ."

You want me to be there when you do it, right?

"Yes, please. For me and for Sue."

She looked around the garage, rubbed her hand on the hood of the taxi, then looked back at me.

Here?

I nodded.

"I want it to be private."

Until you do it, the Centre is yours. I'll make those arrangements. But I hope you will let Sam and Will, a few others, you'll let them be here too. We're your friends, Harry. We all want to help you and Sue.

"I'm sorry. Wasn't thinking. Of course, I'd want you all with us. Sue would too."

Harry, it's not going to be easy. You know that. You think you can do it now, but when the moment comes . . . I'm just saying . . . you have to be absolutely sure you're doing the right thing. And so will she. You have to be absolutely sure you'll see her again. I did my part, getting her up onstage. And I need to tell you something else. It won't happen immediately. She will die, but she won't be one of us immediately. I can't explain it, or predict how long it will take, but she will eventually come back to you. You'll be stuck with just us for a while. That's the bad news. But here's the good. She will come back with all her memories. All the past with you, but also with everyone else, all those years of her other life. And then she'll be giving you hell about your own old man memory problems. Me and the others have joked with each other about us eventually watching her deal with the old guy she loves.

"I can live with that, deal with it."

Okay then, Harry Mason, tell me your plan. We both have work to do.

A week to go. The stages of grief? Not the grief about someone else's death. But, accepting your own death? To be terminal. Am I saying this right? Sue was dying, but so was I? The last stage must be the same for both situations, right? Acceptance. I told Sue that I was going to keep my promise. Why was she so happy? Not even a moment of skepticism, not a "Really?" moment. She was totally at peace.

"Thank you, Harry. I knew I could depend on you."

"You'll just go to sleep, okay?"

"And then I'll come back to you? I mean, I was ready to die a long time ago, wanted to die, but now that I know I'll come back here and be with you . . . isn't this all so perfect."

It was not a question.

Marilyn, Sam and John, Will Rogers, and Harry Chapin . . . shipmates on the S.S. Centre. As Chapin said, *We're the dance band.*

We had movies every night, music afterwards. Everybody talked about their lives, their loves and losses. Old folks in a home for old folks, that's what we were. And, in honor of Sue's departure and her eventual return, we had a party in Peyton's Library. Late December in Oklahoma City, it was almost freezing outside, but balmy in the Library.

"You know, I tried to find this place when you guys were gone for that week after Houdini went away, but I couldn't even find the door. What's the deal with that?"

Marilyn, almost tipsy, was standing next to the open fireplace, a glass of Dom Perignon in her hand.

Good question, Harry.

Everybody laughed, knowing how I hated that response, even Sue.

Here's to you and Sue, my friend. A toast.

Everyone raised their glasses. Me, I was drinking water.

I love this champagne. My friend Bert Stern gave me a bottle right before we did a photo shoot at the Bel-Air. Me and Dom here and just a scarf for a wardrobe. Some of my favorite photos of me. Bert had a magic camera.

I looked up at the Library sky. Sue was next to me on the couch. I was trying to remember the exact date I took the Centre tour with Dwight.

You ask too many questions, Harry. You're going to have to just let it all slide. You wanted to know about why you couldn't find the door to this place. Wrong question. You really want to know about Peyton Davis himself. He's here right now, somewhere in this room, always has been. We all knew him when he was alive, coming and going as we did. But here's the spooky thing. He knew we were here, but he ignored us. He didn't talk to us. Sometimes we would catch him staring at us, but I always got the creepy feeling that he was looking at me and thinking about something else. We might as well have been furniture. A man lives with ghosts . . . with me, my ghost, for chrissakes. . . and he is simply . . . indifferent? There were no rules until Dwight showed up. And that's when Peyton became a myth. No, no, I'm wrong. I can understand a myth. Peyton is just a mystery, and none of us have the answer.

"But you knew all that. You could have told me."

Harry, as hard as it might be for you to believe, we all knew that Peyton was here, but none of us . . . pointing to the others . . . ever saw him after he died . . . the others nodded. *A few of us actually heard him speak to us for the first time . . . after he died. It was his voice that told us to never touch the screen. It was his voice that told me about this room. It was his voice that told me that I was in charge of it. In so many words, I was working for him. I suppose that's another rule we don't understand. Who, after all, is Peyton? Me, I have the feeling that any story that Dwight told about him, the things that supposedly happened when we weren't around . . . that was not who he was. I mean, think about it, we can all be here in his library, if I allow it, but Dwight was banned from ever entering this room. Peyton's rule, and even I, Marilyn Monroe, had to obey it. You think maybe that there's some history between those two men that we'll never know. Was Dwight sweet on Peyton? Did Dwight not realize that Peyton was still here? And the Cori thing. Where the hell is Cori now? Is she here and Peyton is keeping her to himself? Keeping her away from Dwight for some reason. Why are you here, Harry, replacing Dwight, and not some other Joe off the street? Lots of questions, Harry. And here's the real deal, the real question. Even if we understood Peyton and Dwight, would that explain all this . . .* pointing to the sky, the endless rows of books, the fireplace, the world of Peyton's Library. *Hell, Harry, I'm a ghost, I shouldn't be surprised by anything, but all . . . this . . . is beyond me.*

All the others nodded in agreement.

"But you all seemed to know him. I mean, for god's sake Marilyn, you kissed his hand."

Yea, that was odd, even at the time. It just seemed like I should do that. And then he told me to start the countdown. I guess it's just Peyton's world and we live in it. Him showing up that night made no sense and all the sense.

"That's not good enough, Marilyn."

She gave me one of those *You're lucky that I'm a patient woman* looks.

That's all you get, Harry. That's all any of us get. A little bit, not everything. And, in the long run, the only thing you and Sue better not forget is . . . pointing to the others, who answered in unison.

Don't touch the screen.

Everyone seemed to be having a good time, but I still wanted answers. It was then that Sam stood, flicking the ashes from a cigar with one hand and motioning for everyone else to be quiet with the other. He looked at me, looked around at the group, and then looked back at me.

Harry, my young friend, here is the truth that all of us here know. You will learn soon enough. Death makes no more sense than life. Inhaling and exhaling his cigar, puffing clouds of smoke, clearing his throat, looking at the cigar as if he had never seen one before. *Great designs, rational thought, purpose ... did you find it in life? But you expect it in death? The best thing about being dead? There are no answers, so questions are irrelevant. But, the great contradiction, Harry? You can still be happier dead than when you were alive.*

"But, too much of this . . . "

Marilyn kept glaring at me until I shrugged, giving up.

Harry here still wants answers. Fair enough. But I have easier questions. Everybody here has to answer this one for me. I think we've all answered this privately, but now it's time to go public with each other. What do you wish you had done in your past that you did not do, your big regret? Me, I'll go first. I wish I had shot off Harry Cohn's pecker. And I know that Harry wishes he had gone with Sue to Hollywood, but the rest of you? How about you ...

Before Marilyn could choose somebody, Sue raised her hand.

"I wish that I had married Harry."

Marilyn blinked and shook her head. The others were looking at me. Marilyn recovered.

You still have time.

I raised one hand and held on to Sue with the other.

"Marilyn, you do see the obvious problem here, right?"

Sue, a serious question for you . . . not Harry . . . he's not a factor here. If I can arrange it, would you marry him tonight, right here?

"Marilyn . . ."

Did you not hear me, Harry? My question is for Sue. Oh, I know what you're about to say, all that stuff about her already being married right now to somebody else. Right? That's a rule in your world, not mine, not here in this place. If you don't want to marry her, tell me now.

Sue saved me.

"Marilyn, stop it. You're being unfair to Harry. Please stop." It was not really a request. "You know the only thing I remember about my first marriage? I don't even remember his name now. But I do remember the one moment at the altar when I looked behind me, looking for Harry. I believed all those stories about that part when the preacher says 'If anyone here objects,' . . . so on so forth . . . some sort of words like that . . . and I stood there hoping that Harry would run down the aisle and stop me. I wanted him to save me. I wanted that fairy tale to be true. So, yes, Marilyn, I would marry him right now, right here, if he would have me."

Everyone looked at me again.

"Of course, I would."

Did they applaud? Stand up and rush over to hug me and Sue? Did Marilyn start crying? I don't remember exactly, but I think they did.

Okay, folks, give me a few minutes. Marilyn was her organizing-self again. *Truth be told, I underestimated Sue and Harry both. I'll be back in a jif. Gotta find me a preacher. But I am making the arrangements. And, for the record, I'm the Maid of Honor. Harry, your pickings are slim, but one of these guys is going to be your Best Man.*

I looked toward Harry Chapin. He gave me a thumbs-up.

HARRY GETS MARRIED AND THEN GOES TO SLEEP

I'm not a philosopher, probably not even a deep thinker. But as I sat there in Peyton's Library with Sue next to me, I kept trying to make sense of my life. I know you've been there, your own *how did I get here* moment. Was this all a cliché, the thing about second chances? Surely, *this* was my second chance. I was living in a theatre full of ghosts. I was about to marry a married woman who I would then help to die. Of course, it all made perfect sense and was in the cards when I was born, right? Or, it was the inevitable result of decisions made in the past, poetic roads not taken. Sometimes I wish I could talk to my parents again. I know the right questions now. Forget about me. I wish I knew them better. How did they see their children, Slacker Harry and Crazy Frank, growing up? Did they love us? I think they did, in their own parent way. Did they love each other? I never saw them kiss, not even a peck on the cheek. Did that mean anything? They both died before Frank went totally bonkers, but did they see it coming? When they were alone, what did they say to each other about their children? Somebody once told me that a person never understands themselves until they raise their own children, and doing that, raising your own kids, makes you understand your own parents and then you understand yourself. I think my parents would have liked to be grandparents. I'm not sure, but I think so. Too late for that, me and Sue having a child. Too late to see me and Sue in someone else. Too late for a lot of things.

Ladies and gentlemen, the lights are dimming, the curtain is rising. We are gathered here today in the House of the Lord.

Marilyn was back. She had found a preacher. More precisely, she had found a priest and a nun. Father Bill and Sister Jeannine.

Harry and Sue, come on down.

"Marilyn, we're right here."

Right, right. Sorry. You know, Sam is right, sometimes I enjoy being dead more than I did being alive. More fun. But I'm now going to turn things over to the padre here.

Father Bill was evidently one of those priests who was not offended by mockery from skeptics and ghosts. He was comfortable in his faith, generous toward those without. He motioned for me and Sue to step forward, and then he gave us and our wedding party our ritual instructions.

Sue and Harry, would you both please kneel? Marilyn, if you and my good friend Harry Chapin would please stand behind them and put your hand on their shoulder, we can begin.

The foursome was arranged, but I could not stop myself from asking one more question as I knelt in front of him.

"Father, are you sure you can do this?"

This?

"I mean, you're about to marry a woman who has been divorced twice and is now married to somebody else."

Do you love each other?

"And neither of us is Catholic."

The Church is not God. So, I repeat: Do you love each other?

"And I'm an atheist."

Marilyn reached over and slapped me on the head.

Harry, stop being yourself.

Father Bill smiled.

Harry, your lack of faith does not erase God.

"But . . ."

Do you love each other?

"Yes."

God is love, Harry. You and Sue are God.

I was in over my head.

We are gathered here today to witness God in his glory. To consecrate this union, I would ask Sue Alden and Harry Mason to respond to these questions. First, do thee take each other in sickness and health?

"We do"

Do thee promise to honor and cherish each other?

"We do."

Until death do thee part?

"We do."

And forever?

It was the final question. Sue and I were not expecting it, but we knew the answer. We both looked up at Father Bill and nodded.

You may now exchange the rings which are a symbol of your love and faith in each other.

Sue and I held our breaths. Rings? We didn't have any rings.

Marilyn tapped me and Sue, handing each of us a ring. I looked at her and read her mind: *Never forget, Harry. I am Marilyn Monroe.*

Father Bill waited patiently.

I now pronounce you husband and wife. In the presence of this congregation, in the eyes of God.

Sue and I kissed.

An hour later, as we wound down our celebration, Harry Chapin told me one of his plans that did not materialize.

I wanted to find Karen and have her sing "For All We Know," but Marilyn nixed the idea. She said that you would turn into a blubbering idiot.

A last meal, aren't the condemned allowed a last meal? The soon-to-be-free?

Their choice? Sue wanted shrimp and cheese grits.

"You want what?"

"Harry, you said I could have anything I wanted. I want shrimp and cheese grits."

It seems to me that is it bad form to make an offer and then try to negotiate the other person's acceptance. *You want a soft drink? I can do that. You want a Coke, you say? All I can give you is Pepsi. Will that do?* It was obvious that Coca-Cola was shrimp and cheese grits. Pepsi was . . . fish sticks?

"Harry, is this a problem?"

For someone about to die, Sue was in an upbeat mood, and she was also much calmer than I was. We were spending our last day together. We had spent hours going through all the old photos and cards, talking about the distant past, and then we talked about our life after I found her at the 7-Eleven.

"I'll talk to Marilyn."

"You better find a ghost chef you can talk to."

I found Marilyn in the lobby.

Harry, that's it? That's all she wants? And you hesitated? And we expect you to take care of this building for us? Harry, shrimp and grits is not a problem. Bring her to the stage at eight tonight. It won't be a party, and I will shoot myself if I slip up and call it a last supper, but I am telling you now . . . everybody will be there.

I suppose I will never run out of questions, but her mentioning me taking care of the building forced me to ask a question whose answer I was avoiding.

"Marilyn, sooner or later, this building is going to be torn down. Urban progress, remember? What happens then? To you and the others, to Sue, to me? Where do we live?"

I thought I had asked another question she could not or would not answer. I was wrong. She looked around the lobby as we both heard Sue singing upstairs.

Harry, I once slept with a big-time evangelist, and after I had sucked every ounce of life out of him, I asked him sorta the same question. Along the lines of what does heaven look like, where all the angels lived, since he talked about it so much on the radio. He was clueless, get down to it, clueless. I was young then, clueless myself. But I got older, read a lot of books, and then I slept with a poet. I always think of that poet when I come back here.

"Are you making this up?"

Harry, shut the hell up. I'm a ghost. Why should I lie?

"You're an actress?"

I am Marilyn Monroe, Harry. Never forget that. And remember this too. I asked him about life after death. I was twenty-five, and Johnny Hyde had died the year before. I missed him terribly. My poet got out of bed and left me naked under the sheets. He came back with a book and read a poem to me, not one of his. A Walt Whitman poem about crossing a river. It took him awhile to read that poem, letting each line touch me. I was naked, still warm from the sex, and he and Walt Whitman were telling me that Time and Distance and Place . . . avail not, something like that. He read two lines like he was . . . don't you dare blush, Harry . . . like he was slow fucking me. "What is it then between us? What is the count of the scores or hundreds of years between us?" I could have fallen in love with him right then, but when he was finished, and I was aroused again, he said something strange, but it was the thing I always remember when I am here. "I always wanted to write my own version of this poem," he told me. "Whitman always talked about the souls of the dead always being around us, forever. Where we are in this physical world has been occupied by others before us. We are existing together. But he assumed that the physical world was itself permanent. But we know that's not true. I want to write a poem about how that world itself is eventually a ghost. Every room we lived in, everything we touched, become ghosts. I think this room we are in now will always exist even after it is gone. I want to write about that." Something like that, as best I can remember, maybe I'm paraphrasing or adding lines, but I now know what he was talking about. Harry, I never understood it until I came here. *The future can tear this building down, but it will always be here, a ghost of itself. And anybody who was here in life can be here in death. There's your answer, the Centre will always be here. We will always be here. It is always now.*

She stopped abruptly.

I'm sorry. I got carried away. I think about things a lot, Harry. I'm actually more than Marilyn Monroe, but most people only want her. Oh, Harry, I wish you were a poet. I'd steal you away from Sue.

Sue was leaning over the mezzanine railing above us, looking down.

"Marilyn, it's okay. I'll share, but we both know that Harry is prose, not poetry."

A thousand ghosts in the auditorium broke bread with us. On stage, only a few were around the table. Sue sat at one end, with Will on one side of her, Whitney on the other; me at the other end, Chapin to my left, Karen Carpenter to my right. Father Bill led off with a secular grace and then sat next to Sister Jeannine. Marilyn, dressed like a chef, complete with toque perched on her head, walked around the table using a giant ladle to scoop out the shrimp and cheese grits. Sam followed her, costumed like a waiter, pouring wine for everyone except Sue. John Lewis followed Sam, a bottle of wine in each hand. Marilyn served Sue from her own special antique wine carafe. Will was in charge of water glasses.

An hour passed. I sipped on my water and savored . . . Marilyn's cooking? . . . somebody's cooking. Everyone took turns proposing toasts, everyone drank too much, ate too much. I watched Sue even when she wasn't watching me. She was surrounded by people who loved her. She knew it. Whenever we exchanged looks, her eyes told me that she was happy.

And so, the end began.

"I'm sorry everybody, but I'm very sleepy."

She said it softly, but Marilyn heard her. She took off her chef's hat and motioned for me to come help Sue out of her seat.

Time for bed, folks. Thank you all for coming. We'll get together again soon enough.

The auditorium ghosts stood, but they did not leave. They remained as silent witnesses as I held on to Sue and left the stage, followed by the other dinner guests. Down we went, through the side stage door to the dark hallway below. I had a flashlight and led the way to my private garage, where my taxi was waiting. It looked like it had that first night when I left the Centre after Dwight had given me a tour. Spotless, glistening, new.

Harry, the wine will make it easier for her, but it will not make her die. That is your promise to keep for her. You turn the key and then go wait on stage. We'll watch over her.

I put Sue in the front passenger seat and got in beside her. She knew what was happening. We had planned it together. She would die. I would live. She would return.

"I'll stay with you until you're asleep, and then when you wake up, I'll be waiting for you onstage."

Her eyes were closed, but she nodded and said, "Thank you, Harry."

We sat for a few more minutes and just when I thought she was asleep, she whispered like a child.

"Harry, I'm afraid."

I looked through the windshield. Marilyn and the others were looking at me. They knew what was supposed to happen next. Supposed to. Marilyn put two fingers against her lips to kiss and then pointed them in my direction.

Harry, it's up to you. We'll be okay.

John Lewis began singing, but Sue and I heard Mr. Tubridy's voice.

I turned the ignition key and stayed in my taxi with Sue, holding her hand, counting very slowly.

HARRY WAKES UP

All I can tell you is that it is nothing like you imagine.

ACKNOWLEDGEMENTS

As always, Steve Semken at Ice Cube Press gets my first thanks. I hope this is the Larry Baker book that finally makes a profit for him.

Mike Lankford was an early reader and critic. I ignored most of his suggestions, as I usually do, but I can still say that he is one of the few writers in America who I will admit is better than I am. Go find his *Becoming Leonardo*. You will be as amazed as I still am.

Dan Campion was an early reader and surgical copy editor. His collection of poetry, *A Playbill for Sunset*, should be on your bookshelf too.

Special thanks to Jason Chapin and the entire Chapin family for their support. Without Harry Chapin, there is no Harry Mason. Thanks also to Pegge Strella at The Chapin Foundation for her long-time consideration.

Early readers included Joyce Botchford, Rita McGartland, Mike Schenker, Patty Friedmann, and Jeannine Ayres. Thanks to all. Special thanks to Jeannine and Bill Ayres for letting me make them ghost characters in the story. Thanks also to Mark Horstmeyer and Rosemary Doto-Gushue for their photo contributions. Judith Matthews, at the Oklahoma City Public Library, led me to pictures of the old Centre Theatre.

The cover photo has its own unique history. I was searching for the perfect picture and Harold George, in St. Augustine, found it for me. Trying to determine its copyright status was its own story. The photographer was probably Hans Knopf, although others have been cited. Two weeks of web searching and emails and phone calls led to conflicting narratives of copyright ownership. Especially helpful in that search were Darren Julien at Julien's Auctions and Scott Fortner, Director of The Marilyn Monroe Collection.

Finally, and most importantly, Ginger.

CAST OF CHARACTERS AND LOCATIONS

Marilyn Monroe
June 1, 1926—August 2, 1962

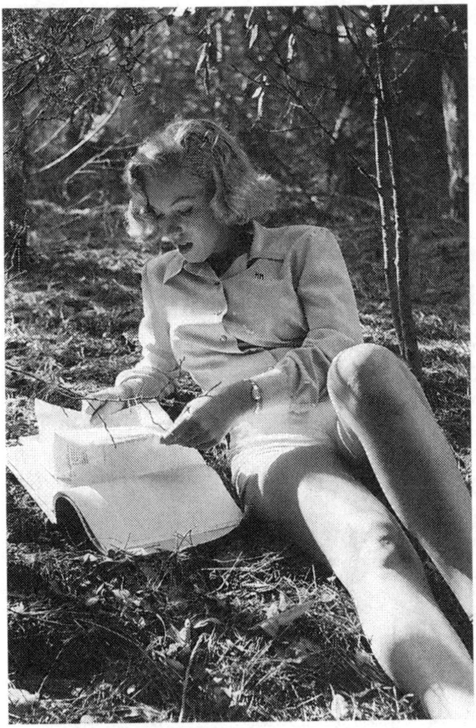

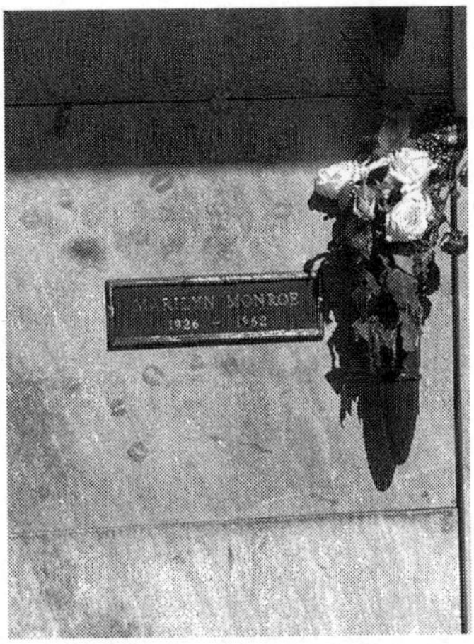
MARILYN MONROE
1926 - 1962

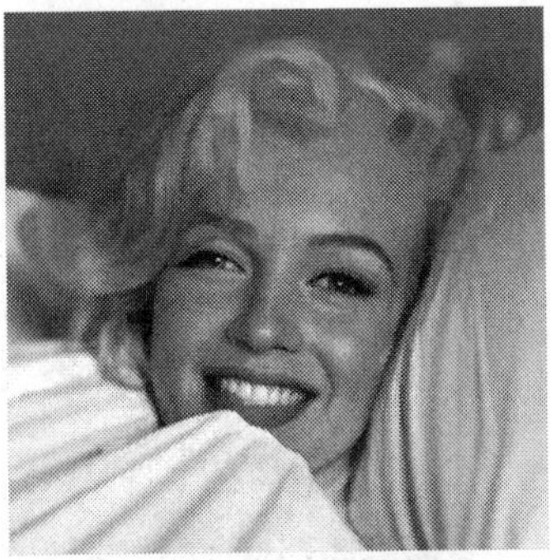

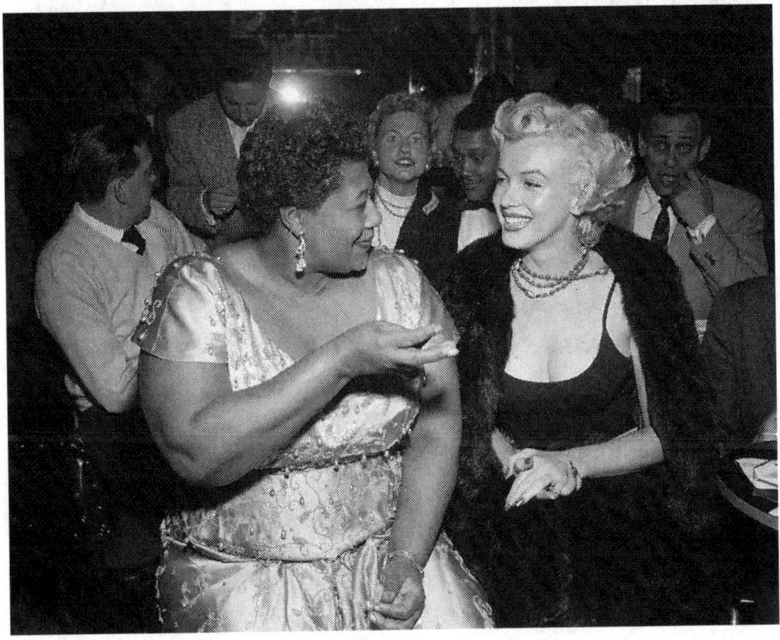

Harry Chapin

December 7, 1942—July 16, 1981

Friday, July 17, 1981 — The Bulletin C7

OBITUARIES — **DEATH NOTICES**

Singer-composer Harry Chapin killed in N.Y. car crash

Bulletin Wire Services

JERICHO, N.Y. — Harry Chapin, the singer-composer who broke onto the recording charts nearly a decade ago with the song "Taxi," was killed yesterday in a traffic accident. He was 38.

Chapin, known for his narrative ballad style and his work to end world hunger, was driving alone in his car when he tried to switch lanes in front of a tractor-trailer at about 12:27 P.M. EDT on the westbound lanes of the Long Island Expressway near Jericho, 15 miles east of New York City.

Nassau County police said Chapin's car, a 1975 Volkswagen Rabbit, was struck from the rear by the tractor-trailer and burst into flames. A police spokesman said the truck driver, who was unhurt, and another driver cut Chapin's seat belt and pulled him from the wreck.

Although the entertainer was not burned, he suffered severe internal injuries and was pronounced dead at the Nassau County Medical Center in East Meadow, where he was flown by police helicopter.

Ed Smith, a spokesman for the center, said Chapin had suffered a massive heart attack and "died of cardiac arrest," but added there was no way of knowing whether it occurred before or after the accident.

Police said no charges are being filed against the driver, 57-year-old Robert Eggleton of South Plainfield, N.J.

A spokesman for Chapin's agent said the singer was en route to a business meeting in New York City. He was scheduled to perform last night at a free concert in the Lakeside Theater in East Meadow.

Chapin was born December 7, 1942 in New York's Greenwich Village. His father, Jim Chapin, was a drummer who worked with bandleaders Tommy Dorsey and Woody Herman. The younger Chapin played the trumpet as a child before taking up guitar. He played folk music during his years at the Air Force Academy and Cornell University.

In 1964, he left school to join his brothers Tom and Stephen and his father in a group called the Chapin Brothers. They made a record, "Chapin Music," but disbanded when Tom and Stephen returned to school.

Chapin applied for a taxi driver's license — which in part inspired "Taxi" — but then turned to film, working his way up from loading reels to editing and then making a number of documentaries. One of them, "Legendary Champions," was nominated for an Oscar in 1969.

The Chapin Brothers got back together in 1970 and recorded an album featuring several songs that would later appear on Chapin's own records. A year later, Chapin formed his own group, which included his brother Steve.

They rented the Village Gate and performed there all summer, after which Chapin signed a recording contract with Elektra-Asylum.

Chapin's first hit was "Taxi," the story of a taxicab driver who longed to be a pilot, which appeared in 1972 on an album called "Heads and Tales." He also was known for "Cat's Cradle," a reflective song about a father who is too busy to devote time to his son.

Chapin also lived in Huntington, N.Y., with his wife, Sandy, whom he married in 1968.

Their family includes Chapin's half sister, Dana, 23, whom they adopted; his wife's children, Jaime, 20, Johno, 17, and Jason, 16; and their own two children, Jennie, 9, and Josh, 8.

The Contemporary Music Almanac lists Chapin as a co-founder of the World Hunger Year project, and a 1975 Tony Award nominee for his multi-media Broadway show, "The Night That Made America Famous." The show was a box-office flop.

In a statement issued in Los Angeles, Neil Bogart, president of Boardwalk Records, called Chapin someone "I was proud to call a friend.

"He understood what it meant to give of himself — to the family and friends he dearly loved and to the fans who enjoyed a decade of his talent and his charm," the statement said.

"But Harry didn't let it stop there. In the fight against world hunger, Harry gave tirelessly of himself and became a great example of what it means to be a true humanitarian. I shall miss him dearly.

"Over the last eight years, Harry raised in excess of $5 million toward that end. He was a commissioner on President Carter's Presidential Commission on Hunger and co-founder of World Hunger Year."

HARRY CHAPIN
1942 — 1981
"OH IF A MAN TRIED
TO TAKE HIS TIME ON EARTH
AND PROVE BEFORE HE DIED
WHAT ONE MAN'S LIFE COULD BE WORTH
WONDER WHAT WOULD HAPPEN
TO THIS WORLD"

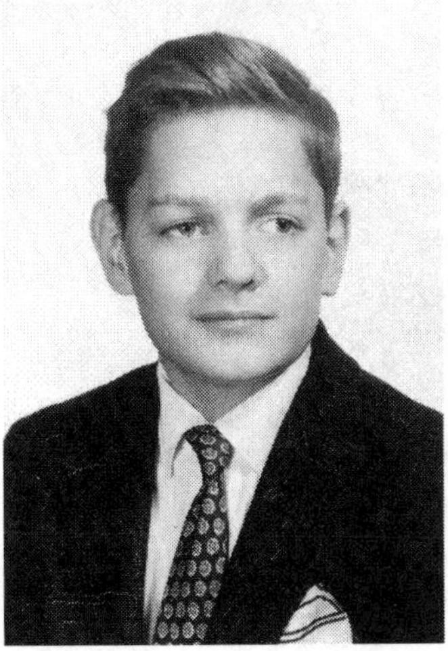

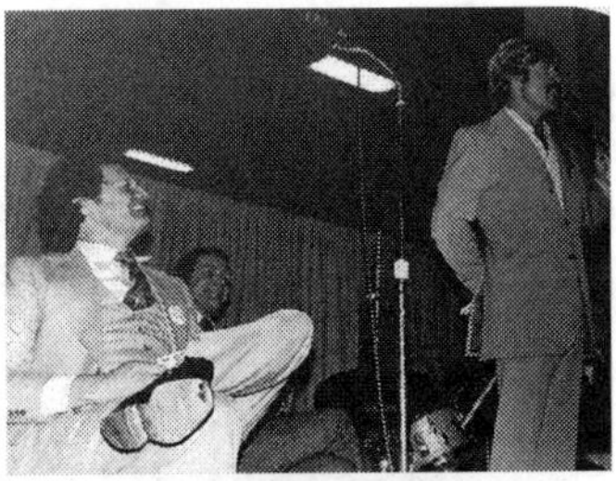

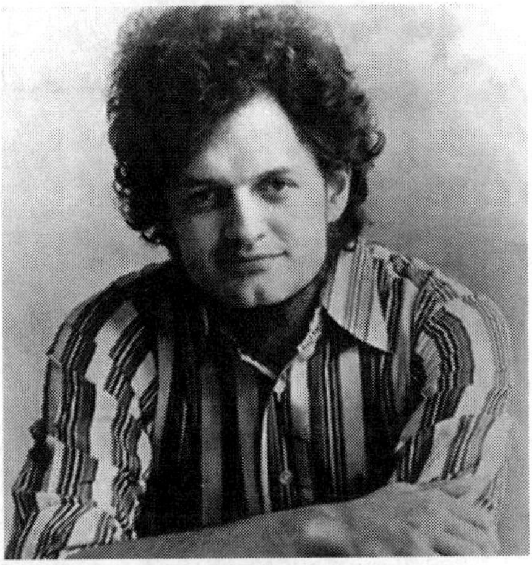

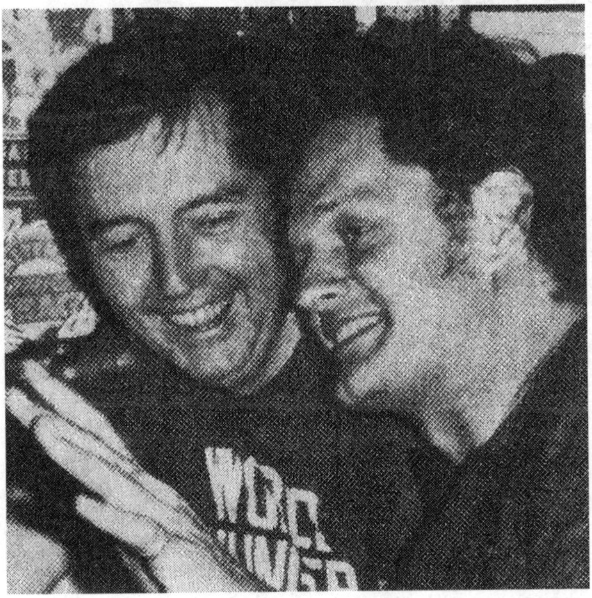

JOHN LEWIS
JANUARY 10, 1835—JULY 23, 1906
SAMUEL CLEMENS
NOVEMBER 30, 1835—APRIL 21, 1910

Harry Houdini
March 24, 1874—October 31, 1926

Will Rogers
November 4, 1879—August 15, 1935

Patsy Cline September 8, 1932—March 5, 1963
Karen Carpenter March 2, 1950—February 4, 1983

HARRY FORSTER DUCHARME

JUNE 28, 1947—NOVEMBER 4, 2008

Bronco Billy Anderson
March 21, 1880—January 20, 1971

Harry Cohn
July 23, 1891—February 27, 1958

MAC DUNCAN

SEPTEMBER 11, 1950— NOVEMBER 18, 2012

PEG LEG BATES

OCTOBER 11, 1907—DECEMBER 8. 1998

Sister Jeannine and Father Bill

Harv Sprafka and Bob Leonard, from Iowa

Centre Theatre
Oklahoma City, Oklahoma

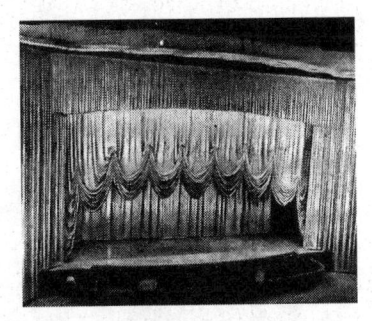

Murrah Building
Oklahoma City, Oklahoma
March 2, 1977—April 19, 1995

Larry Baker is the author of six novels. His first, *The Flamingo Rising*, was a Hallmark movie in 2001. If anybody is interested, he has also written a script for *Harry and Sue*. He currently lives in Iowa City, Iowa, with his wife Ginger and his chihuahua Ellie. He can be reached via email: icwriter@gmail.com

The Ice Cube Press began publishing in 1991 to focus on how to live with the natural world and to better understand how people can best live together in the communities they share and inhabit. Using the literary arts to explore life and experiences in the heartland of the United States we have been recognized by a number of well-known writers including: Bill Bradley, Gary Snyder, Gene Logsdon, Wes Jackson, Patricia Hampl, Greg Brown, Jim Harrison, Annie Dillard, Ken Burns, Roz Chast, Jane Hamilton, Daniel Menaker, Kathleen Norris, Janisse Ray, Craig Lesley, Alison Deming, Harriet Lerner, Richard Lynn Stegner, Richard Rhodes, Michael Pollan, David Abram, David Orr, Scott Russell Sanders, and Barry Lopez... We've published a number of well-known authors including: Mary Swander, Jim Heynen, Mary Pipher, Bill Holm, Connie Mutel, John T. Price, Carol Bly, Marvin Bell, Debra Marquart, Ted Kooser, Stephanie Mills, Bill McKibben, Craig Lesley, Elizabeth McCracken, Derrick Jensen, Dean Bakopoulos, Rick Bass, Linda Hogan, Pam Houston, Paul Gruchow, Bill Moyers, & so many more now... Check out Ice Cube Press books on our web site, join our email list, Facebook group, or follow us on Twitter. Visit booksellers, museum shops, or any place you can find good books and support our truly honest-to-goodness independent publishing projects and discover why we continue striving to hear the other side.

Ice Cube Press, LLC (Est. 1991)
North Liberty, Iowa, Midwest, USA
Resting above the Silurian and Jordan aquifers
steve@icecubepress.com
Check us out on Twitter and Facebook.
order on-line: www.icecubepress.com

Celebrating Thirty-Two Years of Independent Publishing.
2023 Iowa Governor's Art Award